# Praise for *The*

T0007888

"With depth and warmth and w ful, hopeful portrayal of second chances in life and in love. The carefully executed portrayal of anxiety, as well as the wonderfully engrossing love story, make this a pitch-perfect read. I absolutely loved every word. Suzanne Park is a hidden gem in the romance world, and *The Do-Over* is her best book yet."

—Christina Lauren, *New York Times* bestselling author of *The Soulmate Equation*

"A fantastic, empowering second-chance romance that combines wit and charm with an always insightful commentary on imposter syndrome, anxiety, and the challenge of finding ourselves. Suzanne Park wrote a true gem!"

—Ali Hazelwood, *New York Times* bestselling author of *The Love Hypothesis*

"Park's (*So We Meet Again*) latest does an excellent job of navigating topics of anxiety, self-doubt, nepotism, and misogyny through an enjoyable second-chance romance with great characters. This book is an essential read and highly recommended."

—*Library Journal* (starred review)

"A satisfying story of overcoming your fears about expectations—other people's, and your own—and figuring out your own worth. Second-chance romance meets all the other second chances we need to give ourselves."

—KJ Dell'Antonia, *New York Times* bestselling
author of *The Chicken Sisters* and *In Her Boots*

"Suzanne Park hit it out of the park with *The Do-Over*! Park brings her signature humor and heart to this serious (but still lighthearted) story. You'll laugh, you'll swoon, and you'll crave all the sweets as you cheer for Lily Lee to get her second chance—in love and in life."

—Ali Brady, author of *The Beach Trap*

## Praise for *So We Meet Again*

"Funny, romantic, and real-world novel. It centers on Jessie Kim, a young Korean woman who is laid off from her finance job . . . it tackles sexism and racism in gripping ways."

—*Today Show*

"Some books just feel like an old friend, their first pages embracing you with an instant familiarity and warmth you can't help but sink into. Suzanne Park's *So We Meet Again* is that kind of book. . . . A cinematic, charming heart-squeeze-of-a-book that has found its way to my Ultimate Comfort Reads shelf."

—Emily Henry, #1 *New York Times* bestselling author

"A laugh-out-loud comedy with a warm heart. Jess's journey of finding her way amid the noise of the world's expectations will make you smile and sigh and want to chase your dreams."

—Sonali Dev, award-winning author of *Recipe for Persuasion*

# The

# Do-
# Over

## Also by Suzanne Park

*So We Meet Again*
*Loathe at First Sight*

# The
# Do-
# Over

A Novel

# Suzanne Park

AVON

*An Imprint of HarperCollinsPublishers*

P.S.™ is a trademark of HarperCollins Publishers.

THE DO-OVER. Copyright © 2023 by Suzanne Park. All rights reserved. Printed by CPI Group (UK) Ltd, Croydon. No part of this book may be used or reproduced in any manner whatsoever without written permission except in the case of brief quotations embodied in critical articles and reviews. For information, address HarperCollins Publishers, 195 Broadway, New York, NY 10007.

HarperCollins books may be purchased for educational, business, or sales promotional use. For information, please email the Special Markets Department at SPsales@harpercollins.com.

FIRST EDITION

*Designed by Diahann Sturge*

*Illustrations throughout © Smartha; YumyArt; Alice Savina / Shutterstock*

Library of Congress Cataloging-in-Publication Data has been applied for.

ISBN 978-0-06-321605-1

23  24  25  CPI  10  9  8  7  6  5  4  3

*To those still finding their way*

# Author's Note

When I pitched the idea for this novel, I didn't know it would include themes of mental health in the Asian American community. But as I drafted and edited this book, it evolved into a story about a Korean American woman struggling with self-doubt who finds her happily-ever-after in self-love and romance. I rarely see anxiety depicted in fiction centered on Asian American characters, especially not in works of comedy. For a humor writer, it can be a really tough decision to include serious and sensitive topics in a story, but to take on mental health in the Asian community—this was extremely difficult for me. But as the pandemic continued, I was compelled to do it.

Language barriers, stigma, intergenerational trauma, and a "tough it out" mentality are a few of the reasons that the Asian community doesn't like to talk about mental health issues. In this story, I've reflected some of these challenges in ways that are related to my own experience or to those shared by close family members.

Please be aware that this story includes complex and

sensitive topics such as high-functioning anxiety disorder, panic attacks, and imposter syndrome. I tried to write Lily's experience with great care. Although everyone's mental health journey looks different, and Lily's experience isn't the same as everyone else's, I'm hoping people who relate to her journey can feel less alone.

# Chapter One

The call I'd been eagerly waiting for came at the worst time.

Sitting on the reclined, wax-papered examination chair while waiting for my wellness checkup was not the ideal setting for a life-changing phone discussion with an executive headhunter. The nurse had already taken all of my vitals, but my doctor hadn't made her appearance yet. It was only a matter of time.

I swiped to accept the call and whispered, "Um . . . hello?"

"Good morning, Lily. It's Patricia. Did I catch you at a good time?"

I glanced down at my breasts and belly peeking through the opening of the cotton cloth gown. "Yes." After double-checking the screen to make sure it was an audio-only call and not a video one, I added, "It's a great time. I'm out and about. Running errands. Keeping busy. Do you have any updates for me? Did I officially get the job?"

When I had left the final interview with the founder of Swain & Wallace, he asked me when I could start, and soon after that, the company's social media accounts followed me on every platform. In this digital age, that was pretty much the same thing as an offer letter.

I'd left my corporate job a few years back to forge my own professional path—consulting for start-ups and writing a series of career empowerment books—to earn more money so I could save for a down payment on a home. The salary for this executive role at Swain & Wallace was more than double what I was making now. And as a bonus, they had just built a brand-new, in-house gym. Not that I would use it, but it did have a cucumber ice water station near the locker area that I planned to visit every day.

She cleared her throat. "Well, I have good and bad news. Everyone at Swain and Wallace loved you. The hiring manager and his entire team thought you were a slam-dunk hire. The CEO even commented to the HR lead that he could see you in a C-level leadership role there someday. And technically, this morning, you were offered the position."

Dream company. Dream job. Dream team. And an offer of employment. All of this was too good to be true. My body tensed when I noticed she didn't end that positive feedback with a heartfelt "congratulations," and that she had said the last part with a downward inflection. Headhunters like her worked off job-placement commission, so why wasn't she offering to pop champagne bottles with me?

The waxy paper underneath me crinkled loudly as I sat upright. "Is there a problem?"

The sound of air expelling from her nose could mean only one thing. The bad news.

"Swain and Wallace's HR team performed an extensive background check, as is their standard procedure. This step of the hiring process used to take a few days, but with the latest advancements, we've seen these screenings turned around a lot faster. I'm not sure the best way to say this . . . I'm calling to inform you that you didn't pass."

Didn't pass? "Wait, I *failed* the background check?"

How was that possible? I wasn't a criminal. There had to be a mistake. Unless . . . the unpaid parking tickets from Martha's Vineyard from my early twenties had finally caught up with me? I accidentally ran a stop sign at 3 A.M. a few weeks ago in a borrowed car when I thought no one (especially no police cars) had been lurking around . . . but how could that be traced back to me? I'd also discovered I'd been driving with an expired license, but the renewal was paid, processed, and the new card was en route to my Brooklyn apartment. Then there was that angry neighbor incident, someone (not me) had poured birdseed all over his Hummer—a birdwatcher's paradise. Oh! And there was the office package stealer who threatened to press charges when I rigged a glitterbomb explosion a few years ago—

Patricia elaborated, "I hoped it was some kind of mistake, that maybe something was wrong with the vendor's software. We separately ran our *own* background check and it yielded the same results. I hate to ask this, but did you tell the truth about attending Carlthorpe College?"

*That* was the red flag on my record? "*What?* Of course I did! I'm not a *liar.*" The gray-haired nurse popped her head in the room, her eyes widened, and she stepped right back out, closing the door with a thump. Had she come back in because of the ten-pound discrepancy between my stated weight on the medical forms and my actual weigh-in? Because she could single-handedly prove without a doubt that I was, in fact, a liar. But honestly, who didn't lie about those things?

Patricia let out a breath. "That's good news. Maybe it's just a glitch in Carlthorpe's system then."

"I recently paid off my student loans for college, so if I made up that part of my life, I want my money back!" *I'd want all of it, plus interest.*

Patricia chuckled. "Well, okay, I believe you."

I added, "I have graduation photos to prove it."

"Actually, if you have something more official, like a diploma or a college transcript, I think we can submit that to the HR group, argue that their system had a glitch, and this will all go away. I'm afraid photos of you in a cap and gown aren't going to cut it though."

My heartbeat thumped hard in my chest. Ten years since graduation and nothing like this had ever come up before. Then again, I'd worked in only one company and its subsidiaries since college and rose in the ranks there.

Did I have a diploma? Maybe? Actually . . . maybe not. After graduating, I had temporary housing before finding a more permanent living arrangement. Some of my stuff made the move, some didn't. I didn't have a job right away and was couch surfing for a while. It wasn't the best time in my life, and I certainly didn't have my mind laser focused on my diploma's whereabouts. I never thought to get one reissued because I never had any wall space to display it. And who hung up their college diplomas these days anyway?

I took a deep breath in and exhaled slowly. "I'll call the school and get a transcript overnighted to you." If this was all that was standing in between having no job offer and having a *dream* job offer, I needed to act fast.

"Great! We have a plan then. I'll let you go on with your day. Have a great rest of the afternoon."

I hung up and fell back into the crinkly seat just as the nurse reentered the room. "I'm so sorry the doctor's still running behind schedule. Unfortunately, your health profile didn't update when I took your vitals, so I need to get your oxygen levels and BP again."

She put a clip on my finger and wrapped the blood pressure cuff on my upper left biceps. "Try to relax your arm if you can. I'll make sure it uploads to your records this time." The armband puffed and deflated automatically while she took my $O_2$ reading. "Your oxygen levels are excellent, ninety-nine percent. Your blood pressure is . . . whoa, a little high. A lot higher than before, actually. That's strange."

She took my wrist and checked my pulse. "Hmmm. Did anything happen that might spike your blood pressure and heart rate?" Clicking around in my health records, she looked at me and said, "Do we need to change your medications?"

"No," I answered definitively as she removed the Velcro cuff from my arm. "No need. It's nothing to worry about. Only a one-time, minor inconvenience that will get straightened out soon."

She offered me a reassuring smile. "Okay then. The doctor will be here shortly."

I MADE SEVERAL calls to the registrar's office that afternoon, and no one picked up the phone. The on-hold message encouraged me to chat with "Carly" on the college website, Carlthorpe's online virtual assistant beta, but the she-bot couldn't help me because my transcripts were ten years old, past the earliest year in the drop-down menu. Apparently I'd reached the cutoff mark when alumni were "archived." My transcript request would require manual assistance.

Carlthorpe was a leisurely four-and-a-half-hour drive from New York City, or just over three hours if you were driving like a bat out of hell, so relatively close. The train was about the same, but it also required travel to and from the train station. After my fourth attempt to call and speak with a live person, I made a decision to go to campus the next day before the morning rush hour to ask for my paperwork in person. If everything went smoothly, I could be home by dinnertime.

The 7:15 A.M. departure from Grand Central went without a hitch and the train ride was great for my work productivity. I'd managed to organize my notes and had even written a few pages of an outline by the time the train rolled into the station. I checked my watch: 10:45 A.M. Plenty of time to spare.

When my Uber pulled up to the front gates of the campus, an email notification buzzed my phone just as I exited the car. It was a note from Katherine Goodwin, the patient editor of my long-overdue book.

*Good afternoon, Lily,*

*I was thinking more about titles this week, and maybe this new book should have a simple title, like your last one. I loved HOW TO BE A WORK SUPERNOVA, so what do you think about HOW TO LAND YOUR DREAM JOB—it's easy to remember and straightforward, right?*

*How's the research going? Last we spoke you'd been interviewing at some really hot companies and had great insight into researching dream employers. Let me know if you need to run anything by me in the meantime—always open to read any chapters you've written.*

*Also, some good news! I've been promoted to editorial director. I've cc'd Amanda Phillips, our newest team member, who will be working with me as an editorial assistant on your next book. She came over from the contracts department and is a whiz with edits and meticulous with sales and forecast numbers. We're both excited to see what you have for us next!*

*All best,*

*K*

I let out a long sigh. *I'll get back to you soon, Katherine, once I officially have my job offer in hand.*

Immediately, my notifications buzzed.

*Nice to meet you, Lily!*

*As Katherine mentioned, I'll be working with you on your next project. Excited to get started! I took a look at your contract, and it looks like your manuscript is due. Let me know if I can be of any assistance. In the meantime, I'm updating all our authors' bio pages on our website and retail sites. Could you please take a look at your "About the Author" page and let me know if there are any updates to your bio? Also, I see you attended Carlthorpe too! Nice to meet a fellow Carlthorpian!*

*All best,*
*Amanda*

I clicked the link and it redirected to my author page on my publisher's website that hadn't been updated in years. Beneath my headshot was a list of my professional and academic credentials. I replied to Amanda's email, mirroring her enthusiasm, giving her the green light to keep my author blurb the same, adding that I had an exciting new career development and would need another update sometime soon. After clearing up this clerical error with my alma mater, I could include my next position with Swain & Wallace in the marketing materials for my new book. For the author website though, it would have to wait a little bit longer.

I closed the car door and quickly checked my top-half reflection in the passenger-side window before the car pulled away. No flyaway hairs flapping in the wind. A barely wrinkled ivory silk blouse. Smudge-resistant eyeliner still resisting. A presentable, respectable alumna. Lily Lee, business consultant and author of *How to Be a Work Supernova* and the forthcoming second book in the series *How to Land Your Dream Job*, was coming back to where it all started. Carlthorpe College.

In peep-toe heels, I strode along the cobblestone walkway and through the ivy-covered, wrought iron gates of the main campus entrance, where the stationed security guard smiled and nodded at me. The registrar was the first building on the right, which I'd remembered after all these years but was validated by the campus map I'd saved on my phone. I hoped that late morning would be a good time: it was right before the lunch rush and left plenty of time for an administrator to assist me in finding my student file. This didn't leave room for a fun, leisurely day in this quaint college town though. There would be no nostalgic strolls through the courtyard. No casual dining at the cute cafés on Main Street or partaking of the all-afternoon happy hour at the Carlthorpe Tavern. Sadly, not even a visit to the campus bookstore. My plan was to get the transcript and head right back home before the business day ended. I had more résumés to send out, interviews to prepare for, and a book that wasn't going to write itself. My walk down memory lane would have to be another day, under happier, more forgiving circumstances.

The timeworn wooden door leading to the registrar's office gave little resistance to my light push, and I was delighted to see I was the only person in line. It made sense: there wasn't a ton of academic activity during the summer, and fall registration hadn't started yet. Evidence of a birthday celebration lay behind the Plexiglas divider: large catered aluminum trays once filled with fruit salad, home fries, and pasta were now mostly empty. A small wedge of confetti cake sat in a large pink pastry box. Seeing all this food laid out triggered my mouth to water, an involuntary reminder that I needed to eat lunch. Maybe a quick meal at a dining spot on campus would be a nice treat before taking the train back to the city.

The woman at the window pushed her glasses up to the bridge of her nose with her index finger. "Student ID number please." Her fingers were perched above her keyboard, ready to descend and peck.

"I—I'm not a student. I'm an alum." I had to admit, it was somewhat flattering that she thought I could be enrolled here.

"Do you remember your student ID?"

I laughed. Was she serious? I couldn't even remember my own age sometimes. "I graduated ten years ago, I don't recall what it was, I'm sorry." I pasted on a smile. "I'm Lily Lee. College of Arts and Sciences. All I'm looking for is my transcript. I can give you my permanent address, graduation year, pretty much everything else." And I did, I offered her all of this personal information, as well as my social security number and academic advisor's name.

*Tap tap tap.*

*Tap tap tap.*

"Hmmmm. Strange." She tilted her head and squinted at the screen. With a loud, slow exhale, she muttered, "Is Lee your maiden name? Are you married?"

Okay, I didn't expect a "marital status" type of question from her. From my older sister, yes. My mom, yes. But the registrar? No. "Lee was the name I used in college. It's still Lee. Middle name is Ji-Yeon."

"Can you confirm this is your student photo?" She swiveled the screen so I could get a better look at my round, youthful, pimply face and all-gums toothy grin. And by toothy, I mean I actually had fanglike cuspids that were shaved down my first year of college. Sophomore and junior year was when things got better for me. My less canine-like smile. My classes were more interesting. I even dated a charming boy and we were together for over a year, one of the longest relationships I've ever had. Jake Cho. The one who shattered my heart into a million pieces. It never quite fit back together again.

I verified, "Yes, that's me, Lily Ji-Yeon Lee. I wish they had face filters back then."

"Let me share with you what I have here, so we're seeing eye to eye." While the printer hummed and pushed out pages, she typed and tapped some more. She grabbed the stack of paper and slid it toward me. The pile was pleasantly warm to the touch.

"Here's all the academic information we have on file. And your partial transcript."

"Partial?" My stomach lurched as I flipped to the last page. All of my classes were listed from my first semester to my last. Pretty standard stuff until I noticed one thing: in my last semester, two of my classes, Economic Principles and Survey Analysis, were listed as pass/fail. The matriculation date was listed at the top of the transcript, but my graduation date was not. It was blank.

I swallowed hard. Never before had nervousness, nostalgia, and amnesia hit me at the same time.

The registrar cleared her throat. "Ms. Lee, it appears that you didn't obtain enough credits to officially graduate. You're five credits shy, according to your records. Some of those pass/fail credits your last semester don't count toward graduation."

"There must be some mistake. I attended commencement. I walked across the stage." I squeezed my eyes shut, hoping that when I reopened them, this would all be just a dream. But when I fluttered my lashes and peeked, everything was still the same.

"Sometimes academic advisors get the graduation requirements credit tally wrong, but it's rare. In some cases, professors turn in grades the day before graduation and we still let students walk because most of the time the kids pass, even if they get D minuses. It's showing in our system that you switched two classes to pass/fail, which is highly unusual because typically a student is allowed only one per year. It was a special exemption, but only one of the two classes was approved to apply credits toward your major and degree. Do you remember that?"

Vaguely? My last semester was a miserable blur, and my academic advisor had never explained the full risk of switching my classes to pass/fail. Only that I could, and it was too late to drop the classes and the poor grades would drag my GPA way down. The system would generate an academic probation letter sent to my permanent address, even if it was my last semester. It would go to my parents' home. That was my top concern at the time.

"So . . . I didn't . . . graduate? There's no way to work around this somehow? Like a traffic violation where I watch a whole day of online videos and take a multiple-choice quiz to clear my record?"

She adjusted her glasses again. "I'm afraid not. The good news is, you don't have to reapply for admission. If you want to complete your credit requirements, they're opening up fall registration next week. I don't have much sway, but what I *can* do is ensure you have second semester senior status because of your credit standing. You should need only one, maybe two, courses to reach the graduation requirement, but you'd have to confirm this with your academic advisor."

I grabbed the counter to steady myself. My head whooshed and knees buckled from this avalanche of bad news. The lack of lunch wasn't helping with the light-headedness.

"You'd also need to confirm with your academic advisor if there are any additional requirements needed for your degree given that ten years have passed." A fall course catalog and a heavily frosted piece of cake passed through the opening in the Plexiglas window. "It's my last slice, but I think you could use it more than me. It's from Sassy Girl's. Please, I insist."

Sassy Girl's was a local bakery that made the best buttercream cakes in the Northeast. For the first time in my entire life, I had no desire to eat cake. But because the birthday girl was staring at me with her kind eyes through her oversize tortoiseshell glasses, I had no rational reason to protest. With the accompanying plastic fork, I tore off a sizable chunk of the tender, fluffy white cake and took a bite. A culinary masterpiece. Under different circumstances it would have brought me comfort and happiness. It was then I discovered something new about myself: that it was possible to chew, fake a smile while saying "thank you," and cry at the same time. A latent ability I never wanted to experience again.

## Chapter Two

**M**y phone rang. Then my text messages bleeped. It happened over and over, ring, bleep, ring, bleep, until I finally called my mom back.

She greeted me with, "Ji-yeon-ah, everything okay? You should be awake."

Umma always assumed if I wasn't picking up the phone, I was either sleeping in or napping. As if it was a bad thing to get more rest.

"I'm awake." Technically, I was. I just happened to be lying fully flat on my bed, unshowered, with my pajamas still on. It was 1 P.M.

"I'm buying *steak dinner* to celebrate good news!"

"What good news?" I bolted upright. Maybe my sister was pregnant again. Or she got a job promotion. By *steak dinner*, Umma usually meant the eight-ounce sirloin steak combination dinner at Applebee's. For her, steak dinners were reserved for only the most special of celebrations.

She chuckled. "Your new job. I see you talk about on the Instant Grams."

I clicked over to my Instagram account. Sure enough, a couple of weeks ago I had teased that I was looking for a career change and things were going well with my job interviews. I shared an old video of me on a basketball court, making an effortless shot from the three-point line. After my Swain & Wallace interviews, I took a photo of me in my interview suit in front of the company's high-rise building in Midtown and uploaded it too. Maybe I should have deleted that.

"Last time you tell me your interviews were good. I tell all our church friends that you working at big global business soon and also writing new book! They ask if your company have office in Seoul, and I checked internet, and tell them yes!" she chirped.

My stomach sank. How could I tell my mom the truth now? If I did, she would worry herself sick about my finances, and be horribly shamed when people in the church community asked about my job or my possibly never-forthcoming book.

But was this an opportunity to unshackle and free myself from the burden of being a people pleaser, especially to my parents? Because of our money problems growing up, my whole adult life I tried to be fiscally independent. I took a job with a good salary and decent health insurance to compensate for my parents' past financial hardship, just so they wouldn't worry about me. I attained academic success, or so I thought, and used the Carlthorpe name for networking purposes and to buoy my job candidacy. Then I took a risk by doing what I had always wanted to do: I quit the corporate grind to go out on my own. All along the way, nonstop, crippling guilt plagued me, because my parents gave up their lives and their own professional dreams in Korea so my sister and I could have a better future, and I was risking it all by choosing a more entrepreneurial path.

And look where I was now.

Tears that Umma couldn't see flowed down my cheeks, as she expressed her own gesture of pride by offering me a top sirloin steak at her favorite chain restaurant. This was a big deal for her, so I made the decision to keep my secret close to my chest instead of admitting the truth, hoping this choice wouldn't be one I would regret later.

"Can I get a raincheck on dinner? I'm going to be busy the next few months," I explained vaguely.

Confusion clouded her voice. "You starting job right away?"

I swallowed hard. "Not exactly. I'm starting a new job after four months." *Not untrue. I would be starting some kind of job at some point after four months.* "In the meantime, I'm going to take some classes to help educate me for my new job. Digital marketing and the tech landscape have changed so much. I thought by taking some special classes offered at Carlthorpe I could get ahead at work—maybe it could mean more money down the road." Swain & Wallace's HR lead told me that once I cleared the background check they would reconsider me for the position, if it was still available. It wasn't a guarantee, but I needed to do everything within my power to get that job back.

Perhaps suspecting something, she questioned, "Are you sure nothing is wrong?"

She was older now and retired, and over time we'd bick-
ered less, mainly because I'd found ways to distance myself from my parents when they were causing stress. These
were her golden years. I didn't want to burden her with any
of this.

I replied confidently, "Geokjeong haji maseyo." *Don't
worry, Umma. It'll be okay.*

"Algesseo. In four months, then I promise steak dinner!"

I smiled. In four months I would have my degree. My life
would go back the way it was. And then there would be
plenty of reason to celebrate.

## Chapter Three

On my last day in New York City, I choked on my iced coffee while reading an article in *Publishers Digest*. My drink had gone down my windpipe into my lungs, triggering a choking and gagging reflex. It would have been far more preferable if I had been at home, but no, I happened to be at Café LaLa, where my coughs were met with long, harsh stares by other judgy patrons who peered at me over their aviators and trendy, round plastic frames. *C'mon, like none of you have ever sucked a drink into your breathing tube instead of your food and drink pipe?*

Eyes all around me rolled in unison. *Geez, I know I'm fucking up the ambiance and aesthetic of this place, but still. I'm having a bad day, people.*

"You okay? Am I supposed to pat your back? Or would that make things worse? Is the coffee *that* shitty? For these prices, it better not be." Mia closed her laptop and leaned forward. "Please don't make me do mouth-to-mouth."

I laughed. And coughed.

She examined my face. "Okay, laughing is good. That means no Heimlich maneuver."

Mia always knew how to make things a little better, even when my life was swirling down the drain. She'd been my rock since the first days of college, and somehow over all the years she still stuck by my side. And I stuck by hers.

"Look." Cough.

"At." Cough.

"This." Cough.

I handed her my phone and her eyes bugged as she scrolled the article. "Hey! They make you sound like you have your shit together. It's all pretty good actually," she chirped, then paused. "Well, okay, until the end part."

I took the phone back and read the article a second time.

## PUBLISHERS DIGEST EXCLUSIVE
## CRACKING THE GLASS CEILING

Lily Lee, former communications executive, now business strategy consultant and author, didn't expect to write a book about women reaching greater heights in the business world and obtaining career satisfaction.

But when Lee made the *Forbes* 30 Under 30 list a few years ago and was asked to speak at alumni and professional events across the country about her career success, she realized that many young women wanted advice on job promotions, presenting themselves in the workplace, and how to seize opportunities. This led to writing her highly praised business book for women, now consistently topping the self-help and business charts. Her first book in the series, **HOW TO BE A WORK SUPERNOVA**, was recently named a Best Business Book of the Year by *The Washington Post* and *The Wall Street Journal*. Over the years, Lee has learned that people want to read grassroots success stories like hers, and young women all over the country are trusting her authentic business and career advice. Lee has big-name endorsements too: Suze Orman, Sheryl Sandberg, and Shonda Rhimes have all expressed love for her work.

When she was in her early twenties, Lee was promoted into a senior role, putting her on the fast track. "My boss had abruptly left the company, and I was the only one who knew how to do his job. Sure, on paper there were so many people who had more seniority at the company . . . but I had great relationships with my teammates and with our clients, and I had the industry knowledge that other people didn't. I put in the work, combing through trend reports, going to trade shows, and reading everything on the cloud drive I could get my hands on my first few weeks of employment. Because of this, I was able to influence people to get things done, and soon I was able to move up the ranks quickly."

Quickly is an understatement. She was promoted to account lead, then vaulted from director to VP to eventually EVP at the award-winning Splash Communications over a span of six years, leading and growing the Apex Mobile and Homegirl Entertainment accounts. She left two years ago to consult for new tech companies, assisting them in creating breakthrough brand identities and go-to-market strategies for new products. At that time, she came up with the idea for **HOW TO BE A WORK SUPERNOVA**, secured a literary agent, and landed a multi-book publishing deal.

Lily Lee has inspired others to forge similar paths. Twins Cameron John O'Hara and Mary Louise O'Hara, of the prominent O'Hara family in the Boston area, received a whopping deal in an undisclosed preempt for **YOU GO, GIRL!** and it's rumored to be in the high six figures. This book is also about ways women can find success in the workplace, focusing on similar themes to Lee's debut book and interweaving the authors' own work-related anecdotes, starting with internships at the family's billion-dollar beer and spirits business. **YOU GO, GIRL!** will be releasing in the fall, followed by Lee's next book (currently untitled), which will release sometime the following year. The O'Haras announced their deal on their Instagram accounts, where they each have approximately 150K followers. In the coming weeks, Cameron and Mary will appear on CNN to talk about their debut.

You can preorder books by the authors <u>here.</u>

The last paragraph of the article was the cause of my near-choking caffeine death.

I wiped away the cough-induced tears from my face and took another sip of iced coffee, this time swallowing it properly. "Can someone tell me what experience Cameron, the king bro of all bros, has to be able to write a book about women overcoming obstacles in the workplace? Do Cam and Mary even work? Everyone knows they were handed a plum job by their dad out of college and they didn't have to do anything to earn it . . . It's the corporate equivalent of being born into royalty. Can you imagine getting a job without even interviewing? And then they had access to the elite O'Hara network . . . so of course they'll be able to get any job they want for the rest of their lives."

Mia sighed. "I wish I had a rich dad. Or at the very least, a sugar daddy with mad LinkedIn connections."

I exhaled loudly out my nose. "Watch Mary and Cam's book sell, like, a gajillion copies. Their dad will probably buy thousands of them and give the books out to the employees as holiday gifts. Sometimes I feel like publishing is like a high-risk game of musical chairs, and everyone other than me is given a heads-up on when the music will stop."

Mia's eyes widened. "You're starting to sound jaded like me. I don't need a doomsday twin, I want my even-keeled Lily back! Begone, you horrible monster!"

Mia knew all about working her fingers to the bone, and the chip on her shoulder against the Camerons and Marys of the world was larger than mine. Mia and I were among the have-nots who needed to do work study or have part-time jobs in order to attend. We couldn't afford tutors, off-campus party-pad apartments, or spring breaks at high-end resorts in the Caribbean like everyone else. When my classmates asked me where I "summered" before going to college, they looked at me like I'd committed a felony when I admitted I worked in retail and hadn't traveled. "It was Brooks Brothers," I added, thinking that would help. But it didn't: they were wondering if I was a Hamptons, Nantucket, or European villa second-home person, not a paid-by-the-hour type. I'd committed a social faux pas and didn't even know it at the time. But the universe eventually graced me with meeting "my people" in college, lifelong friends like Mia, so it didn't matter.

Escaping "lesser-than" status was a huge motivator and we were both determined to change our futures. Taking a time machine jump to present day: we were now sipping eight-dollar iced coffee drinks at a place that served your beverages on pale pink napkins with inscriptions that reminded us to "Be kind," letting patrons know "You are enough" on the napkin dispensers. You wouldn't know it by looking at her petite frame swimming in an oversize gray hoodie, sporting a messy black ponytail, and sitting with both legs propped on a nearby chair, but Mia was incredibly successful at PR and publicity. So successful in fact that she'd quit her job, founded her own company, Mia Chang Communications (known officially as MCC), and built a lucrative freelancing business from the ground up, mainly working for start-ups and up-and-coming fashion brands.

"Sorry I'm not rich and powerful. You know if I had a billion dollars like the O'Haras, I would have given you all the free jobs." Mia broke off a piece of ginger cookie and stuffed it in her mouth. She had no fixed 9-to-5 schedule, so she'd offered to help me move into my bedroom in a shared apartment near campus, under the condition that I would be her first author client, and that she'd help me with publicity for my new book to broaden her portfolio. I agreed and treated us to this nice café breakfast the day before we set out on my "College, take two!" adventure.

She broke off another piece and handed it to me. "For what it's worth, I think your book will speak to more people, not like *You Go, Girl!* by the O'Haras. Yours is about how real people get jobs and climb their way up. It's not this fairy godmother shit that never happens to regular folks. You offer realistic shit."

I sighed. "People don't want realistic shit."

She snorted. "What? Of course they do."

I chewed the cookie and stared at my coffee cup. "They want to see success without all the grittiness, ugliness, and struggles behind the scenes. They want fairy-tale stories about prosperous, beautiful women who have the means to climb higher, and then do. I guess it's more aspirational that way, and predictable. Or they want to live vicariously maybe, like in a fantasy world . . . who knows. But I don't know that kind of life. I only know mine."

Mia tapped on my hand so I would look up at her. "Your books speak to so many women. Your audience is growing. People need stories with real adversity, like yours. Fuck the twins and their Daddy Warbucks money. And their mansion. And private island. Don't let 'em get to you."

*Yeah.* "Screw their money and mansion and private island," I said with a slight smirk.

"And all because you didn't actually graduate college, and technically each of the O'Haras has that on you—plus billions of dollars and easy access to beauty professionals and plastic surgeons who make them look perfect—don't let 'em bring you down. They've rattled you bad and you can't let that happen." Mia paused and winced. "Did the whole 'didn't actually graduate college' thing go too far?"

"And the other stuff didn't?" I barked out a laugh. "Nah. I'm used to how the world is. It's like one long string of unlucky breaks with occasional blips of hope. Sometimes I feel like a down-and-out gambler, hoping to finally catch my break." Throwing my wadded napkin on the table, I said, "But I'm used to it. So let's go. I need to go home and pack."

She scooted her chair back. "As the O'Hara twins would say, YOU GO, GIRL!" Mia paused and stifled a laugh. "Too far again?"

I nodded. "Yep. Too far and too soon."

We gulped down the last of our coffees and walked outside into a light mist. A quick rainfall had come and gone while we were inside the café. Mia pointed down the street. "Is that a double rainbow?" Sure enough, it was. The first one I'd ever seen. I wouldn't have noticed it at all if she hadn't mentioned it.

Maybe I was looking at life all wrong, seeing the world through shit-colored glasses, and I'd missed out on good things right in front of me. It was something to think about as I started my college life journey . . . again. Maybe everything was looking up, opportunities awaiting me, and I just didn't know it yet.

# Chapter Four

Y ou had six weeks to pack and purge, and you still brought way too much crap," Mia yelled out the truck window.

She was right. All of my stuff weighed down the U-Haul, which resulted in me needing to fill up on gas earlier than expected as we sputtered into the greater Carlthorpe metropolitan area. The pump chugged along and clicked, and then the display showed the final damage. Eighty-five dollars. We still had fifteen miles left to go, and to my knowledge, this was the only gas station in the area.

Mia leaned her head out again as I recapped the gas tank. "Can you run across the street to the grocery store and buy some more snacks? I finished our stash, sorry. I'll wash the windows with the squeegee while you shop. We can divide and conquer."

If given the choice between grocery shopping and washing windows, I was definitely all for #teamgrocery. I hated everything about the window-washing process. Pulling out the long stick with the questionably hygienic handle from the murky liquid . . . so gross. Was it even cleaning fluid in the first place? There were no bubbles or disinfectant smells, not that I ever stuck my nose in there to confirm. The spongy head inevitably dripped brownish-gray barf water onto my shoes, even when I tried to avoid it at any cost. I hoped Mia would keep it to the front windshield only—I could see her getting carried away and squeegeeing our entire truck just to make it look uniform.

Looking both ways and crossing the street, I was feeling good about my decision to shop, until Mia shouted out her wish list.

"Sparkling water! Doritos! Salted almonds! Sour Patch Kids! Chex Mix! And alcohol!"

"That's all?" I shouted back.

"Oh, and a shitload of condoms!"

I'd already crossed the street and wasn't about to bellow across the busy intersection, "WHAT DO YOU MEAN, SHITLOAD OF CONDOMS?"

I texted her, Condoms??? Really??? and proceeded to enter the market through the double automatic doors, grabbing a red plastic basket along the way.

Grand Central Market still looked exactly the same, and was as overpriced as ever, but they also managed to have everything I needed. Including condoms. As a joke, at least I think it was a joke, I bought Mia the entire inventory, which wasn't actually that vast, but by my standards, it was a shitload: four boxes of various sizes, textures, and thickness. Then I proceeded to buy the rest of Mia's wish list, along with a diet Dr Pepper, a bag of Bugles, and a small bottle of Jack Daniel's for myself. Passing the dairy case with my full basket, I stopped abruptly and a deep craving, a culinary pang in my very core, kept me standing there. The small tubs of sour cream were on sale, half off. The Lipton onion dip mix was right behind me, on an end display.

Serendipity.

I grabbed the container and packet and made my way to the next row: Ruffles with French onion dip were my absolute worst vice, and I only bought them when I was stressed beyond belief: during finals, after a breakup, while I was on a writing or editing deadline. It was a dietary disaster I'd picked up in college during Res Life study breaks. As I continued browsing the chip options, I considered my present-day existence—that I was Thelma and Louise road-tripping with my friend from college who had managed to graduate ten years ago while I had not—that I was moving back to Carlthorpe to finish my undergraduate degree in my thirties. My *thirties*, for God's sake. Yes, these unprecedented times called for chips and dip.

I grabbed an extra bottle of vodka on sale and added it to my basket too. Because why not?

The basket handle stretched oblongly from all the weight as I waddled to the checkout line, carrying my goods two-handed. With both arms straining, I put the basket down on the floor and waited for the guy in front of me to unload his items onto the counter at a sloth's pace.

The cashier activated the conveyor belt, leaving me room to put down my groceries as it moved. My face flushed when I witnessed the assortment of items belonging to the customer in front of me rumbling toward the cashier's scanner: Pepcid AC, toilet paper, TUMS, two Monster Energy drinks, two cases of Sam Adams . . . and to my surprise, Ruffles, sour cream, and Lipton onion dip mix.

*Damn, he's literally the reason they invented self-checkout. This secondhand embarrassment is killing me.* I stared hard at the floor. His white-and-black Adidas were pretty ordinary. Probably a size ten. Olive-green cargo shorts, not too much of a surprise. I snuck a quick glance upward to see what he looked like, but immediately averted my eyes down to the floor again, remembering that this was a college town, and the last thing I needed was to know who exactly this was who needed all the gastro relief, and I *definitely* didn't want to appear to be interested in him by accidentally staring too long. This was *not* the time to be labeled the Carlthorpe Campus Cougar™.

As he chatted with the cashier, curiosity got the best of me, and I peeked once more, but he had dipped his chin so low I couldn't get a good look. His frayed red baseball cap embroidered with a large "C" for Carlthorpe on the front hid most of his face: it was a nondescript hat, the color so washed out it was arguably more pink than crimson. All that was visible from beneath his vintage cap was his mesmerizing, gorgeous smile.

*Snap out of the hypnotic trance, Lily. Bad cougar. Bad.*

I methodically unloaded my items, separating the groceries into refrigerated and dry goods, continuing to avoid eye contact with this Sam Adams and Ruffles party maniac with gastrointestinal distress.

My entire body froze when I looked down at my basket. The four condom boxes were all that were left. Red Hat Guy was almost done, with only some beer left to scan, and Mia hadn't texted back why exactly she needed all the condoms, although I had my guesses. I quickly unloaded them and grabbed an *Us Weekly* with Harry Styles on the cover to blanket my various prophylactics.

I heard him chuckle and then say, "Good times ahead, eh?" My breath hitched with a quick inhale as I realized he wasn't just laughing at the condoms: he was reacting to my glass vodka bottle that had tipped over when the conveyor belt reengaged. It rolled all the way up to his beer cases, and then barreled back when the belt stopped moving, crashing into the boxes of condoms like a bowling ball splitting pins down the middle of the lane.

*CLINK!* The vodka bottle continued rolling and slammed into the Jack Daniel's. Hard.

"Cheers!" Red Hat Guy spoke with a hint of amusement in his voice.

My face grew hot as I separated the bottles with the family-size Ruffles bag as a buffer and let out a long, exasperated breath. I hadn't even made it to campus yet and I was already stressed out of my mind about a simple store trip. And it didn't help that my first encounter with a Carlthorpian was turning into a cringy sitcom disaster.

"Hope you enjoy your family-size Ruffles and onion dip."

Excuse me? Was he being sarcastic? Or envious? It was hard to tell at first, but I remembered he'd made the same purchase. He'd made that comment in solidarity.

Red Hat Guy walked away with a plastic bag and a case of beer in each hand. "Thank you," I muttered, watching him exit the store. His salt-and-pepper hair peeked from under his cap, suggesting he was older than he acted. He had an athletic build, put on visual display as his gray T-shirt pulled tightly across his broad shoulders while he hauled his heavy load. I pulled my attention back to my groceries and the cashier, then paid and walked out with two heavy brown bags.

I couldn't shake a prickle of familiarity with the Red Hat Guy. Was it simply instant attraction? I did enjoy his gruff, "just woke up" voice . . . his confident stance as he swiped his credit card and bagged some items himself . . . and his ease in just being okay with his embarrassing purchases without the need to hide them with a tabloid magazine.

Still . . . there was something, a je ne sais quoi—

HONNNNKKKKK!

Mia's head shot out of the passenger-side window of the U-Haul. She shouted, "Could you be any slower? What are you, ancient? Like thirty-two?" A pause. "Sorry, too far again? Or too soon?"

"Yep. Both." I handed her the groceries and entered the driver's side. She looked inside the bags as I turned on the ignition and restarted the navigation on my phone.

She squealed and dove into the Bugles bag. "I didn't even ask for these! You know me so well!"

I smiled and put the truck into reverse. Thirty minutes left to go in this leg of the trip. Then the truly dreaded part of the journey would begin.

Or rebegin, depending how you looked at it.

I held out my hand and Mia handed me a fistful of salty corn cone treats. After shoving them into my mouth one by one, I pulled out of the parking lot and barreled down the newly paved, tree-lined street toward Carlthorpe's campus.

# Chapter Five

R OOMIE!"
The apartment door flung open and a young twenty-something with a swishy golden ponytail tackle-hugged me. She reminded me of a golden retriever I had dog-walked once. The puppy had the habit of enthusiastically smelling the crotches of anyone we passed on the sidewalk. Fingers crossed my new roommate wouldn't share this trait.

She loosened her firm grip around my upper torso and took a step back. "You're very huggable, you know that? Like an adorable poppin' fresh Pillsbury Doughgirl, but the dough isn't all over, it's just in your boobs. They're great though, your boobs, don't get me wrong. I mean that in the best way possible, my nana had a nice set too. I'm Beth, but you can call me Roomie, Roomie!"

Holy shit. My roommate was a female Ted Lasso.

So. Much. Energy.

And yes, I had a size D chest, which came with all sorts of problems other than being huggable, such as unwanted leering stares, ill-fitting tops, and chronic back pain. But I'd never *ever* been told my boobs were poppin' fresh. This was a first. And hopefully the last.

Mia peeked over my shoulder and whispered into my ear, "Do I need to book us an Airbnb? This could be a disaster. Just say the word and I'll get it done."

"It's fine." The truth was, I kind of liked her. Aside from Mia, I'd had some terrible roommates; the worst one was from freshman year. Erika, who always set her phone alarm at full blast at 5 A.M. to hit the gym, and then snoozed it a dozen times, and never actually made it to any of her spin classes. Ever.

Beth's arms wildly gestured as she spoke about the walkability of the neighborhood, like her body created caffeine as a by-product. She was nice though, and that went a long way with me. I didn't originally plan to have a roommate, but there were no studio apartments available to rent around campus, and one-bedrooms in town were scarce and in high demand. I'd missed the campus housing lottery, which was maybe a blessing—it was far better for me to be a senior living off campus and commuting instead.

Usually people who were in apartments were transfers or those who had been booted out of Res Life for noncompliance, and the thought crossed my mind when she made a distinction between *those dorm kids* and *people off campus*.

Mia had been subliminally following my train of thought about off-campus living, because she asked Beth point-blank, "So what's your deal? Are you a transfer? Or did you get kicked out of housing?"

Beth didn't change her puppy-dog eager demeanor one bit. "Well, it depends who you ask. If you ask *me*, I'd say there was a gross misunderstanding and I'm still waiting to clear my name with the Carlthorpe judicial committee. If you ask the director of Residential Life, she might say that someone fitting my description *allegedly* provided prescription drugs as an illegal study aid, but in reality a bunch of floormates broke into my room and stole an old bottle of my expired Adderall last year during finals. It was their word against mine. They were trustee families, if you catch my drift."

I took her at her word and let it go. "Well, I'm sorry to hear that. But I'm happy to meet you, Beth. This is Mia, she's my good friend, a Carlthorpe alumna helping me move in. She graduated ten years ago."

"Oh! You don't look ten years older than us!" Beth maneuvered around me to hug-tackle Mia. "Any friend of Roomie's is a friend of mine. Nice to meet you! Are you stayin' long? I'm fixin' to put a roasted chicken in the oven. Well, it's not roasted now, it's uncooked and fleshy pink at the moment, but give me forty-five minutes and I'll fix that problem!"

My roomie squeezed Mia hard, and I exchanged glances with her over Beth's head. Mia's face was priceless. A dead-even mix of expressions: half amusement, half revulsion. "To be clear, I'm ten years older than *you*, not Lily. She's my age, though she doesn't look it. There's the saying 'Asian don't raisin' and she's living proof of that. And although I do love chicken, I need to help my friend here unload her shit and then I gotta head back to the truck rental before they charge us an extra day. We've got plenty of boxes and containers to unload, like this one."

My new roomie's eyes rounded when she noticed one of the clear plastic stackable containers Mia had placed on the floor by her feet, packed with tampons, pads, essential K-beauty products, and, of course, condoms. She'd put the four boxes in plain view. *Thanks for that, Mia.*

Mia wheezed in Beth's arms, "I'll be visiting often, don't you worry. So chicken raincheck?"

Beth loosened her grip and Mia took in a deep breath of relief.

"Abso-freakin-lutely! If I know you're coming, I can make a feast for all of us too. I love cooking for a group! I make a mean bread pudding. I love baking pretty much everything, except for popovers. Or Yorkshire pudding, depending on where you're from."

"How can you be anti-popover?" I asked, mildly horrified. Popovers were so crowd-pleasingly simple.

"Well, they're beige, flavorless, and as boring as my uncle Jude. And, most importantly, they're too light and airy. I hope you two love butter, it's a Beth Reynolds staple!" She lightly punched Mia in the upper arm.

Mia looked at me and shrugged. "I mean, seriously, who doesn't love butter?"

Indeed. God bless butter.

"Alrighty! I have to run to the bookstore real quick to grab a workbook, but holler if you need anything. I can help you unpack when I get back. And by the way, everything of mine is ours to share. Well, except for my boyfriend, who goes to Georgetown and who I plan to marry, he's strictly off-limits. But other than him, what's mine is yours! Mi casa es su casa, literally! Oh, and except for razors, deodorant, and toothbrushes, because sharing those would be downright nasty. Nice to meet ya both!" Beth and her ponytail swished past us, leaving Mia and me standing in the entryway, mouths agape, as the front door closed.

I pointed to the doorway. "It's going to take me a while to process what just happened there."

Mia's eyes bulged. "That was like listening to a podcast at 2X speed."

I laughed and clapped my hands. "Okay, let's find my bedroom and start unloading before it gets dark."

The entire apartment was decorated farmhouse shabby chic, in true Beth Reynolds style, with heavy emphasis on *farm* and *shabby*. Although there was an absence of hay on the floor, the living room and kitchen had a vintage quality that paid homage to an older era. Beth was clearly an aspiring antiques collector or, maybe more accurately, an old junk amasser. Old wooden milk crates were used as bookshelves and side tables. Glass milk bottles and mason jars doubled as drinkware. Cow, pig, and rooster wooden art populated the walls, as did metal John Deere tractor signs. It was more kitschy than tacky, but barely.

This was no time to throw stones at any glass house, even a tacky farm-themed one, because I could relate. In my college days, and even a few years after, I used to browse and buy all of my decor and furniture in thrift shops and consignment stores to save money and to blow off steam through low-end retail therapy. The thrill of finding my next "trash treasure" was incomparable to any pleasure I derived from grown-up purchases I'd made in my more successful years. I still had my greatest finds somewhere in storage: a vintage Nirvana shirt, a hand-painted porcelain rooster, and a set of cast-iron skillets that were heavy as fuck to lug home but were only ten dollars thanks to a red tag special. These were my most prized possessions.

Mia pursed her lips, like she needed to say something or she'd explode. Then she finally did.

"How in the hell are you supposed to invite anyone over with all that crazy country crap all around? You could hang a box of condoms with a FREE SEX! sign around your neck and get them to the door, but they'll one-hundred-eighty-degree spin when they see all that fucked-up farm fuckery inside. You're not seriously going to live here, right?"

I shrugged. "I guess I'll have to cross that bridge later, if it ever comes." We entered my large square bedroom as she ended her rant. I put down my satchel and phone by the door. "Aha! Now I know why you had me buy all those condoms. You want me to be an STD lure, to which I must say no thank you. But as for your main concern, I think it'll be fine. Beth's got a boyfriend, and I can just focus on my studies, get my stupid credits, and get the hell out of here after one semester. I don't need to invite people over and be social."

Mia cocked her head. "Seriously? You're doing this all wrong. That's why you're lucky to have me here as your orgasm oracle. The condoms are strictly for just-in-case use, like if you hook up with another student from class or have a party and want to get all naked with some dude. Maybe this is just the thing to get you to date more and put yourself out there." She dropped the bags of snacks from the store onto the carpeted floor. "This is your second chance to do college! Surely there are things you'll want to try again this time around. Or do for the first time. So many of my friends are jealous of this opportunity."

I pulled the closet door open and flicked on the light. "You're all jealous of me screwing up my life so badly that I didn't get enough credits? Jealous of me being in danger of looking like a fraud if anyone exposes me before my next book comes out? My life right now is hardly enviable."

She took the boxes of condoms from the container and stacked them in the empty dresser's top drawer, all nice and orderly. "*Noooo, chingoo,* that's not what I meant. College is the last stage of metamorphosis before becoming a real adult. Then you get burdened by loans and mortgages and 401(k)s. Everyone we know is getting married or is already married. They're having babies. Some are peaking at work and some are hitting plateaus in their jobs. You're getting a chance to relive a time when most people have no worries."

*Most people. But you know as well as I do that wasn't true for me in college.*

She patted my arm. "Okay, aside from the fact that you almost failed out of two classes and then messed up the whole major pass/fail thing to graduate, remember some of those fun times we had together? You'd dumped your shitty and boring long-distance high school boyfriend, the guy who would make a stick in the mud look interesting. We went all

Beyoncé 'Run the World (Girls)' right after that—we went dancing and had those fake IDs and went to diners on the weekend at one A.M. to share cheese fries." She sighed wistfully. "And you even dated that cute guy for a while . . . Jake. Jake Cho from ASA? The guy who always wore summer clothes, even when it was snowing?"

Yes, he was in the Asian Student Association with Mia and me. Jake and I were club officers our sophomore and junior years. We had both broken off long-distance relationships and then we started dating the night we went out of town to attend Columbia's Korean Student Association culture show. But it was supposed to be just a casual thing, with my friends egging me on to hook up with him because he was available and looking for a good time, and we had both broken up with our high school sweethearts. We actually started dating but things were not perfect, and it led to mutually assured emotional destruction.

Jake Cho. My friend turned friend-with-benefits, turned boyfriend, turned . . . messy. Actually devastating. Not exactly one of those *good ol' college days* memories. "I looked him up a while back but he's not online." His internet existence disappeared a few years ago. The last I'd seen from him was a personal blog of his random musings and carefree drives across the country. After college, I'd moved to a high-rise in NYC with a bunch of friends and never left. I was the opposite of a digital nomad. I was tethered to my job. Shackled, actually, for less pay than I was worth. It wasn't until I left the company to start consulting and secured a book deal that I had more financial freedom.

Mia pulled out her phone. Type, type, type. *Click. Click. Tap. Tap.* "I'll be damned. You're right. Jake Cho went totally off the grid a few years after graduation. But there are a bunch of Jake Chos online, maybe he's lost in the sea of them. Or maybe he's in witness protection. Or maybe he died." Mia tapped on her screen. "Okay, there are no obits for any Jake Chos. But if he was in witness protection, it's possible he's not listed in the obituary under his real name—"

"Hey, this conversation has gone noticeably morbid and I don't really feel like talking about Jake right now. Can we just unpack and not talk about witness protection and dying?" Mia's conspiracy theories usually ended with murder and death. It wasn't just Jake.

Seeing my ex now would be mortifying. When you encounter someone after ten years, you hope to God you're in a better place professionally, socially, emotionally, and mentally since your last encounter. I didn't want Jake to see me like this. Not when my professional life was in shambles. While jobless. With no husband. No kids. No advanced degrees, or even a college one for that matter. Even my author career was stagnating with a deadline now past due.

Mia knocked on my forehead, pulling me out of my downward spiral of thoughts.

"What the hell?" I asked, swiping her hand away like it was a flurry of spiders.

"I'm trying to crack that hard shell of yours. This isn't reliving college again exactly as it was. This is giving it another go, on your terms. So yes, please study, but also remember that you know how to prioritize projects now and get shit done because you kicked ass at work for so many years. Have fun when you're not studying! You've been given an enviable gift!" She nodded her head toward the stack of containers. "Now, let's move you in so you can get your damn degree."

"But this time I'm going to be that weird, mysterious mature student who all the regular undergrads notice and silently judge." My shoulders slumped as I took my toiletry bag out of my roller bag. "Remember when you were twenty-two, thinking that thirty-two was so old? In my previous job we looked at customer preferences by age, so adults would be split up into ranges of eighteen to twenty-four, then twenty-five to thirty-four. I'm in a completely different demographic than everyone here!" I sighed loudly. "Maybe it's too late to try something exciting and new. Maybe I'll just take whatever class is the easiest instead of trying to be adventurous."

"I'm telling you, that would be a shame. You don't think you can teach an old dog new tricks, is that it? What about the time when we were drunk and I taught you how to properly line a trash can? And didn't you show me last year that you could burp the alphabet?"

I narrowed my eyes. "Yes to the trash thing, and the alphabet was something I learned in high school, and it doesn't count. And it should never, ever be mentioned again. Also, remember that over the last decade, I've watched, like, a hundred videos on how to fold a fitted bedsheet and I still can't do it."

"Okay, fine. But maybe this is all a good thing for you. You were go-go-go for ten years. At the same company and on the same team for most of that time. You never took classes or traveled like you said you would." Mia wagged her finger at me. "It could be a time for reinvention! Anyway, grab your shit so I can return the truck." Before I could protest any more, Mia had marched out of my bedroom, swinging the U-Haul keys in circles on her finger.

My first year of college it had been my mom and dad moving me into the dorms. That day was miserable because we argued about every little thing. Which bank to use for opening a checking account. Whether to take the stairs or the elevator. How to organize my dresser and closets. And that was just the first hour. But over the years, Mia had become the person to fill in the emotional cracks and holes that my parents had left gaping and never bothered to mend or repair. I grew into my own person, and Mia was there for that. She had my back and was willing to fight for me no matter what. She was my family, and I was hers, and it was fitting that she was the one with me now. She'd literally fight for me if she had to, like in the olden days when you had a duel with pistols and fought for someone's honor. Mia would be up for a physical takedown anytime, which was a little scary. But also endearing.

If I was ever accused of a crime, Mia would be my auto-dial. My mom and dad would be too worried about the word getting out in our gossipy Korean community, more concerned by that than my well-being. It was just how my

relationship with my parents was. We had different priorities and values, and it wasn't until I was living on my own
and had sought out mental health support that I finally came
to terms with it.

And maybe Mia was right about getting another shot at
college. I'd watched those comedic movies like *Never Been
Kissed* and *Life of the Party,* where the main character goes
back to school, gets a second chance, and it ends with a
happily-ever-after. Maybe when all this college drama finally blew over, that would happen for me too.

# Chapter Six

It was early September, orientation week had just ended, and the hustle and bustle of fall semester was in full swing. According to my reenrollment packet, I needed to get final signoff from my academic advisor, Dean Balmer-Collins. The same woman who misguided me my last semester ten years ago, approving my pass/fail credits without warning me about what the trade-off would be. She had hyphenated her name, wore a wedding ring with a diamond the size of a Hershey's Kiss, and had upgraded her office to one with a window. She'd found good fortune the last ten years.

"Please, come in. Apologies for running late." She gestured for me to take a seat. Dean Balmer-Collins's stoic demeanor and chin-length bob had remained the same over the years, as did the slight disdain in her voice.

I sat in the plush, worn guest chair, my hands overlapping on my right crossed knee, and took deep breaths in and out. All I needed from her was a signature. Then I would never see her again. No need to mention that I'd known her in my previous life, and that she was the main reason I was sitting here in the first place. Bygones, and all that.

"We have a slight problem, Miss Lee." She took her glasses off and placed them in front of her on her mahogany desk.

*Surely the problem couldn't be worse than you screwing up my college graduation the first time around?*

"It appears that your major is no longer one we offer. As such, I'm loath to say that you will need to pick a new major."

My stomach dropped to my feet. "But . . . Carlthorpe was the first college to offer a combined sociology-anthropology major."

She nodded. "Yes, and it was popular for a long time, but we phased it out several years ago in favor of streamlining our majors and added ones more technologically forward in thinking. The good thing is, most of your credits apply to either a sociology or anthropology major, and if you choose either of those, you can very well be on your way to finishing your degree in one semester or, depending on your work-load, two semesters. I don't want to say this is bad news nec-essarily, because I'd like to see this as an exciting learning opportunity more than anything else."

Learning opportunity? I scoured her face for some kind of sign that she was feeding me a load of bullshit, but she had a good poker face.

The dean rested her hands on her desk. "We've added additional STEM requirements to all liberal arts majors, so in addition to your coursework needed to graduate, you'll need to take calculus, statistics, or computer science, or any of the sciences on the approved list. For the first two, there are math classes that are more qualitative and designed specifically for the humanities. For example, the stats classes are tailored toward survey implementation, collection, and analysis, and although those classes are currently full, you can try to put yourself on the waitlist. It's my understanding that the statistics class has one big project assignment plus a final, so it's a good bet for a late-term admittance. But it looks like the Introductory Computer Science class has an open spot." She scribbled her signature on my coursework. "So just update your major, add the extra STEM class, and hopefully you'll be graduating in no time, Liana. Thank you for stopping in."

*Liana?*

She scooted the piece of paper over to me and turned her full attention to her laptop, as if I'd instantly turned invisible.

*Hello? I'm still here!*

My pulse quickened as I considered what to do next. Getting my name wrong warranted a correction, but did I bother telling her what had happened all those years ago, and that her bad advice led me here? Would she even care?

I stood from my chair, then sat back down. *Yes, I need to set her straight.*

Then stood again. *She doesn't care. She can't even get my name right. And she's completely ignoring me. In fact, she turned up the volume on her computer and it's pumping out Debussy.*

I sat once more. *Lily, you need to confront her. You can't let her get away with this.*

"Is there anything else you'd like to discuss?" She tipped her head down and raised an eyebrow. "Clearly you're conflicted about leaving this room, that much is obvious." The dean let out a bored sigh. "Most kids can't wait to leave my office."

*No shit, I wonder why.*

She tapped her fingers on the desk like she was playing a five-note arpeggio. Over and over. "Liana, what else do you need from me?"

I balled my fists. "It's Lily, actually. Ten years ago you were Dean Balmer, assistant dean of the Arts and Sciences?"

She pursed her lips and nodded.

"Ten years ago you gave me academic advice that has now come back to haunt me. You were the one who advised me to take more than one class pass/fail. I didn't graduate that year, based on insufficient credits."

Her eye twitched. "I beg your pardon? Ten years ago I was just granted tenure, so clearly I was doing my job. Admittedly, I was planning my wedding and had a full plate at that time. If you slipped through the cracks, well, this is just as much your fault. Your generation is always looking to blame others. Accountability for your future, well, that was and is something you need to accept, *especially* an adult." She squinted at me. "At best, I suppose I could have offered advice that you either misinterpreted or ignored. At worst, you made some bad life choices and are looking to find someone else to blame other than yourself."

*The gall of this lady.* "Look, I accept that this is something I needed to own up to, but I was in a crisis then and you fed me misinformation. What happened ten years ago can't be changed and there's nothing I can do about it now. I'm owning up to that and I've grown as a person. What's done is done. But you gave me shitty advice back then that resulted in me never graduating, and I wanted you to know that I'm here at least partly because of that. I'm not asking for special favors, or for you to be my mentor, no thanks to that. Kids here are depending on you, and you can't go around ruining lives by not having your eye on the ball."

I grabbed my laptop bag and turned before I opened the door. "You are a dean of Student Affairs now. Not assistant dean, or associate dean. And you've had ten more years of work experience since I last saw you. You're leading by example and the word *students* is in your title. I'm being accountable for my actions, and you should do the same."

I slammed the door closed behind me, ending my commentary with an exclamation point. I never wanted to see her judgy, scrunched face again. Had she ruined the lives of anyone else? My well-being did not even seem to register to her, not then, and not now. Ten years ago I was much more lost, and sure, I was still lost now, but one thing I'd learned in my decade of working is that some people really don't give a rat's ass about others. I called her out, which younger Lily would have been too scared to do. Honestly, it felt great, like I'd just checked something off my bucket list, but mine was more of a list of grievances and grudges. This probably wasn't what Mia was raving about when she went on and on about my opportunities for second chances.

I took my final schedule to the registrar and paid my tuition in full. I had no financial aid, so my bank account took a huge hit. The one bright side was that my return to school didn't dip into my 401(k). Hopefully I wouldn't need to take out any of those savings.

I put myself on the waitlist for the statistics class and enrolled in the computer science one, taking the last available slot. Then I added the popular, groundbreaking class I'd read about that only Carlthorpe offered, Building a Global Audience and Influencer Culture, the class my parents thought I was returning to campus for to help me advance at work. With my courses approved and paid for, all I needed to do was attend my sessions, get decent grades, and earn my diploma. And then I could get right back to the life I left in New York.

## Chapter Seven

The scorching rays from the afternoon sun seared through my long-sleeve cotton tee as I ran down the cobblestone path. I'd brought clothes for college that were suited for fall weather, it being early September and all, but I hadn't anticipated an eighty-five-degree heat wave that would cause buckets of sweat to drench my forehead, chest, and upper back, then pool in the front of my underwire bra as I bolted down the central campus walkway. Being late on the first day of classes as a second-time-around student? Unacceptable. But also inescapable, because two things that hadn't changed over the years were my poor sense of direction and my inability to interpret campus signs with arrows pointing all over the place.

The Computer Science Hall was new to me, situated near the science buildings, which I hadn't spent much time in during my college years. The structure was mostly metal and glass, a sharp contrast to the adjacent set of ivy-clad brown brick buildings, where the music and art classes were held. The building planner had cleverly named all the classrooms in the CS Hall in binary code: turns out that two-symbol systems humor isn't all that amusing when you're late for class and the 0s and 1s above the doors aren't in sequential numerical order. At least not one that I could tell.

I found the location in the east wing of the second floor, Room 101011, which turned out to be Room 43. This classroom looked more like a large conference hall you'd find at some of the large tech companies, mixed with collegiate heritage furnishings: the chalkboards from long ago had been replaced with slick whiteboard walls, which contrasted sharply with the dark brown wood trim throughout the auditorium. The flip-down seats were the same, though they were modernized with padded cushions. And the best lecture hall upgrade in ten years? Fast Wi-Fi with a strong signal.

Even after all these years, the magnetic draw to the back row of seats was strong, like the gravity of the moon pulling the seas toward it. I fought my urge to fade away into the outer ring by opting to sit toward the middle of the pack of students. Maybe that would be the key to better grades this go-around.

A man in his late fifties jogged down the center aisle and plopped his leather satchel down next to the wooden podium embossed with a brass Carlthorpe insignia. The sparse, stringy gray-haired ponytail gave him an appearance of an aged musician, but his oversize black tee with the words I'M JUST AN OKAY BOOMER suggested he was not the rock-star type.

He cleared his throat. "I'm Dr. Stevenson. You can call me Doc, even though I have a PhD in computer science and not medicine. Or you can simply call me Professor." He wrote

"Doc" and "Professor" on the whiteboard wall, as if those would be hard to remember and we should jot them down. I found myself leaning forward and squinting a little. Was this because I wasn't used to reading someone's handwriting from so far away? Or did I need new contacts? I forced my brain to not go down the "maybe it's what happens to older people" rabbit hole thought spiral.

"Welcome to the Fundamentals of Code. What I want to do here is teach the basics of computer science, but in such a way that's less academic and more practical and usable in the outside world. You might not leave here a programmer, but if you ever find yourself in a technical role, or a technically adjacent one, you'll be able to understand and speak a common language with your product and dev teams." His eyes shifted from his podium notes over to the door, which creaked open. "Perfect timing! Class, please say hello to the unusually punctual Jacob Cho, your teaching assistant. He's a doctoral candidate and has been studying with me for, what, five, maybe six years?"

I nearly spat out my coffee. And I say nearly, because I was in the process of swallowing my iced drink as Jacob walked through the entryway, and it went down the wrong pipe instead, just as it did at Café LaLa. I drew loads of attention to myself with all the coughing, including the wide-eyed stare of the TA.

The TA who had on a red frayed baseball cap with a Carlthorpe "C."

The TA Jacob Cho, also known as Jake Cho from my college days.

Ex-boyfriend Jake Cho, to be exact.

The same guy from the market, who was now staring at me quizzically while I tried to control my incessant hacking. It was impossible to not notice that he had transformed from scrawny to brawny over the years. And his unexpected head of salt-and-pepper hair made my senses spin. Everything about him—the broad shoulders, boyish smile, and unruly dark hair flecked with silver—stirred something inside me that I hated to admit. His khaki shorts showed off his taut, muscular legs, another unexpected discovery.

Jake Cho had grown into a hot older guy.

*No, no, no. Lily . . . no. You can't be hot for teacher.*

A spark of recognition lit up his face as my coughing subsided. I could still read his expressions, even after all these years. The raised brow. The slight smirk. *What on Earth are you doing here, Lily Lee?*

And he could read mine. *You're in a computer science PhD program? But you were a liberal arts major, like me, Jake Cho. It's Jacob now?*

He shrugged.

Blood rushed to my head, making me dizzy. I looked down at my spiral notebook and focused on the horizontal college-ruled lines.

The professor continued chattering away about the expectations for the class while my heart resumed beating after temporarily seizing.

A confirmed Jake Cho sighting after nearly a decade. Did he still have a million hobbies and side hustles—or had he changed over the years to be less scattered and more focused? I had dreaded this day, when I would run into my ex. I'd had ten years to think it through: if I saw him—maybe at an airport, on a subway, or on the street—I made a promise to myself to avoid him. Never once had I ever played out a scenario in which I would be back in college as an undergraduate student in my thirties and have Jake as my TA.

He came to me in my dreams sometimes. Usually in nightmare form, like running into him at a wedding, or at a reunion, or once, at a Weight Watchers studio that I was leaving while he was walking into the boxing gym next door. But even with the occasional good dream, when my unconscious imaginings were happy, or romantic, or even hot-damn steamy, it always ended the same way. With Jake turning away and leaving me. Cue sad K-drama ballad music sequence.

Physically speaking, and to my absolute dismay, he'd changed for the better. While the professor continued with his lecture, I couldn't help but steal quick looks at Jake. Damn, that thick, wavy hair. Curse his lean, broad, and tall body, and that boyish face with full lips accented with two sharp peaks . . . and those crinkly, flirty eyes with creases underneath that made him look expressive rather than exhausted . . .

I stared hard at my shoes while the professor spoke. *I can't take this class. It's JAKE, for God's sake. Must talk to the registrar to beg my way into the stats class, stat.*

". . . Our goal is to teach students how to think algorithmically and solve real-world problems efficiently. Languages included in the coursework will be C, Python, SQL, and JavaScript, plus CSS and HTML, but not all of them will be on your midterms or finals. To make things interesting, those who rank top of the class after key projects are turned in will be eligible for highly coveted summer-internship opportunities at Solv Technologies, one of the companies I advise. They're looking for people who major in social sciences but are programmably inclined. Jacob, why don't you introduce yourself and tell them more about Solv."

I didn't think "programmably" was a word but it wasn't a hill I was willing to die on.

Jake/Jacob put on a serious face as he addressed the class. "I'm Jacob, a Carlthorpe alum. Recruiters from Solv will be on campus this semester to find top talent, so as long as you turn in homework on time, study for exams, and earn a top spot in the class, this could turn into a lucrative career opportunity." The entire class ooohed and ahhed, me included. Solv was one of those reputable tech companies that offered catered lunches, had team off-sites at ski resorts, and lived and breathed diversity and inclusion. They had been at the top of *Fortune*'s 100 Best Companies to Work For list, for three years straight. The word on the street was that each job opening there had a thousand or more applicants. What a dream it would be to even get an invitation to interview there.

*Pssst, Lily, he's talking to these twenty-something-year-olds, not you. YOU have a career that you're trying to get back to, remember? It's too late for someone like you to start over like this. Plus, you're going to statistics anyway.*

Right. I needed to get as far away from this class as possible. Specifically, away from my ex, Jake. And Jacob Cho, his hotter grad student persona.

One of the girls in front of me leaned to her left, whispering loudly to her friends, "I hope Jacob has office hours, I need to pay him a visit."

Her friend laughed and elbowed her. "If I'd known CS grad students looked like him, I'd have started taking these classes first semester first year. He's a little broody too. My favorite."

I slunk down in my chair, avoiding any eye contact with the professor or with Jacob. My plan was to get through this class period, and then go to the registrar immediately afterward to get transferred into stats. Or calc. Even quantum mechanics and nuclear physics. Honestly, any class but this one. Reliving college was bad enough, but what in the fresh hell kind of nightmare was I living in now? My college ex was in a position where he could fail me out of school again if he wanted to. This was something someone at Netflix could adapt into an eight-episode horror miniseries.

The professor chirped, "And this marks the end of the first lecture. So now let's get to the heart of what programming is, shall we? Jacob, would you please take these two boxes of chocolate and hand them to a couple of people in the room?"

Jake put his backpack down next to the professor and took the candy from his hands. He proceeded to walk down my aisle. Toward me. With each step he took, my heart rate jacked up higher and higher, like I had just started an intense cardio-heavy workout on too hard of a level.

He handed a candy box to one of the Jacob-obsessed groupies in front of me. Their entire squad squealed in delight. Jake continued down the aisle, passing my row, and I didn't bother to turn around to see who else received the chocolates. Didn't matter . . . I'd already set my mind on transferring out.

The professor said, "Okay, let's begin. Mr. Cho, stay where you are." Smiling at the audience, he explained the exercise to the class. "Please give Jacob a set of verbal instructions that will have him go to either one of the candy stations, take the box back into his hands, and return it to me. If you can do that, or contribute significantly to this exercise, you will not only get the candy, but you'll get an automatic A on the first assignment."

My classmates shouted out a wide range of instructions, which Jacob took literally. "Move forward" made Jacob walk all the way down the aisle and out the door. "Turn right!" caused Jacob to spin in circles clockwise. Our directions became more nitpickingly specific as Jacob twisted, turned, and ran all over the room. Eventually, the class offered instructions that resulted in Jacob moving in teeny tiny increments to eventually work his way to the fangirl one row ahead of me.

My chest tightened as he drew closer and closer. I didn't want him to get her chocolates.

Was this ridiculous? Yes.

Petty? Absolutely.

But something inside me kicked into gear. Adrenaline? Grit? Maybe just good old-fashioned jealousy? Good grief, whatever it was, it made me want to win this thing.

I glanced over my shoulder and saw a brawny dude near the aisle holding the other box of candy. Only one or two commands were needed to get Jake over to the girl, but I'd never been known to take the easy way out.

Clearing my throat, I projected my voice and gave my instructions. "Turn one hundred eighty degrees to the right and stop. Walk twenty-five paces forward and stop. Turn ninety degrees to the left. Walk three paces ahead and stop." I knew Jake's shoe size from college. And his underwear size, but that wasn't needed for this exercise.

Jacob walked away from his fangirl and, with my commands, ended up right next to the guy who held the other box of chocolates. I couldn't help but grin at my tiny nerdy achievement.

Soon, others in the class offered instructions to have Jacob pick up the candy and deliver the box of sweets straight down the aisle to the professor.

Doc nodded as he received the candies from his TA. "Well done. This was by far the best attempt in all my years of teaching this exercise about how computers take things literally." He moved his head right and left, scanning the lecture hall. "The young gentleman in the Red Sox shirt, please stand." It was the guy who gave the instructions after mine, the ones that made Jacob reach out and take the candy box. "The young woman in the black-and-white stripes?" She was the one who "programmed" my ex to walk down the aisle and stop next to the professor. "And the woman dressed in the black long-sleeve tee, with just past shoulder-length black hair."

Me. That was me. And he didn't call me young. Damn it. I stood slowly.

"Attention, students, these three will be the ones receiving the first As this week. As for everyone else, you'll have to earn your first assignment grades the old-fashioned way."

I avoided looking at Jake's face. I knew the moment I gazed into his eyes, my life would change in an instant. Kind of like what would happen to people when they saw Medusa. One of my worst fears could come true that as soon as I laid my eyes on Jake, my heart would melt and I would fall for him all over again.

The moment class ended, my glance swept over to my ex. I saw with clear eyes what he'd become: a brainy, attractive man who had successfully reinvented himself. Did I mention attractive? It was like I had googled "How do you fill out a shirt?" and all these hot 3D renderings of Jake appeared. No wonder those female students in front of me had gone gaga over him. He was hot.

The Jake I knew back then was directionless. Cute, but gangly. Tall, lean, and wiry.

This was Jacob 2.0. Still tall, but now he had an athletic, trim body, and he was looking right at me.

Holy hammer curls.

*Lily, under no circumstances are you allowed to fall for Jacob Cho. Stop it.*

Doc waved to students as they exited. "See you at the next class!" He turned around and wiped "Doc" and "Professor" from the whiteboard. "We've got a good group this year, don't you think, Jacob? That exercise went really well for this group in particular, thanks for coming up with it."

Jake looked in my direction and said to his advisor, "I'm curious to see how this class goes."

Did he absolutely, positively recognize me? He had to, right? At my last high school reunion, everyone pretty much looked the same after ten years. Sure, I could maybe use some HIIT classes or a few thousand burpees to bring me closer to how I looked back then, but everyone from high school knew it was me. But then again, I was only one of four other Asians in my class, and I was the shortest one, so maybe that was partly why.

But did I want him to recognize me? No, I definitely did *not* want to walk down memory lane with Jake after class. It was humiliating enough to have to come back to Carlthorpe to complete my bachelor's degree. And to have Jake be my TA, having that leverage over me? Jake Cho? He'd seen me naked, for God's sake.

NO. THANK. YOU. My cheeks burned as I grabbed my TUMI bag and ran out the back door.

Over at the registrar, the line moved as quickly as anything else with the same level of democratized, bureaucratic inefficiency. The DMV. Post office. The non–TSA PreCheck line at the airport. One by one, students ahead of me reached the front of the line and talked to administrators behind the Plexiglas windows. When it was close to my turn, my phone buzzed with an email notification.

A message from my editor. Subject line: Checking In. *How's the book coming along? —K.*

Oh no.

My stomach lurched as I snoozed the email. I could deal with it later in the evening. What was I supposed to say to her?

*Dear Katherine,*

*I owe you a longer update, which will come at a later date, but I'm thinking we might need to switch the title from* **HOW TO LAND YOUR DREAM JOB** *to* **HOW TO LAND YOUR DREAM JOB BUT THEN FIND OUT YOU DIDN'T PASS BACKGROUND CHECK AND NEED TO GO BACK TO COLLEGE TO FINISH YOUR DEGREE, PLEASE SEND DOUGHNUTS.**

*If you like the sound of it, I can send you my complete manuscript after I graduate (if I graduate, for real this time) in a few months.*

*Sincerely,*
*Lily the Loser*

"NEXT!" The closest window became available and the woman behind the glass wildly flapped both arms, with the intensity of someone waving down a plane for an island rescue. Her gesticulation ended as soon as I made eye contact and approached.

"I wanted to check my waitlist status . . . I'd like to drop CS and add stats, if that's an option now." I left out the fun fact that the TA was my ex.

She nodded eagerly and typed on her keyboard as I gave

her my student ID info. "I'm afraid you're still on the wait-list for the statistics course." *Click, click, click.* "There aren't any other classes with open spots that meet your degree requirement. Stats is your best bet because you're number two on the list. My advice to you is to attend the classes you want and wait it out. We usually have a few students who don't show up at all for class and drop courses right before midterms. Spots *will* open up, it's just a question of when and how many."

I knew what she said logically made sense. In fact, I remember dropping a class or two myself throughout college under the same circumstances. The main issue was that I didn't want to attend another class if I wasn't guaranteed a spot, but I knew that it wasn't something in her control.

She offered a sympathetic smile. "Mark the date in your calendar, six weeks from today. That's the last day class registration can be changed without penalty. Good luck to you."

I thanked her for her time and sighed as I left the building.

Six weeks.

The cobblestone walkway leading to the main campus gate was lined with folding tables and chairs. Students crowded the path, so it was practically impossible to cut through. As I squeezed by, I had time to read the tabletop signs and posterboard signs on display.

COME JOIN THE DEBATE TEAM!

QUEENS GAMBIT IRL! FIRST CHESS CLUB MEETING THIS THURSDAY!

THE *CARLTHORPE COURIER* NEEDS YOU! WE'RE LOOKING FOR SPORTS, ENTERTAINMENT/LIFESTYLE, AND CAMPUS LIFE REPORTERS!

A snort escaped my nose when I passed by the Asian Student Association table. I didn't mean to laugh, but it was just funny to me that more than a decade ago I was sitting in this exact spot, trying to recruit new members. And that Jake was helping me do it.

K-pop blared from the Bluetooth speakers as the club recruiters cried out, "All are welcome! You don't have to be Asian!"

A tap on my shoulder got my attention. "Hey! Would you be interested in joining? Our first meeting is tonight, and we'll have pizza and snacks."

I thought about making a racial profiling joke, but I held my tongue. "No thank you." Though I was curious about how the organization had evolved since I left school, I was not in the mood to crash the club to find out.

One of the guys approached. "We have a fashion show in the winter. We need models for that."

That comment actually made me burst into a fit of laughter. The fashion show was not something we had back in the day. And I wasn't qualified to model anything other than pajamas and sweatpants.

"I'm sorry, I could have sworn you said you wanted me to model."

He grinned. "I did. My name is Ethan. And you are?"

Were we really doing this? "I'm—" I hadn't thought about this before. Did I use my real name in college? People could easily google me and discover my backstory. Too risky. "Lil."

Worst. Spontaneous. Name. Ever.

"Lil?"

"Yeah, it's my rapper name," I joked.

"Like Lil Nas X? Lil' Kim? I like it." Well, he laughed at least.

It occurred to me that "Lil" paired with my last name, Lee, would end up with "Lil Lee"—pronounced . . . Lily.

Boy, was I an idiot.

Ethan pitched me on the Asian Student Association, the very organization in which I was VP of communications over a decade ago. Back then, we didn't have enough of an Asian population to form subgroups, such as Korean, Chinese, Japanese, and Filipino organizations, like other big universities had. I had hoped by now that those individual groups would have come to fruition.

I looked down the row of tables and didn't see a Korean Student Association. "So is the Asian Student Association the only Asian group at Carlthorpe?"

He shrugged. "Sort of? There's an official Chinese Culture Appreciation group. We have unofficial clubs like the Korean Pop Culture Stan Club, which I helped cocreate, and the Taiwanese Foodie Club, which I also founded—I'm half Korean, half Taiwanese. These smaller clubs don't have the numbers yet to secure organizational funding. We've been pushing hard to get that changed the last few years. I'm a fourth-year student now." Ethan smiled. "Are you a senior too? I haven't seen you around before."

And the first of the awkward conversations about my undergrad status had arrived: Did I come clean with my real situation, or play along that I was indeed a senior, with-out revealing more? On the most technical level, I was a fourteenth-year student. Omission wasn't necessarily lying, especially if it was for something minor and nonharmful like taking classes on campus to complete a degree, right?

"I took time off. It's my last year here, hoping to graduate this semester." All of this was true.

He grinned. Ethan was really cute for a young twenty-something-year-old. He was at the age where most guys were in peak form. Thick black hair, lean but muscular phy-sique, chiseled jaw, and bold fashion choices. He wore a fit-ted tee to reveal his dedication to the campus gym. If I was in college, I would be starry-eyed smitten. Well, I *was* in college, but you know, not like—

"Wait, aren't you in that CS class with Doc? I thought you looked familiar."

Oh wow, that had come right back to haunt me like a mur-derous machete boomerang. "Yeah, but . . . I'm trying to transfer into stats instead. CS isn't for me." *More specifically, awkward encounters with Jake Cho weren't for me.*

His right eyebrow shot up. "Wait, why? You got that free pass already for your first assignment. I was actually won-dering if you wanted to be my group partner. Well, one of my group partners. I have some friends in that class and we'd love to have you join. Please?"

I mean, how could I say no to this college-aged Daniel Dae Kim clone? "I'll think about it, I just came from the reg-istrar, the stats class is full anyway."

"Well, if you'd join us, I bet you'd want to stay. We have

study sessions in the Commons. Give me your number and I'll make sure you have the meet-up info."

I didn't remember making friends—or groupmates—so easily the first time around. Non beginner's luck, I guess.

"And while you're here, you sure you don't want to join ASA? We have our first meeting soon," he added with a smirk.

I blurted the words, "Maybe another time," even though *OH HELL NO!* was screaming in my head.

My phone buzzed with a text. Hi. It's Ethan. I'm standing right here heyyyoooooo

I tried to swallow a laugh but it came out anyway. He had an easygoing, goofy sense of humor.

Ethan smirked. "That's me. Oh, take a T-shirt. I can tell by your face that you're leaning toward no, but that doesn't mean you can't still enjoy free stuff." He handed me an XL men's tee.

I held the shirt by the shoulders and shook out the fabric. A gasp escaped me.

"What's wrong?"

I shook my head. "It's nothing. It's just that this tee is so soft and the logo is, um, neat." *Neat? Did college kids even say that?* I certainly didn't, unless I was at a bar and ordering a whiskey for Mia, which was why it was so bizarre it came out of my mouth.

The ASA logo featured prominently on the shirt was over ten years old. I knew, because I designed it.

Ethan examined the tee. "Yeah. The color logo is nice too. A few guys tried to redesign it, but the original looked better. It's simple but still stylized. A classic."

He held out his hand. Unsure of how to handle this inter-action, I extended my hand and timidly shook his. Ethan explained, "That's our handshake agreement that you'll be our group member in CS, at least until you officially aban-don us for stats. You'll round out our group to four people. It's a good number. And a good group."

I didn't see any harm in that. "Sounds neat. See you around." My shoulders scrunched to my ears as I walked away. *Neat? Again, Lily?*

Could I survive being in Jake's CS class? Not taking com-puter science in undergrad was always something I regret-ted, mainly because there were so many job opportunities for graduates with CS backgrounds. Was it possible to take the course and try to compartmentalize it, separating the class from my ex? Maybe this could be a good learning ex-perience. And a personal growth experience. So what if Jake was there? I didn't have to talk to him—back in college, I never talked to my TAs. I never went to office hours. And I still made okay grades . . . well, until senior year. Could Ethan and his friends ease my discomfort in a way that be-ing a lone person couldn't? So what if Jake was likely one of those nurturing, helpful, encouraging teaching types and I was missing out on my education by not engaging with him? All I needed was a passing grade.

It was nice to be asked to be part of a group. Throughout my entire life, being asked to join a group or team was al-ways flattering in some way. Someone wanted to be in my company, or, like in this case, wanted me for my brains. But maybe this was what I was missing out on the last time I was a senior.

I texted Ethan: When's the first group meeting?

Next week after class.
Welcome aboard!

With a slow smile spreading across my face, I headed back to the apartment.

# Chapter Eight

*Fourteen Years Ago*

**M**ore than anyone I knew, Mia was motivated by food. Specifically, free food, offered at organization and club meetings around campus. In one night, we had stopped by the Pre-Law Group, Anime Society, Christian Fellowship, and Irish Dance Troupe—chatting, mingling, grazing—and then left these get-togethers with our Tupperware containers and gallon-size Ziploc bags filled with enough snacks and pizza slices to last a full week, maybe even two. And that was the point: to supplement our meals so we didn't need to pay extra food expenses outside of the dining plan.

She looked at her notes on her phone. "One more to go. This way." Mia adjusted the shoulder straps on her overstuffed backpack and nodded toward the walkway, signaling me to follow her.

My messenger bag weighed down my right shoulder. I switched it over to the left one. "Don't you think we have enough? This two-liter you took from the LSAT study break session is taking up so much space. And the doctor at the Student Health Clinic says for me to lay off soda or anything acidic; he thinks that can help calm some of my stomach pain."

She stopped and looked at me. "They still don't know what it is?"

I waved my hand like I was shooing a fly. "The doctor basically said it could be an ulcer. Or GI distress from stress."

She asked, "Is that serious? Ulcers sound pretty bad."

"He said to pop antacids if it happens again, and to lay off coffee and alcohol. That sounds shitty, but manageable. Oh, and he told me to stop drinking my two Cokes a day." I pulled out the bottle and held it in my arms like a two-liter newborn. "I miss my baby."

Mia bit her lip. "Okay then, I'll carry it."

"Really?"

She nodded. "Unless you have urgent plans to drop Mentos in a perfectly good bottle of soda to make it explode in all your spare time? Yes, give it to me. I'll hold it, so you won't be tempted to drink any. We can use your bag for the ASA snacks. They're the best ones anyway. I heard they get their chips and candy from legit Asian markets. One of the parents drives them in once a month from New Jersey."

It was true, the Asian Student Association had the best snacks. Shrimp chips and soy sauce rice crackers were my favorites. The ski team met only once a month, but they had the next best, with their high-end baked goods and heated, snackable hors d'oeuvres.

She pointed to her right. "Peabody Hall. We're here. And we're a little early."

Mia took off her jacket and covered the bottle of Coke, which she cradled in her left arm. "Let's be quick with this one . . . sneak in and out so we can get back soon. I need to turn in some classwork tonight."

Fine with me. It was always Mia who was the one lingering longer than we needed to: maybe deep down she wanted to be a member of all of these clubs but didn't have the time to commit or the membership dues to join.

Because we had arrived before the meeting began, we were obligated to chat with other students and the nominated board members. Mia and I eyed the table in the back where they were just setting up refreshments.

"Hi, Mia. Lily. Glad you could join us today! We're kicking off the culture show planning. Would love for you to participate this year." Emily Chin, the ASA president, was a year above us but looked and acted ten years older. Or maybe Mia and I acted ten years younger, the way we smuggled snacks like two elementary school pranksters.

A hand reached over mine to grab the unopened cuttlefish chips at the same time I touched the bag. We both tugged. Neither party would let go. Cuttlefish chips were the ultimate prize snack, and there was only one package. That meant one winner of this tug-of-war.

I responded to the stare of my opponent with a glower. "Should we do rock paper scissors then?"

He laughed. "Can I declare a thumb war instead?"

I pursed my lips to suppress a smile. "I prefer a dance-off."

Though we were joking around, neither of us were loosening our grip. This standoff might last all night.

Mia came by with a roll of kimbap and fried mandu on a paper napkin in one hand. The two-liter was still in the crook of her left arm. "Want some?" she asked me.

I shook my head no. Other ASA members were stopping by the snack table, opening bags of chips and crackers and pouring small portions on their plates.

"We could share," he said. "If you let go, I promise to pour only a few on my plate. You can have the rest."

I made eye contact with Mia. She shrugged. Apparently she wasn't as dead set on getting these snacks into my messenger bag as we'd originally planned. She'd gotten sidetracked by the prepared food. Understandable. But cuttlefish chips were my favorite, and I hadn't had them in a few months.

"I'm Jake Cho by the way. Originally from Dallas, but grew up in New Haven. A first-year student." The way he was speaking to me reminded me of how people try to talk to serial killers to humanize themselves so they don't become the next murder victim.

I answered softly. "I'm Lily Lee. I'm a first-year too."

It worked. Maybe it was his calm words. Or his lopsided smile, which paired really well with his boyish face. I eased my grip and Jake pulled, or rather yanked, the bag from my hand. After quickly tearing open the package, he poured a handful of chips into a paper bowl.

"Lily Lee, the rest are yours. As promised." He grinned and handed me the bag of approximately five remaining servings. "I'm a man of my word."

I happily ate my chips straight from the bag as the meeting came to order. "Should we leave now?" I asked Mia.

She wadded up her napkin and opened the bottle of room-temp Coke. As it expelled a long, menacing hiss, I winced and hid behind her.

"Want a small sip? Are you allowed?"

"Nah." We stayed through the meeting and after it ended, she and I looked at the sign-up form for the culture show. We weren't involved in many campus life activities—we were too busy floating by numerous organizations and clubs in our limited spare time, but for dietary and culinary reasons only. When I saw the list of volunteers and noticed Jake Cho's name on it, something inside me changed. A pull. A tug. Then a gentle easing of the tight grip around my heart. I pulled out a pen and added my name and email address to the form.

Mia skimmed the sign-up sheet and smiled at me. "Ah. I gotcha. You can add me too if you want."

# Chapter Nine

S tupid key.
 Stupid lock.

After thirty seconds of jiggling, wiggling, and profanity-shouting, the door flung open.

"ROOMIE! How've you been? The weather is so nice today!"

"Hey. Sorry for all my racket. Had trouble with the key again." I moved past Beth and plopped down on the couch.

"Two things, Roomie. One, we're backpack twins! I can't believe we have the same one! Let me guess, Amazon's top choice for back-to-school? Gray JanSport for the win! A school classic, like good old-fashioned Coca-Cola, am I right?"

When I didn't reply and got up from the couch, she followed me all the way to my room. "Second thing, your friend is here. Mia, the Awkwafina look-alike. And I'm not saying that because I don't know what I'm talking about, she dead-on looks like my girl Nora."

It was true, Mia was mistaken for Awkwafina all the time. She loved it, or hated it, depending on her mood.

"Mia's here?" I pulled out the free ASA T-shirt from my backpack and handed it to Beth. "Here, you can have this."

She unrolled the tee and then hugged it to her body. "I appreciate your generosity. Thank you."

What she didn't know yet was that I had a nearly identical shirt that I slept in, albeit rattier and worn in the ringed collar, left over from my college days. It was one of my few mementos from that era. My heart swelled with pride knowing that my T-shirt design had lasted so many years and the logo was still used by the organization.

Beth asked, "Do you think having the same backpack is like a personality test? Because it combines a lot of things, like color affinity, price sensitivity, and other attributes. Personally, I think if anything, it means we're a lot alike and meant to be BFFs."

I shrugged. "Or it could simply mean that Amazon served us the same ad that we both clicked on, right?"

She tilted her head. "But that also would mean that we had a similar profile for the Amazon algorithms to say, 'Aha! These people are likely to click on this because we have a shit ton of data on them and they basically have the same tastes.'"

Beth had a point. Damn, she was right about how algorithms work. I bought my backpack a few weeks ago, so we weren't even sharing the same IP address, therefore I couldn't explain it with that. Beth was smart and insightful for such a young person. Who knew, she could possibly be my white soul sister backpack twin. A shiver traveled down my spine as I literally shuddered at the notion that boisterous Beth was more like me than I had thought. She veered away to the bathroom as I turned the doorknob to my room. Mia sat cross-legged on my bed, drinking a White Claw. "How was school, dear? Did you make any new friends?"

I groaned. "You wouldn't believe me if I told you. I need that drink."

She handed it to me. "You hate White Claw. That bad, eh? Now I'm curious."

"I saw Jake." I took a swig and burped, remembering why I hated the Claw.

Her jaw hung open. "What? How? Did you kick him where it counts? Did he not finish his degree either?"

I coughed on my next sip. "No, I took the high road and didn't punch him in the nuts. Not finishing college is uniquely my failure. But yeah, I saw him, and somehow restrained myself from ball kicking."

"So . . . what's he look like now? Hot or not? Swipe left or right?"

My memories flashed from earlier that day. His handsome face. Muscular chest. Sardonic smile. That hair I badly wanted to tangle my fingers in, and those ripped arms pushing against the fabric of his T-shirt.

"Your scrunched face suggests he's either super attractive or the exact opposite. I'm guessing . . . hot . . . or you would be in a much better mood. Did you catch up with him? Why is he on campus?"

"He's my TA," I squeaked.

She yelped. "For your TikTok class?"

I rolled my eyes. "It's called Building a Global Audience and Influencer Culture, thank you very much, and I told my mom I'd take this course to help my career. But the Jake class is for the new STEM requirement for liberal arts majors, and if I pass, it happens to complete my degree. He's the TA for the computer science class, and getting a PhD, if you can believe it. I actually saw him at the market the other day but didn't realize it was him."

"Holy shit." She fell back into a cushion. "That's a lot to take in." She grabbed the White Claw can from me and chugged. "Random question, does he dress like a grown-up now? He wore sleeveless shirts and basketball shorts year-round. I can't picture him in khakis, or whatever wannabe professors wear."

A laugh burst out of me. "He's going with a half glow up. He wears regular adult clothing on top, but still rocks his shorts on the bottom."

She grinned. "Good for him."

"I'm hoping he'll ignore me and not acknowledge that I'm in his class. But I might drop it anyway. I think it's going to be hard." I sighed.

"Taking a CS class *does* sound hard, but I know you'll do well in your courses. You know what they say about graduating, right? Cs get degrees. So don't stress yourself out. I know how you can get, overworking and winding yourself into a tight ball of worry, and you need to make sure you keep things in check, per your therapist's orders."

She was right, of course. According to my therapist, I needed to try to find balance. My external validation mental model affected my self-esteem, which as of late was in a precarious state thanks to my incapability of meeting my next book deadline and being so wrongfully confident in my Carlthorpe alumna status. I needed to work on getting my life back in order, in as mentally healthy a way as possible.

Mia asked, "So back to Jake, are you two good? Did you make up after . . . you know? I honestly don't remember how you eventually left things."

How did we leave things? Badly. That's how. He quit on me when I needed him the most, and I could never forgive him for that. I never returned his calls or emails when he wanted to apologize later. Maybe I should have responded, because now karma was truly being a supreme bitch. I closed my eyes and took a deep breath, which came out as an annoyed sigh.

"So not good." Mia read me like a book.

"Not good," I confirmed. "Let's change the subject and change locations." We stood and she followed me to the living room.

I asked, "Remind me why you're here? I thought you were coming here only on weekends."

"I wanted to be your emotional support animal your first week, and I miss having you around. Also, my apartment is being painted and I didn't realize how disruptive that could be. There are all these plastic sheets everywhere, like a fucked-up serial killer set up shop. And something else, I was just about to message you. The O'Hara twins are going to be on CNN tonight."

Mia grabbed the remote from the coffee table, pressed the Live TV button, and set it back down.

"And why are we watching this? To torture me?" I took the can from her hand again and chugged the rest of the White Claw.

"Other than to hate-watch, we need to do research on your competition and figure out how they're pitching the book so you can learn from it."

I leaned forward and pulled a few Ruffles from the nearly empty bag in Mia's lap. Delicious, but way better with French onion dip, which I'd polished off earlier in the week.

"And what if I still don't want to watch, even as a learning opportunity?" I asked.

She sighed. "Okay, full confession, I was planning for this to be, like, ten percent learning exercise, the rest . . . a petty bitch snark session. You know, a pick-me-up."

"Is this really what we've come to? Eating chips, drinking White Claw, and making fun of the O'Haras?"

"Yes!" Mia said with zero hesitation. "Especially if they're being featured on TV using a book concept that's nearly identical to yours, basically stealing your idea, saying *you* inspired them. And *especially* if one of the coauthors is a mansplainy dude writing about women in the workplace."

Beth came out of her bedroom and sat on the nearby rocking chair. "I have to agree with Mia, if they really stole your idea, that's savage." She smiled at me. "Sorry, I was eavesdropping. I'm so glad you're my roomie. I know you're all famous and all, but I'm relieved you're, like, a normal person. And so what if you have friends who visit us unannounced." She looked over at Mia. "I mean that in the best way possible, you're like the neighborhood stray cat who shows up on the porch. But everyone feeds her, because we all love her and could use her company, because let's face it, we're all a little bit lonely sometimes."

And with that bizarre yet profound comment, she turned up the volume on the remote just as Cameron O'Hara appeared on-screen with the caption "Cameron O'Hara, co-author of the trailblazing *You Go, Girl!* book, up next" running along the bottom.

My phone buzzed with a notification. It was Amanda, with a late-night friendly reminder about my overdue manuscript. She also attached the original contract, with highlighted excerpts of all the paragraphs related to the deliverable dates cut and pasted in the email, making it painfully clear I had missed the deadline. As I quickly skimmed the document to see if there was any wiggle room with the date, my heart nearly stopped when I came to the indemnities section, which I hadn't paid attention to before because it hadn't been a concern . . . until now. Specifically, the part that read in bold: **The Author has not misrepresented academic or other credentials and will not provide any false or materially misleading documents concerning the work . . .**

My stomach dropped. "Ohhhhhh shit-shit-shit-shit-fuck."

Mia grabbed the phone from my hand. Her eyes widened

when she came across the same section. "Ohhhhhh shit-shit-shit-shit-fuck is right. Does your editor know anything about what's going on with you?"

I shook my head, speechless from this discovery.

She read the email. "Okay, well, it doesn't look like this Amanda person knows about your situation and isn't calling you out on this. Maybe no one has to know. Maybe you can lay low and say you're at some kind of solo writing retreat and unreachable to the outside world. I can update your social media so it says you're taking a break or something."

My shoulders sagged. Amanda was a stickler for the rules, and if she found out I never actually graduated from Carlthorpe, the publisher could take back my advance and cancel my contract. It said so in bold Times New Roman twelve-point font. The other big problem, other than the sheer embarrassment of being a career advice expert and not having a Carlthorpe degree to my name, was that I'd used my entire advance to pay for these college classes. If they took that back, I would go into serious debt, and that in turn would affect my credit score, and . . . oh God . . .

Mia looked me straight in the eyes. "Look, it's only four months. You can come clean and tell your publisher what's happening, but honestly I think you can manage to not draw attention to yourself in that time, right? Just get through your classes and focus on passing them, turn in some pages and ask for feedback, and stall a bit. If you don't get your degree, everything you've built these years will blow up big-time. No advance, no contract, no career."

I swallowed hard and nodded. As a PR professional, Mia

was an expert in crisis management. She was right, that focusing on my schoolwork would get me my degree, and then my background check would clear. Leaning back into the couch, I briefly contemplated coming clean to my editor. But the contract I signed was crystal clear, and I'd recently committed a blatant violation by approving my author bio for the publisher's website.

It was only four months. Then I could tackle all the issues other than the completion of my college degree. Dealing with one problem at a time was a reasonable approach. Maybe I'd get lucky and in four months all these problems would go away.

Beth handed me a fresh can of White Claw. "You'll probably need that more than me."

Mia booed when the O'Haras came on-screen for the interview. "They called them *trailblazing* in their introductions. Trailblazing, my ass!"

A perfect distraction to my "damned if I do, damned if I don't" dilemma. The O'Haras. People like Cameron O'Hara were born to be on national cable news shows. Poised and perfectly groomed, he answered the interviewer's questions with polish and ease, something I wished came naturally to me. And when asked the question I hoped would stump him, it didn't. "You want to know why this book is groundbreaking? Well, for one, you get a glimpse into the O'Hara mogul life, which we've closed off for the sake of privacy up until now. We rarely even have Warren and Mark over to talk shop. Oh, that's Warren *Buffett* and Mark *Zuckerberg*, for your viewers. The other way our book is revolutionary is that we share the perspective of women via my sister's point of view, and then you have mine, someone who cares deeply about helping people like my sister succeed."

Mia shouted at the television. "Gross, you just admitted to nepotism, you loser!"

I couldn't help but laugh at her outburst. "Can we turn this off please? I've heard enough, and seeing as how you pounded the bag of chips with both fists so there are merely potato particles now, you may have hit your douche bro limit today."

We all scrambled to find the remote, which each of us swore we were not in possession of, and my ears perked up at Cameron's casual mentioning of my name.

"Lily Lee's book really got our attention, making us realize there are so many people Mary and I can help, and we didn't know there was a market for it until Lily's book came along and so many people bought it. We loved her 'everyday woman' approach to content, with interviews and surveys of women in middle and upper management, and cute graphics on every page. But we wanted to create motivational books for *serious* women invested in taking their careers to the next level. Not that there's anything wrong with Lily's fun approach." His words made my stomach lurch and drop. My book was frothy and frivolous in his mind, whereas his was a canon masterpiece.

But then his next comments slapped me in the face. "Our book includes sections about prominent thought leaders, written by, well, thought leaders. You want a career guide written by successful, leading business experts. That's the main difference between our book and others on the shelves."

It was clear that by *others*, he meant mine.

Yes . . . in the first book of my series I included surveys and interviews with highlights and sound bites. I added voices other than my own to offer perspective and experiences about management and leadership broader than just mine. And yes, there were graphics and eye-catching designs within the pages, which the publisher thought would draw in a lot of new readers, and they were right. But what Cameron had just said on the evening news in front of millions of viewers was essentially "Lily Lee is a nobody. And she wrote a book for nobodies."

I shook my head. "That dirty little—"

Beth let out a primal scream into one of her I'M 100% SUNSHINE & CAFFEINE cross-stitched throw pillows. Then she lodged all the cushions on the couch at Cameron's face. "I'm never one to talk trash about a person, but that guy is a huge bona fide butthole. And trust me, coming from me that's saying something."

"Bona fide butthole is right." Mia managed to find the remote under her ass and turned off the television. "Well, if that's not motivation to get back out in the work world and write your next book, Lily, I don't know what is. Fuck that guy."

Yeah. Fuck that guy. "You're right. If you'll excuse me, I have a homework set to do tonight and a book to write."

I thought Jake being my TA would be challenging enough,

but even more problematic would be stepping away from publishing and letting the O'Haras be the loudest career expert voices out there.

No. I couldn't let that happen. Shutting my bedroom door, I downloaded the CS textbook onto my computer and started the required reading.

## Chapter Ten

E ach time I stepped foot on campus, I marveled at how different its picturesque scenery was from the hustle and bustle of Manhattan. The abundance of oak, maple, and ginkgo trees lining the main pathway made for an idyllic campus setting. Some of the green leaves had dulled, turning a soft yellow, and the mingling of orange, red, and brown would soon follow.

I zipped up my jacket. Fall had officially arrived.

Heading to class early gave me time to refamiliarize myself with and appreciate the campus setting: the inscriptions in Latin on the Corinthian columns of the library; the bas-relief carvings of Athena, Demeter, and Zeus in the central fountain; and the weather-worn pale green copper roofs of the oldest brick buildings that had made me fall in love with the school the first time around. Seeing them now as a super senior (the super-est in all of Carlthorpe history, probably) filled me with a complicated mix of pride, humility, and shame. I liked being back on campus, but also hated it. As classes approached the end of the second week, I had settled into the idea that there were nearly fifteen more weeks remaining of this temporary life diversion, and then I could go back to the way things were.

Fifteen more weeks of my overly excitable roommate.

Fifteen more weeks of homework and studying.

Fifteen more weeks of circumnavigating Jake Cho.

*You can do this.*

I found a seat near Ethan, who had arrived just before me. "Is this taken?" I asked.

He smiled. "It's all yours. Saving these other ones." To his right, he had his sweatshirt in the next spot and a flannel button-down two seats over.

"Do you normally disrobe this much for the sake of your friends?" I looked at the shirt draped over a wooden seat and back to his short-sleeved black tee. "Aren't you cold?"

He laughed. "Yes and yes. I'm lucky I wore enough layers today but they better show up soon or I might get hypothermia. And you're lucky I have only two friends in this class other than you. It could have gotten ugly. There's not much clothing left." Ethan's brown, sparkling eyes crinkled on the outer edges, giving him a more mature look. But older in, like, a twenty-six-year-old way.

He pulled an extra-large energy drink from the side pocket of his backpack, along with an individually wrapped cinnamon roll. "Want a bite?"

Ah, to have the metabolism of my younger self. "No thank you, appreciate the offer. I just had a big breakfast." It was a bowl of overnight oats plus a handful of blueberries. Because that was what thirty-two-year-old women ate who were well past the energy drink and store-bought iced pastry days.

If he had offered me a travel cup of coffee, I would have accepted. Beth didn't have a coffee machine, and in New York I had always gotten my caffeine fix from the breakfast truck stationed outside my apartment in the mornings. Oscar knew my order: iced coffee, two pumps of chocolate syrup, with enough 2% milk till it turned beige. Never once did Oscar judge me for my coffee, which was essentially coffee-flavored chocolate milk. He had it ready for me every day at eight thirty Monday through Friday, rain or shine, sleet or snow. Oscar was more reliable than the mailman. When I told him I was moving away for a few months, he teared up, wished me well, and offered me a free blueberry muffin as a parting gift.

It suddenly occurred to me that Oscar was one of the few people I'd spoken to candidly about my departure. I hadn't even come clean to my editor yet. Or to my parents. Why had I confided in this man I barely knew, but not in those people closer to me? What did that say about them? And . . . what did that say about me?

I reached into my bag and pulled out my phone. Missed messages from Mia.

Have you thought about doing college activities? I'm looking on the Student Life webpage and they have pickleball. YOU MUST DO PICKLEBALL

NO PICKLEBALL

Broomball? Inner tube water polo?

NO and NO

Well think about your options.
You've been given a second
chance. We're hoping you
won't get a third lol

She added: Give it a good ol' college try. Har har. Okay I'll
shut up now

I sent her an eyeroll emoji and put my phone away.

Out the classroom window, you could see the grassy central lawn, where dozens of college kids sat in small groups
on blankets, eating, lounging, and conducting outdoor seminars, just as students had when I was an undergrad. It was
a strange feeling to be back at campus now, seeing firsthand
how different college was in some ways, and how entirely
unchanged it was in others.

"Hey." The smooth tenor voice coming from the aisle
caused me to freeze. I knew who it was without looking up.

"Oh God," I accidentally muttered aloud.

"Miss Lee, can you meet with me after class today, if
you're free?"

Chin still tucked and looking down at my backpack, I
bobbed my head and avoided direct eye contact, focusing

more on steadying my breathing rather than watching Jake whisk himself away.

Inhale. Hold. Long exhale.

Ethan joked, "Hey, teacher's pet! After you meet with the TA, come by the Commons so we can grab an early lunch with the rest of the group. We're going to talk about the first group assignment."

I looked up to see Jake sprinting to the front of the classroom. As he set up the computer and projected the first slide on the pull-down screen, I studied his pensive face, his swift movements, his confident stature while he logged in to the class portal. What did he want to talk to me about, and why had he singled me out the way he did?

Well, I could think of reasons. Like asking me why I was a student in his class.

Why I hadn't tried to communicate with him after all these years.

Why I had reentered and disrupted his orbit and why he'd come crashing into mine.

You know, just a few off-the-cuff thoughts flooding my brain.

Ethan jumped to his feet, abruptly breaking my Jake-induced trance. His hand shot up, signaling to two people who had just walked through the back doors to join him. After putting his flannel shirt back on, he took his backpack off the neighboring seat.

I asked, "Oooh. Am I about to meet the people you're willing to strip for?"

He chuckled. "Yes! Finally, you get to meet your group project buds." He reached out, grabbed the hand of the guy walking toward him, and pulled his friend in for a hug, like he hadn't seen him in ages. I pictured Jake and me doing this after class and laughed out loud.

"Sorry, was just thinking about something stupid." Remembering I had to stick with the dumb name I'd given Ethan, I added, "I'm Lil, Ethan's new friend."

"I'm Princeton. Princeton Li." He shook my hand and noted my surprise. "My parents named me after their alma mater. Naming a kid after an Ivy League school to fulfill their own dreams and then getting waitlisted there isn't all too great for the ol' self-esteem, I have to admit. And Li is spelled L-I, like Long Island." He said that last part with an exaggerated New York accent.

"I'm sorry, can we actually go back to the Princeton thing? I'm still needing to process that. That's on your birth certificate and everything?" I asked.

He laughed at my reaction. "It's okay, I'm surprisingly fine with it now. I've been going by PJ too, because people get all weird about saying Princeton over and over. Either works."

"What's the 'J' stand for? Johns Hopkins?" I joked.

"Jing actually," he sassed back. "Thank God it's not Johns Hopkins . . . I'll save that for my own children."

I chuckled. "Your first and last name sounds like a fancy adverb. Princetonly. He handled his numerous social engagements in a *princetonly* fashion."

He laughed. PJ was such a good sport.

"I'm Grace." The girl next to him squeezed my hand and offered a firmer handshake than PJ's.

Ethan noted, "They're in ASA with me. And we promise not to keep trying to recruit you, although the more Asians, the merrier."

PJ groaned at Ethan's comment, which made me grin.

Grace asked, "Are you a transfer?"

I had toyed with the idea of acting like I'd transferred to Carlthorpe from somewhere else as a viable cover story, but I didn't want to add any more complexity to my life, seeing as how I had to go by Lil now because I couldn't think on my feet. How did pathological liars make stuff up so well and stay committed?

"It's a long story, but I used to go here, and now I'm back."

PJ said, "Oh, so you transferred out and returned."

Not at all. But I didn't want to explain myself. Luckily, I didn't have to, because while we were chatting, the professor had entered the room.

"Let's get settled so we can start on time, class!" Doc huffed as he made his way to the podium.

I had to admit, the first CS classes about making code easy to understand were interesting, and I couldn't wait to learn more. I loved how the professor was such a passionate teacher and gave interesting, real-world examples. Time flew by, and it wasn't until he checked his watch and said, "Oops, I've gone over, sorry about that. Class dismissed!" that I realized the hour-long class had ended. That's how good of a professor he was.

Ethan packed up quickly. "See you at the Commons, we'll

be in the back corner table working on this week's problem set. If the TA gives you any tips or cheats, you have to tell us, okay?"

The room dispersed, and I checked how I looked in selfie-mode on my phone before rising to my feet. I'd seen better days, but I looked presentable at least. Trudging toward the door, I thought about how there was no way to avoid my past while taking classes here again, and I knew it had potential to get messy. But Jake Cho as my TA . . . really? This was the universe giving me two middle fingers. One for Jake. One for Cho.

He was waiting for me right outside the auditorium.

To my surprise, he offered a wide smile when we made eye contact. Like, the corners of his mouth pulled up to his sparkling eyes, making my heart squeeze a little.

"My God, it really *is* you," he breathed.

"Yeah." My cheeks surged with heat from both anger and embarrassment.

We stood still, not knowing how to physically greet each other. A handshake would be awkward between two people who had seen each other naked. No hug—it would be too familiar and intimate.

And that left nothing, so we did that. Nothing. It was a huge relief.

He said, "I have so many questions. Wanna walk next door to the Commons and grab a coffee?"

"That seems fine," I answered. Our walking strides started out at different paces but after a few seconds he walked in sync with me.

Jake held open the door to the café. "I noticed your name when the class roster was published, but I never in a million years thought it would actually be you. I assumed it was another Lily Lee, but then I saw you with my own eyes." He gulped. "So . . . you're back at Carlthorpe? Is this for a new book project or something for your series?"

Wow, he'd revealed so much in just a few sentences. He'd kept track of me and my career this whole time?

I paused before passing through the entryway. What was the point in chitchatting like this? Surely this was as painful for him as it was for me. Why not be like two coworkers who accidentally hooked up at a holiday party and then had to see each other at work the next day? *Let's not do this, Jake.*

"It's a really *long* story. You might need to cancel classes for the week to hear the abridged version," I replied.

He smiled. "I have time." He got himself a black coffee and added a packet of sugar. "You still drink that coffee-flavored chocolate milk?"

He still remembered?

"I like my coffee that way." It was how I coped with not having two Cokes every day in college, and I never shook the habit.

Jake smirked. "It's very gross and endearing, which makes it memorable."

I couldn't resist a little dig. "And I see you're still keeping up with the latest shorts fashion?"

He stuck his right foot out. "This pair I'm wearing was on sale at REI. It has so many pockets that I lose everything in them."

"It's like the game Memory? Always opening and closing all the pockets?"

"Exactly." When the conversation drifted to awkward silence, he asked again, "So . . . you're here . . . because?"

I stared at the menu on the wall and took a while to order my drink. It gave me time to think about my answer. *It's none of your business*, I wanted to say, but the truth was, it *was* his business once I landed on his class roster. But until I could switch out of his CS course and into another STEM class, I was stuck with Jake as my TA. My goal at the moment was to end this conversation as soon as possible without seeming rude, and never talk to him again. And ideally also score a free iced coffee if I played this right.

The barista called out "Lila!" before I could respond to Jake. She placed my iced coffee on the counter. I took it and walked to the checkout line.

"Let me get it," he said, fumbling for his wallet for a few seconds too long.

"It's okay, I'll pay."

The clerk keyed in the codes for our drinks and I swiped my temporary ID.

BUZZ.

A giant X appeared on the card swiper. I swiped again, and was denied a second time.

She swiveled the monitor so I could see why the ID was rejected. "Photo expired." Pointing to the image on the screen, she commented, "You need to get another ID picture at the registrar."

Jake looked over my shoulder. "Oh wow, that's from over ten years ago."

It was a color photo from my senior year, when I had thick bangs, a smattering of forehead acne from said thick bangs, and a pre-Invisalign smile. At least I looked happy. Like someone who didn't know she would have to repeat college.

I couldn't even play this off. I was mortified, and I had no cash on hand.

Jake skirted around me and, with one quick move, swiped his card, and shoved his ID in his pocket. The monitor flashed with his TA credentials and a gorgeous photo of Jake 2.0 appeared. Strong jaw. Mischievous, borderline naughty smile. And God, that hair.

He grabbed both of our drinks before I could say anything. I followed him as the checkout clerk called out to me, "Don't forget to get a new picture, or this will keep happening to you."

*Trust me, lady, I'm getting this fixed right away. The last thing I needed was my senior year cherub, pimply face haunting me every time I used my dining points.*

"Don't feel bad. When I became a PhD student, they used my old undergrad photo for a while. Apparently the ID picture expires after a certain number of years, like a driver's license or passport. Needless to say, my picture wasn't nearly as flattering as yours." He was saying this to be nice, because he was not only cute in college, like he was now, but he was also one of those insanely photogenic people. He had angular features that weren't too sharp. Unlike me, where over time, my baby face had not only disappeared, but my jawline also never appeared. I had thought for so many years that when the baby fat on my cheeks melted away, my chin and jawline would reveal themselves. Ta-da! Well, no such luck.

Jake found a bistro table with two chairs situated near the front window. "Do you have time to sit? Only for five minutes, I know you're busy with your book stuff." For him to think I was here for research was certainly better than me explaining my actual situation, so I left it alone and didn't correct him.

To avoid staring into Jake's eyes, I took in the Commons surroundings as I drank my caffeinated chocolate milk. The Carlthorpe Commons was new, meaning it had been built over the last ten years, like the CS building. "This wasn't always here, right? What did it replace?"

"Yeah, it's newish. It replaced the old student center, remember that brick building that looked like a prison? This new complex is so much nicer: it's where most of the clubs meet now. You can book rooms using an online reservation system and there's plenty of space." I glanced at him while he took a long sip. His proximity sent chills down my spine, which I wasn't expecting at all after so many years. Meetings like this needed to be avoided at all costs.

One minute had passed. Just four more to go. Then it was adios, Jake.

He fidgeted with the coffee cup sleeve and stared intensely at the QR code on his drink. "I don't even know where to start, I actually rehearsed this last night and this morning, in case you said yes to meeting with me." He took a deep breath in and then spoke really fast. "I'm sorry about how we left things. How *I* left things. It's been over a decade and I . . . I'm just hoping that you can find a way to forgive me. And I know an iced coffee doesn't cut it, but it's a start, and I'm prepared to grovel and apologize and do whatever I can to get you to not hate me."

My fingers tingled, then went numb. I had no idea how to respond to this unexpected apology. My brain went blank and I couldn't think of anything to say. How was I supposed to answer after so many years of ignoring his calls and emails?

"J-just know that I've had a lot of time to think about everything between us and I feel like a total asshole. So if you can't find it in your heart to forgive me, I'd love to be able to have a cordial TA and student relationship. Again, I know that's a lot to ask. I'm rambling. I'm sorry."

The long, weighty pause that followed made me feel like my next words should really count.

"Okay."

"Okay, meaning . . . you're okay with forgiving me? Or okay to being genial this semester?"

"I don't know," I mumbled. This was a lot to take in, and he finally took notice.

"I didn't mean to put you on the spot. But thanks, Lily, for letting me speak my piece. I know I just sprung a lot on you." He offered an apologetic smile. "I'm glad to see you're doing well. After graduation I was so lost. I actually became an Uber driver using my friend's mom's minivan, if you can believe it."

His changing the subject was a relief. I let out a long breath while he continued. "For a while I made decent money too, but it got weird when people booked me to drop off large courier deliveries around town. At one point I was pretty sure I was transporting human organs or something, because the customer kept texting me and checking the whereabouts of the time-sensitive delivery of an Igloo container. That's when I decided to get a more stable job in data mining and data science."

"That's quite a jump, from organ delivery to data analysis. It's a hot field though," I noted. "Data analysis, not the organ transportation. How'd you even do that?"

"I started out at the bottom. First for a small start-up company, which used AI predictive language to help dudes write breakup letters or texts to their girlfriends so they would sound more loving and heartfelt. I wish I were joking."

My jaw fell. I didn't want to be interested in his past, but I couldn't help being intrigued by this. "That's despicable . . . but fascinating. So, like, a guy would pay for a service to help them craft these letters so they weren't so asshole-y?"

He nodded. "I worked on the apologetic language auto-completion. It's not my proudest professional moment. Breaking up that way would be shitty."

I shifted uncomfortably in my seat. *Speaking of that, are we really talking about breakups right now?*

My face must've read murderous because he changed the subject again. "After a few months I moved on to a junior data analyst role at a mattress company."

"Customer data? Or product data?"

His eyes widened. "I didn't expect you to be such a numbers nerd. Usually when I say I worked at a mattress company people make sleeping and snoring jokes."

I shrugged. "I'm a well-rounded nerd, thank you very much, I'm both a qualitative and quant type. And I always love bed talk."

As soon as I said it, I blushed.

Jake's cheeks reddened but he didn't look away. His dark brown eyes glinted as he smirked at my comment.

I cleared my throat. "So anyway, a mattress company. I would say tell me more about the business, but you're right, that actually sounds boring."

He leaned forward. "Well, hear me out. All of their mattresses were custom and used smart technology. So you could set preferences on firmness, base positions, temperature controls, you name it."

"That still sounds boring."

His eyes twinkled as he leaned forward, signaling there was more to come. "I knew everything about the customer. Sleeping habits, duration of rest, and even when they were having sex."

I nearly spat out my coffee. "You mean, how many times?"

He cocked his head. "Yes. And think about the type of data a mattress company could collect other than frequency."

"Duration?"

He raised a suggestive eyebrow.

"Um . . . vigor?"

His mouth pressed tight. "I shot up the ranks at that company because I was the best sex analyst around."

From the first moment I laid my eyes on Jake, long ago when we both grabbed a bag of cuttlefish chips at an ASA meeting, I'd been attracted to him. He was charming and boyishly handsome, and knew how to make me laugh, which was by far one of the most attractive features in a man. But as soon as he said "sex analyst," something inside me flicked the "on" switch, and just like that, he almost reeled me back in.

*No, Lily. No.*

He continued. "I learned a lot about security and privacy then, which is why I never put anything on the internet."

Well, this explained why he was essentially a ghost online.

"That's where I learned SQL and taught myself how to code. But I learned in an unstructured environment, where I had to do everything myself. I was good at what I did, but it was all homegrown. I knew that with proper instruction and guidance, I could do so much more."

"You want to dream big and be the best sex analyst in the universe," I said dryly, managing to keep a straight face.

He put the lid back on his drink. "Something like that. I'm good at it! I want to be the very best, and I want to teach the next generation of sex analysts."

I hated to admit it, but it felt good to joke around like in the old days. And for a fleeting moment, I'd forgotten why we'd broken up in the first place. Forgotten why I hadn't contacted him for all these years. But then I remembered he was my TA, and scooted back farther into my seat.

He tore a corner off his napkin and wadded it into a tiny ball. "There's also a selfish reason I'm back in school. I'm tired of working in the real world. All of my friends are married and having kids, or really far into their careers, and I felt like I was drifting. Not in an aimless, confused way. But I wanted to accomplish something and claim it as mine." He sighed. "Even with a PhD though, I still don't think I know what to do until I retire."

Did everyone our age feel like they weren't quite where they were supposed to be? I could definitely relate. "It's weird how you graduate and then they thrust you into the real world without any practical skills. And then before you know it, you're thirty-something, or older even, and wonder where all the time went. Wondering if you were doing what you were put on this Earth to do. Learning skills and hoping you're getting paid what you're worth."

He nodded. "That's why I was so happy to see that you became an author after vaulting to the top of the corporate ladder. I don't remember you taking English or journalism classes. And you definitely weren't a staff writer nerd for the college paper like I was."

He failed to mention he quit the paper after two semesters as he continued. "It's impressive, everything you're doing. Makes me think that it's okay to not just do one thing in life. Or that it's okay to try new things long after you graduate." His lips quirked up as he took a sip from his cup.

I sighed. "The career rat race is mostly just a rusty, squeaky old hamster wheel going nowhere."

He responded, "Truth."

Being an adult was hard, and you didn't get many chances to try different paths once you were on one. Sometimes changing meant giving something up, or being penalized by having to start at the bottom again. And as years passed, these trade-offs became less appealing, not to mention it was much harder to change direction after you turned thirty. I knew about this firsthand.

I assured him, "You might think it's cowardly to duck out of the never-ending corporate slog and try something new, but I think you're brave with your career change."

"Well, I think you're brave too."

My gaze traveled the room for any onlookers, to make sure no one was getting the wrong idea. Not that there was anything between us. Not anymore at least.

Most of the tables were occupied with clusters of students who were on their phones, not only ignoring Jake and me, but also disregarding one another. Over in the far back corner, I made eye contact with Ethan.

Oh no. I'd forgotten about him. Them. My CS group.

Icy cold prickles flooded my body, making me involuntarily shiver as a sense of guilt swept over me. I couldn't tell from Ethan's expression how he was reading this situation. Was it clear we were just TA and pupil, and nothing more? Was there anything to misconstrue? In any case, I needed to end my conversation immediately with Jake. It would be a bad idea to keep things too friendly and familiar between us. The last thing I needed to do was to kick up rumors and draw attention to myself.

I scooted back my chair and rose to my feet. "Thanks for the coffee and the walk down memory lane. I need to meet up with my group to work on the next assignment."

His smile fell. "Oh, I was hoping we could—" Jake saw me nervously glance over at Ethan's table. "Well, maybe another time. It was really nice seeing you again. If you need any help on the homework let me know. And if your group has questions about using VS Code on the SEASnet Windows Server, you can text me. Or stop by my office hours tomorrow. Room 1001011."

Right, I forgot about the binary code.

He texted his contact info and we pushed our chairs under the table. After saying our quick goodbyes, we parted ways.

I nearly tripped over my own feet as I rushed over to Ethan's table. "So sorry I'm late. I met up with Jake . . . er . . . Jacob. I knew him from a long time ago, we go way back. It's wild seeing him here at Carlthorpe. Anyway, what'd I miss?" I spoke with too much enthusiasm, a sign I was hiding something, or flat-out lying. *Calm the eff down, Lily.*

"We were just building the executable from the program," Grace said, smiling at me. "Except PJ, he was watching YouTube."

"Hey! I was browsing videos to see if anyone had posted content about this assignment or something similar, thank you very much. I'm sad to report that we're on our own for this one." He slammed his laptop shut and groaned.

Grace sighed. "Not every class is going to have a teacher's

edition textbook or video with answers." She rolled her eyes. "Can we just get this done so I can have the weekend free?"

Ethan cleared a section of the table so I could sit. "Have you had a chance to look at the assignment? It's harder than I thought it would be."

I flipped open my laptop, skimmed the syllabus, and clicked the link to the homework. "Looks like he's a stickler on the requirements. We can't include any extra files or misspell anything in our final deliverable. Yes, I understand what he's looking for."

PJ's eyes widened. "Wow, well, I'm glad you're with us. I think I'm in over my head."

We spent the next hour going over the assignment and making sure we were all meticulous and on the same page. The four of us worked really well together and each of us added something to the conversation. Although as far as comprehension went, I had the strongest affinity for the materials covered in the lesson, probably because one of the many hats I'd worn at my last corporate job was working as a liaison between the product and dev teams. One of the programmers had written their mantra on their depart-ment hallway: "We write slick, tight code!" It rang vaguely offensive to a few people at the company so they had to take it down, but I knew what they meant. And this class was all about simplicity, efficiency, and attention to detail. These were three things that I valued highly, especially in a work setting. The class material clicked with me, more than any coursework had in the past.

Ethan closed his laptop. "Homework done. Weekend free. This is amazing."

Grace asked me, "Do you mind if I ask you a few questions?"

I shrugged. "Sure, fire away."

She prompted, "So . . . are you getting a post-bac degree? I'm not saying you're old but—"

PJ sniggered while playing a mobile shooter game on his phone. "Wow, that's a rude question. And you kind of just did."

Ethan said unconvincingly, "Age is just a number, Grace."

Honestly, you'd think I was fifty-two and not thirty-two by the way they were talking. I was only ten years older, maybe eleven. When I was at my last company, I'd worked with interns and recent college grads every day and would like to think I could still carry myself in a nongeriatric fashion. They'd invited me to lunch and happy hours sometimes, which was the ultimate nod of approval, right?

Grace held up her hand to PJ's face, signaling for him to shut his trap. "Let me explain where I'm going with this, without your mansplaining."

PJ mimed that he was zipping his mouth, and he and Grace laughed together. Clearly they had a good relationship, and she could put him in his place when needed.

"Maybe you're right and my words came out wrong, let me try again with adding context. I went to Seoul International Prep, one of the expat schools in Korea where most of the teachers are from the States. I was born in Florida but moved to Seoul when I was four. I see myself as equally Korean and American, and I wanted to know if I should call you Lil or sunbae or unnie." She shot a look at PJ. "My question comes from a place of respect, not insult."

I'd been around Korean American people my entire life, mostly peers and elders, and I'd never been in such an awkward position where my being the oldest in a group would need clarity around honorific titles. Just as she didn't know whether to call me "older sister" or her "senior," I didn't know if calling all of them hubae, my junior, was appropriate now that this hierarchy issue had come up.

Mia was going to laugh her ass off when I told her about this. I couldn't believe this was happening to me.

"Well, I'm open to whatever you'd want, but I personally like to think of myself as a peer. And I know I've been pretty quiet about my reasons for being in the class, and I can share my long story another time, maybe over lunch soon? I promise it's innocuous, and not because I murdered someone at my last school and transferred here."

We continued to joke around, my answer seeming to placate the three of them. And it bought me some time to think about what parts of my background I was willing to offer up to people I didn't know well. The more people who knew about my circumstances, the riskier it was.

Grace said, "I'll call you Lil then!"

I let out a small groan. "Actually, could you all please call me Lily? That's also another part of the story that I'll explain later."

She smiled. "I'm okay with that. Are you taking classes in the college or in the School of Professional Studies?"

"Just college. I have the CS class with all of you, the sta-tistics course I've been auditing is in the college program too, and so is my Building a Global Audience and Influencer Culture elective sociology class." It wasn't as rigorous for me as my other coursework, and I figured I could keep it as a buffer in case the dean was wrong again about my degree completion requirements.

Grace asked, "Why are you auditing the stats class?"

I bit my lip and looked at Ethan. How forthcoming could I be with these new classmates? "I'm hoping someone drops out so I can enroll. It's a course that covers things I al-ready know from my last corporate job—surveys and data analysis—so it would probably be an easy A." What I left out was that I would drop out of CS if I got into stats. No need to alarm anyone.

PJ threw his phone on the table. "My battery died." He looked at Ethan. "So I guess we meet up for the next assign-ment next week? Same time, same place?"

Ethan stacked our trash on his tray. "Yes, unless you have something better to do."

As I got up from the table, my knees cracked loudly, like the first kernel exploding inside a microwave bag of pop-corn. They never did that in my twenties. I was officially "snap-crackle-pop joints" years old.

When someone's stomach growls, people usually pretend they don't hear, and these new friends of mine extended the same courtesy with my cracking knees. Not only did my buddies have quiet joints, but all three also had sky-high metabolisms. Ethan and PJ had each inhaled two slices of pizza and a jumbo Coke, leaving only a few bites of crust, while Grace ate a full burrito with sour cream and guacamole, then washed it all down with a strawberry lemonade.

Outside, I waved to them. "I'll see you in class." Ethan and PJ went to the library, Grace headed to the gym, and I walked to the registrar to take a new photo and get a new ID.

On my way home, I snapped a picture of my new badge and sent it to Mia. It was so bad I knew she'd get a kick out of it. It was like they took my cringy old senior year ID photo and used age progression software to add ten prison years. As I turned the key for the front door, my phone buzzed.

Mia. Hottest 32 yo undergrad student on campus!

Mia again. Eat your heart out, Jake Cho

*Yes, eat your heart out, Jacob.*

## Chapter Eleven

The kitchen countertops were entirely covered with dirty dishes, used pots, and Pyrex casserole containers. An absolute mess. The Brita water pitcher I needed was nowhere to be found, so I filled my water bottle from the sink instead.

"Do we need to talk about this, Roomie?" I joked, gawking at the disarray.

Beth wiped her hands on her SPIRITUAL GANGSTER apron and lifted a glass baking pan to show me her latest culinary masterpiece. "I made cherry yum yum. It's a Southern and Midwestern thing." She had also made oatmeal chocolate chip cookies. Pecan bars. Chex Mix muddy buddies. All littering the kitchen table and stovetop. "I'm procrasti-baking," she explained. "Feel free to have whatever you want. The rest will be for my friends, my study groups, and for the variety treat packs I sell on campus. People love them, especially around exam time."

I could see why homemade treats would go over well with college students. Especially those who stress-snacked or smoked weed and consequentially had voracious appetites.

"Try my latest creation!" She grabbed a bowl and a giant metal spoon and scooped some of the fruity, fluffy dessert from the rectangular glass container. I couldn't help but notice a corner section was missing. Beth was probably taste-testing. "This is a no-bake recipe, and it needs to be refrigerated, so eat it up fast!"

I was so used to being around people my age who were heavily focused on extreme health consciousness and dietary limitations, so this was such a treat for me. I grabbed a fork from the dish rack and stabbed at the dessert with the prongs. It was soft, with the consistency of tiramisu.

On the far end of the counter, she had already started bagging and tagging her baked treats in cellophane. Looking at the vast number of baked goods around me and the rate at which she was packaging them, it was evident that Beth was no novice in monetarily beneficial baking.

I took a big bite. Mmmm, creamy, delicious goodness, like a cherry cheesecake and a cream pie had a tasty baby. My favorite pie is key lime, mainly because I love graham cracker crusts, and this dessert had that too. Basically, this was the perfect dessert.

As if she could read my mind, Beth said, "It's easy to make too. You don't need to bake anything so I can make it anytime. I knew you'd love it!"

I did. And because I loved it, I devoured the entire bowl.

She sealed the glass dish with a lid and placed the cherry yum yum on the bottom shelf of the fridge. I eyed the location for future reference. "It should last three or four days. My boyfriend comes this weekend and he can finish off what you don't eat."

"Thanks for making that for us. It was so good."

"Mia said the same thing. That makes me so happy!"

I raised an eyebrow. "Wait, Mia had some? She's here again?"

As if on cue, Mia walked in, yawning with her arms stretched above her head. She was wearing a crop top with the words I'M A FUCKING POLLYANNA across her chest. She grabbed a pecan bar and chewed away, not providing any explanation as to why she was here during the school week.

I cleared my throat, hoping I wouldn't have to verbalize my "why the hell are you here on a weekday, BFF?" confusion.

Mia held up her last pecan bar morsel, like she was toasting the room. "These are fucking amazing." She popped it in her mouth and rubbed her hands together, signaling that she'd finished it off. "Anyway, to answer your telepathic question, I came here to ask you to write some essays about job hunting and career limitations that I could pitch to magazines and newspapers. My fashion and tech start-up founder clients don't like writing as much as you do, but these print and online opinion pieces help build their credibility. I think you should try it. Even if your book isn't ready, and won't be for a while, we can continue to establish you as a subject matter expert to those who might not have discovered your books yet."

The egg timer dinged and Beth took brownies out of the oven. While setting down the baking pan, she said,

"Confession . . . I finally googled you. Well, I looked you up before when I found out I was getting a new roomie, but at the time it didn't really sink in that I would be sharing an apartment with a critically acclaimed nonfiction author. But I looked up your book and to Mia's point, no one in my generation has heard of you. No offense."

Mia poured herself a glass of water from the Brita that had miraculously reappeared. "And that's exactly the right point. The O'Haras might have their audience figured out, but you have room to expand your readership into this younger market—the people who are just starting out rather than seasoned professionals. You can provide guidance for the younger folks early in their careers so they're prepared for what's ahead."

I nodded. "Makes sense. But my ESP is telling me that's not the only reason you're here. You could have easily messaged that to me or hopped on a video call."

She waved an oatmeal chocolate chip cookie at me. "Okay, fine. I missed you, okay? We've basically been joined at the hip in New York for a whole decade and you leaving me was like sending a kid off to college or something." She nibbled her treat. "And this one here"—she nodded her head toward Beth—"you always have good eats. And I know what you're thinking, and yes, I am driving a long way to hang out with you and currently freeloading, but in exchange I offered Beth a *lite* version of my PR services, and she agreed. I'm designing flyers and getting a QR code set up for her foodie enterprise."

Mia was hard-edged and gave off cranky-pants vibes

twenty-four/seven, but she was like a wild porcupine: a misunderstood creature, because it was actually possible to pet one, as long as there is mutual trust, gentleness . . . and food. Mia had a heart of gold, and the stomach of a college heavyweight wrestler. And now she was helping Beth build her business too, even though she had a lot on her plate.

"Well, I guess I should actually finish up homework that's due tomorrow. Then I can see about those things you want me to write."

While Mia and I chatted, Beth put aluminum foil on all the baked goodies and let out a long breath when she was done. Then her face perked up. "Oh! I forgot to tell you, the Wi-Fi is better and cheaper now. I banded together with other students who live in this building and we all chipped in for Verizon Fios. So now we are on a crazy-fast fiberoptic network with way better reliability. I put the password on a sticky note on your bedroom door. We also share Google Home and Nest camera networking too." There was a Google Home device already in my room when I arrived but I hadn't asked it to do anything. I never tried to talk to it. I didn't even know if it worked. Back in New York, I used to ask mine what time it was, what the weather was like, and sometimes to play music from my playlists. It would be good to have that set up again.

Mia refilled the water pitcher. "I hope it's okay that I brought my overnight duffel. And a sleeping bag. And my pillow."

I laughed. "Mi casa es su casa is the apartment motto, according to Beth."

Mia's lips upturned into a wide grin. "I'll be quiet while

you both do homework, I have some work to do tonight for
a client's launch next month."

We took a few cookies and headed back to my bedroom.
The handwritten Wi-Fi password on the Post-it was almost
thirty characters long, and a mix of uppercase, lowercase,
and numerals. And zeros that looked like O's. And ones that
looked like I's. It took a few tries, but I finally connected to
the network. I handed Mia the sticky note but she shook her
head.

"I already entered it earlier today when I arrived. I'm
connected already."

*Mi casa es Mia's casa.*

For a couple of hours, all you could hear was our typing.
After being on my own for a couple of years, it was almost
like being back in an office setting, sitting in the same area
with a coworker. A coworker who happened to be my best
friend. And an office that happened to have an internet con-
nection with screaming-fast speeds and a really amazing
free bakery down the hall.

I finished answering discussion guide questions for my
influencer class, then printed it out to check for typos. This
assignment wasn't graded, but it would be used for a class
discussion. As the printer clicked and hummed, a barely au-
dible panting grew louder in our room. Mia looked at me.
I shrugged. We both abandoned what we were working on
to investigate: she opened the window to check outside, and
I stood on my bed, thinking the sound might be coming
from our neighbors upstairs through the air vents.

"Is that a dog?" Mia asked me.

"Oh! Ohhhhh! YES!" The panting abruptly stopped, re-placed by shrieking, shouting, moaning.

Mia shook her head and closed the window. I hopped off the bed. The sounds were coming from somewhere in my bedroom!

"YESSSSSS! There! Ohhhhh!" The screams, now unmis-takably close, originated from my dresser. The Google Home device next to my picture frames and jewelry box vibrated as the yelling grew louder and louder.

Someone was playing a porno on my Google Home.

I yelled, "Okay, Google. Knock it off!" and the room fell silent for a moment. But then a ding-dong sound came over the airwaves and the panting resumed.

Mia bellowed, "Okay, Google, stop! For fuck's sake!"

The whimpering, panting, and ass slapping disappeared. I threw open my door and stormed into the kitchen, where Beth was making streusel.

I tried to destress my voice. "Was that you? Playing a prank on Google Home?"

She stopped piping icing and cocked her head. "What are you talking about?" Beth wiped her hands and motioned for me to follow her to her room. Beyond her door, the porn sounds were back. She fumbled with the smart device and asked Siri on her Apple watch to call someone named Grady. But Siri didn't cooperate. Instead, she said, "I don't know what you mean by Grady-Oh-Oh-Oh-Yes-Mmmm-Yes. Right there."

I yanked the plug on her Google Home. Silence never sounded so good.

Beth called Grady on her phone and barked into the speaker, "We know you're watching porn. You're streaming it on Chromecast and it needs to stop NOW."

She kept the phone to her ear a few seconds and then hung up. "Grady apologizes. He's the mastermind behind the account sharing but obviously there are some glitches with our plan. We did it to save money but we might have to reconsider this group networking situation now that we've seen how this could go tragically wrong."

I laughed. "Well, on the bright side, thank God we weren't in a Zoom job interview." I still admired her for trying to find ways to be frugal.

Mia walked in. "Look, it wasn't *that* bad. My roommate from a few years ago tied tube socks to the top of her bed posts to keep them from banging the walls when she was banging her boss."

Beth gasped. "Did the socks work?"

"*That's* your question?" Mia shrugged. "Not really. And the posts made dents in the wall that cost us our entire security deposit. But that experience introduced me to the world of noise-canceling headphones. Best investment ever."

Beth turned to me and asked coyly, "Will *I* need to make a noise-canceling headphone purchase?"

"I don't normally watch porn on speakerphone at top volume," I replied.

"No, I mean, I saw you around lunchtime with a hot guy at the Commons. I didn't want to say anything yet, but now that we're having girl talk—"

I cut her off. "Well, I don't know how we went from Google Home porn to this, but Jake and I are not—"

"Wait, you had a secret lunch with Jake?" Mia slugged my arm. "How did you not tell me about this? I thought you were going to dropkick his ass to Mars! But honestly, if he's just a fling and he's hot, I say *get it*, girl. Seize the fucking day!"

"I'm not having lunch with anyone, secret or otherwise." I crossed my arms. "Jake wanted to grab coffee and apologize. He asked for it to be civil between us, that's all. And I cut it short because of this exact problem, I didn't want people to get the wrong idea."

Mia raised an eyebrow. "I hope there was groveling and a promise of extra credit or something. And no shade if you want to hold this grudge until you die. I'd respect that."

Beth nodded. "Me too. So okay, you and the cute TA are *not* an item. But how about you and that other attractive guy you were in a group with?"

Mia slapped my arm again. "Seriously? Another guy?"

I sighed. I knew who she meant. "That other guy is Ethan. He's just a friend, and the group is only using me for my brains."

Mia looked pensive. "A brainiac angle could work. He uses you for your brain, you use him for his—"

Shaking my head hard, I said, "Nope. He's ten years younger. Not gonna happen."

Beth's eyes widened. "Have you learned nothing from Nick Jonas and Priyanka Chopra Jonas? Age doesn't mean poop these days."

"I don't know how to break this to you, Beth, but I'm no Priyanka Chopra in the looks department. The only thing we have in common is our height and that we both love posting photos of roti. And we both favor our right side in photos. She works her ass off though, which I admire."

Mia peeled up the foil on one of the aluminum trays. "You know way more about Priyanka than I thought. It's a little weird."

She offered me a pecan bar, which I accepted. Beth grabbed a cookie and we all raised our treats to mimic a group "cheers!"

"Bon appétit!" Beth chewed and offered me a pensive look. "Well, Priyanka definitely works hard. But there's no glory in any hard-core grind if it wears you down to a little stub, so I hope it's worth it. I hope she's happy."

My roommate, with another oddly poignant and bizarre life insight.

"Amen to that," I said.

Mia offered prayer hands. "Amen!"

# Chapter Twelve

I needed to get out of the house. Beth was baking up a storm again, tempting me with all the extra calories, and the Google Home speaker was now occasionally broadcasting our neighbor Grady's non-porn ESPN football highlights. But when I made the decision to leave the apartment to study elsewhere, I didn't expect it to be sunny one minute and then raining cats and dogs the next. "Light drizzle" was in the weather forecast, but it wasn't supposed to hit until the evening.

I especially didn't expect to see Jake walking a tiny dog ahead of me on my way to campus. Had he always been a dog person? From my days in New York, a cishet guy walking a tiny dog usually meant there was a girlfriend in the picture. It was almost as certain as other evident truths in life, like how horse dewormers shouldn't be used to cure human viral illnesses, or that drinking beer before liquor would never end well.

In my past life, when PetMania was one of my clients, it was my responsibility to conduct dozens of focus groups with pet owners. Self-professed dog lovers were lively in their discourse, far more energetic and chattier than I expected as they gushed about their pups, and this was definitely *not* how I would describe Jake. Seeing Jake in this slice-of-life moment was perplexing to me.

Simply put, he didn't give off dog-owner energy. Not back then, and not now.

Did he give manic Asian *Back to the Future* Doc Brown vibes in college sometimes? Yes. But bubbly, yippy dog-owner vibes? No.

The rain continued to soak through my clothes, making them cling to me like an octopus clutching its prey. And of course I had on a heavyweight, absorbent cotton hoodie and jeans in the thickest fall denim. My waterlogged sweatshirt turned into a weighted blanket and the pants suctioned to my thighs, making my stride heavier and slower with each step. The only thing that was waterproof was my backpack, and thank goodness for that, because my laptop and reading materials were inside.

Jake veered off the path as his doggy contemplated a bathroom break next to a spindly maple. I drew closer and he saw me. "Hey, Lily! Wanna share? It's a golf umbrella. Those backpacks are good but they're water resistant, not waterproof."

My sneakers squished as I continued walking. "No thanks."

Jake cocked his head, and his dog mirrored his head tilt. Great, even this dog thought it was idiotic to turn down rain protection. "But the rain's getting worse." He was right, it was pouring now. And my refusing to take shelter under his umbrella was nothing more than me being petty. I sometimes wondered if holding long grudges was hereditary, because my parents did the same. If it was a sport, the Lee family would be Olympians. Maybe it was in our DNA, and as Kylo Ren tells Rey, "The dark side is in our blood." It was just how we were. How *I* was.

But maybe just once I could resist it for the sake of self-preservation.

"Okay," I conceded, while pushing my sopping wet curtain bangs from my eyes. I took steps toward him and the dog growled. "I'm headed to Cobbs Library, if you're headed that way."

"I'm going to my office, so it's no trouble. And don't worry about her. She's just territorial. Thinks you're trying to steal her favorite pee spot." More snarling. "Sasha, no! She's just sharing the umbrella with us."

I swear, Sasha rolled her eyes at me as she squatted. There was more than enough room for the two of us plus Sasha under his umbrella. It was practically the size of a pop-up tent. "Thank you for the coverage. Is Sasha your dog?"

He nodded. "Yup."

Silence fell between us. That's it? No more info? No backstory on why a grown-ass man would have such a tiny-ass dog?

After a few seconds he asked, "Do you like dogs?"

Back when we were dating, this sort of thing never came up. We had other priorities besides discussing pet affinity.

I scrunched my nose. "I had dogs growing up."

"That's not the same thing as liking them."

"It's not?"

He answered, "It's not. That's like me asking, 'Do you like popcorn, specifically those tins with caramel and cheese?' and you saying, 'I have some in my pantry.' It doesn't mean you like it, or even eat it. It could be your roommate's, or a long-forgotten present."

"People give popcorn as a present?" I gaped.

"Anyone gifting me popcorn would be my soul mate." He stopped walking. "Garrett's is the best."

"I have a sweet tooth. I'd want perfectly baked chocolate chip cookies. Crispy on the outer rim, chewy on the inside. A hint of brown butter and vanilla flavor. My roommate makes them and they're close to perfect."

He turned to face me as we approached the campus grounds. "I bake cookies."

"You do?" Who *was* this man?

"I preheat the oven, cut the cookie dough log, and let them cook for ten to twelve minutes until they turn a golden brown." He showed a hint of a smile.

A snort escaped me. "That's not baking. I can't believe you said that. That's offensive to all home bakers around the world."

He pointed out, "Technically, it *is* baking, because I'm pressing the *bake* button on my oven. That makes me a baker, aka a person who bakes. And I'm afraid my human-walking services end here. No dogs allowed around the main campus library."

While we chatted, I forgot that the rain had soaked every inch of me. Even my bra and underwear were drenched, and my running shoes made slurping sounds as I walked. Not too sad about leaving the downpour, but my heart fluttered inside my chest as Jake and Sasha waited for me to leave their umbrella canopy and enter the library building.

Jake's eyes sparkled and his lips turned upward into a smirk, making me suspicious.

"Why are you smiling?"

"She likes you."

He pointed to my feet. Sasha had finished sniffing me and sat on my right sneaker. "She hates everyone. Including my ex, her former owner."

*Aha! Thank you, Sasha, for drawing out Jake's origin story. I owe you one for that.*

I squatted down to pet her, and my knees popped, scaring her into a standing, teeth-snarling position, which made Jake burst into uncontrollable laughter.

"She gets this way only on the Fourth of July when the neighborhood goes berserk with illegal fireworks." He wiped his eyes with the back of his hand. "I'm sorry for laughing. My knees pop like that too. Seeing her trying to act ferocious, as if her Chihuahua and Jack Russell terrier genes were not an impediment, is just so funny to me."

Sasha's ears pricked up, then she flopped down on my shoe again and rolled to her side.

He explained, "Now she wants you to rub her belly, even on the wet sidewalk. Man, I've really spoiled her." Jake pulled gently on her leash, but Sasha wouldn't budge.

With my knees already loosened, I attempted a second squat. After about ten seconds of petting, I resumed standing. Sasha rolled to her feet and barked. A soft, quick yip.

Jake tilted the umbrella and scooped her up. "That's her way of showing appreciation. Thanks for the fun walk. And look! The rain is slowing."

I hadn't noticed it had transitioned from a cascade to a hard drizzle to a sprinkle. I'd missed the entire progression.

"So I'll see you tomorrow, in class?" he asked.

"Yeah. And thanks again for the umbrella coverage."

Taking a few steps, I turned to see if they'd already turned to leave, only to find Jake staring right at me. His face turned tomato red and he jerked his head down to speak to Sasha.

I continued my journey to the library. What had I learned?

That Jake was still nice enough to share his umbrella.

He was a dog person. Surprising to me, but maybe he always had been.

He had an ex who no longer had joint pet custody.

His ornery dog liked me.

When he blushed, his ears blazed bright pink.

And huh. I enjoyed the company. Mainly Sasha's, of course.

Hiking up my waterlogged jeans, I entered the library and inhaled the smell of bound books and the aroma of aged wood from the bookshelves, floors, and tables. The combination of scents triggered a pleasing feeling of nostalgia from my earliest college memories, hanging out in the libraries with friends I'd made in the dorms. I found an isolated desk away from the crowds and placed my bag on an adjacent chair. The seats had low backs, which meant hanging my sweatshirt would result in half of it bunched up on the floor, which was hardly desirable. I kept everything on and hoped that the warm air pumping through the ventilation system would eventually dry me.

I laid out my textbook, notebook, and rainbow assortment of felt-tip pens as a golden stream of sunlight flooded through the window, casting an overexposed glow on all my belongings. Of course the sun would reappear the moment I entered the library. I sighed and glanced outside, observing the youthful crop of Carlthorpe students walking in and out of the surrounding buildings. It was a strange feeling to no longer be among the youngest generation of adults anymore. I had to be the oldest undergrad student on campus, and I'd never felt so out of place in my entire life.

*Get it together, Lily. Age is not your identity and you don't have an expiration date. It's just an artificial limitation in your mind.*

I had just zipped my backpack closed when a muffled *WOMP WOMP* sound emitted from the front interior compartment. My textbooks and gym clothes muted the sound of my mom's ringtone as it rang a second time, *WOMP WOM-MMMMP.* It was the sad trombone sound effect, which I'd assigned to Umma after she messaged me for the millionth time, asking about my job and my move back to Carlthorpe.

"Hello?" I whispered. "Is everything okay?"

"I called over and over again."

*Yeah, I noticed.* "Sorry, Umma, but I can't talk right now. I'm in the library. Studying hard." I added the last part because I knew she would consider that more important than almost anything else.

"Did you get package? I send something from Amazon."

I'd gotten a package earlier in the day. Snail mucus K-beauty eye cream to depuff the bags under my eyes, vitamin C supplements, and a box of ginseng tea. Honestly, I thought it was a misdelivery. Good to know it was from my mom. Her version of a care package.

"Yes, thank you. I'll use them soon. I have to go write a paper for that class I'm taking."

"Go study. Don't forget eye cream once a day. Two if you have baggy eye."

"Okay. Gamsahamnida! And geokjeonghaji maseyo." *Don't worry, Umma.*

She ended the call, telling me to take the supplements so I wouldn't get sick.

Once I entered my thirties, my parents and I chatted only once a week, always on Sundays. These calls were more check-ins than actual conversations, rarely lasting longer than five minutes. For the most part, my parents focused primarily on my sister's life, as she started her own medical practice and gave birth to twins. But now, after hearing I was going back to school, my mom was all up in my business. Did she know deep down that something wasn't right? Or was this the only way she knew how to feel useful and "motherly"—by badgering me about my health, studying, and grades, as if we were winding back the clock to a time she and my dad had had a bigger impact on my life? I took a deep breath and exhaled slowly. Hopefully she would chill out soon, because the last thing I needed right now was more pressure from two domineering, meddling parents with priorities that didn't align with mine.

I cracked open the textbook and began reading, with my yellow highlighter in hand. I made it through one chapter without any study breaks or phone notification interruptions, but while skimming more pages to get ahead for the next assignment, my mind drifted back to my rainy-day encounter with my ex. What would it be like to be friends with Jake now? He didn't have to offer to help, but he had, and this act of selflessness had protected me from the torrential rain. It was gentlemanly and thoughtful, but not far beyond what a TA would do for a student in a storm.

I stared out the window, letting my mind continue to drift. I glanced toward the sky, watching more rays of sunshine push through the clouds. The rain had fully stopped and sunlight had finally broken through the heather-gray billows, giving them a metallic shimmer.

There was that popular saying that every cloud has a silver lining. That every bad situation holds some promise or possibility.

Could these clouds be a metaphor for my life? Was there a silver lining? And did Jake Cho represent the cloud or the silver lining?

My mouth twitched into a slight smile as I focused on the words on the page.

# Chapter Thirteen

J ake Cho showed up to the CS class the next day with a cat.

Or it could have been a raccoon. It was hard to see from my seat. It was in a pet carrier, and a little black-masked face with stark blue eyes pressed against the metal grate while Jake pulled the professor aside and explained rather loudly that he had an emergency and couldn't stay. He would be available for office hours later that afternoon after he got back from the vet.

I'd had my doubts before, but this confirmed everything I knew about Jake. Of *course* he would be a dog person *and* a cat person. Most people fall neatly into feline or canine or possibly neither. I'd actually pegged him as neither, being so noncommittal.

Jake was not like most people. Back in college, he was sometimes like an alien to me: the kind of person who preferred non-edge pieces of brownies. Someone who not only loved, but *preferred*, black jelly beans. And the type of traveler who ran to the departure gate at the airport just as the plane doors were closing, cutting it so close that passengers groaned when he boarded.

Were we incompatible or complementary? After all these years, I still didn't know.

Although he had left the classroom, I couldn't help but think about what he was like at home with his two pets. Did he talk to them in goofy voices? Did he give *them* goofy voices? Was his floor covered with squeaky toys?

Someone said my name.

"—Lee, Grace Pak, and Ethan Chang. This group is the only one who followed all the instructions. Class, this is your only warning: starting this week you'll get points docked from your group project grades if you don't follow directions. It's a reflection of your work, and no one wants sloppy, incomplete deliverables. Especially not for this class."

While I didn't always love this type of "showing praise to demonstrate a lesson" approach to teaching, any sort of positive affirmation these days was a win. Ethan sat to my right, and he mouthed, "We got an A plus! Yesssss!" while grinning at me.

Honestly, if I was twenty-two-year-old Lily right now, I would be so into him. His playful dark eyes, purposefully unruly hair, and barely there dimples were to die for . . . damn. The only other guy I'd seen with a face like his was on one of my favorite K-dramas, and he was thousands of miles away living on a different continent. Ethan could seriously be that actor's body double.

"Can you believe the professor knows who we are now?" Ethan whispered.

My lips curved into a wide smile. "Yes, he does!" Even better, we earned this praise without any special help from a certain TA.

When the class ended, Ethan asked, "What are you doing tonight?"

Before I could panic about what exactly he was fishing for, he quickly added, "Because a bunch of us are going to PJ's frat party tonight."

"PJ's in a fraternity?" He was a skateboarding, man-bun-wearing, baggy-clothed guy. Ethan looked more fratty than PJ. Hell, even *I* looked more fratty than PJ.

Ethan grinned. "I know—his brother was the Sigma Mu president a few years ago and PJ kind of had to join. Believe it or not, he fits in well there when he's in his element."

"And what is his element?"

"Drunk." Ethan's eyes glinted with amusement.

I rarely went to Greek parties in college the first time around. The very thought of going ten years later was too Will Ferrell in the movie *Old School* for me.

Nope. Not gonna happen. "I'll pass. But thank you for the offer."

"Well, if you change your mind, it starts tonight at eight. It's the house with blue windows and doors on Brighton Alley. And you can't miss the Sigma Mu letters, they light up like a motel vacancy sign. Gives off bug zapper vibes."

I smiled to myself as we parted ways. Ducking into the Commons to grab a coffee, I texted Jake while waiting in line to pay. After typing, editing, and deleting my message over and over again, I ended up with three brilliant words: How's the cat?

He wrote back quickly. Bandit had an abscessed molar and they removed it. God, so expensive

He added: There's nothing worse than grading homework with a cat wailing by your feet all night. At least it was a legit reason and not her just wanting attention or treats. She's staying the night for observation for infection. Thx for asking ☺

I swiped my ID at the register and my new photo appeared on-screen. Seeing an unfiltered, unedited image of my face on a very high-res monitor was not something I would ever get used to, even if I bought food and drinks on campus multiple times a day and was forced to see myself with every snack and caffeine purchase. I still couldn't get over how this photograph was possibly worse than any high school yearbook image, corporate security badge picture, or double-chin-angled selfie taken by someone with short arms. Definitely worse than my previous student ID photo. My unsmiling passport mugshot looked better than this, and that was saying something.

First, there was the ghastly lighting. Fluorescent of course, with the illumination of maybe one hundred ring lights.

Second, the angle. The camera was positioned so it was directly in front, but it was also slightly lower than my head, and as anyone with a nonexistent jawline could tell you, this is not a universally loved camera position.

And last, my skin. What was going on with my breakouts? My nights toiling over required reading, homework sets, and career research during my study breaks had taken a toll on me. I was probably the only undergrad student here with both wrinkles *and* pimples.

The cashier glanced at the screen and said, "You may need to replenish your dining funds. You're down to one hundred dollars and you're in here a lot."

Already? I hadn't thought about the impact of my daily caffeine habit in New York, but now that I had a fixed budget, with most of my savings funneling toward tuition and housing, I needed to be more careful.

A heartfelt smile spread across her face. "But I do love seeing you. Take care, hon."

I took my iced coffee to a window seat facing the CS building and texted Mia.

> I got invited to a frat party LOL

> YOU HAVE TO GO!
> What's the theme?

> Theme? Binge drinking. Hangovers. Possibly regrettable sex?

> Noooo like Shots and Thots, Bros and Hos, the Great Fratsby

> What are you even talking about? And how do you know so much about Greek party life? Didn't we hang out in college all the time? Were you sneaking out to parties when I went to sleep???

No comment. But figure out
the theme and dress to the
nines if you go. Otherwise
you look like an asshole

> If I GO I'll look like an asshole.
> WHO BROUGHT THEIR
> MOM? —everyone

Okay MILF-types at a frat party
are a plus, not a minus. You
are looking at this all wrong

This conversation had taken a sharp turn, and in fact was barreling down an icy road with shitty brakes. I thought for sure Mia would laugh her ass off knowing that my evening could include kegs of Natty Light. But now I was curious: Was there really a party theme?

I messaged Ethan. What's the theme for the party? I'm curious (but not going)

It's color themed, maybe black
and white? What can I do or
say to convince you to go ;-)

I was well out of practice on college-aged texting but . . . was that a flirty winking face? Or a "har har wink wink we both know you're not really coming soooooo" face?

Like my conversation with Mia, this had potential to derail

quickly. I didn't respond, and placed the phone on the counter while I drank my coffee and stared out the window. A
red-baseball-cap-wearing Jake headed into the CS building, returning for office hours. He was cat-less, and five
minutes early.

I sipped and observed. Steady streams of students walked
out of the science and engineering buildings. It was lunchtime and hordes of undergrads headed toward the two
main dining establishments on campus. I didn't want to be
that old person who went on "back in my day" tirades, but
back in my day, kids looked and behaved differently. We
didn't carry gigantic water flasks, parading them around
like campus status symbols. Nor did we have an extreme di-
chotomy between students wearing pajamas with knock-off
UGGs to class and the fancier ones who wore Moncler
beanies, Canada Goose parkas, and Prada boots when the
weather dropped below fifty degrees some mornings. And
to continue with my clothing complaints, since when did
the larger-size ladies' shirts in the Student Union barely fit
over my boobs? I bought an XL Carlthorpe logo shirt and it
barely fit. When did the XLs get so small?

I caught a glimpse of a trio of gorgeous girls walking into
the CS building, all carrying Chihuahua-size, pastel reus-
able bottles and they were most definitely not wearing XL
anything. These waify college girls looked nothing like my
peers from a decade ago. Style and fashion had obviously
changed over the years, but these young women glowed.
They were plucked and highlighted and microbladed, things I
hadn't even known about until I was thirty. In my old, over-

size black-and-white-striped Madewell boyfriend shirt and high-waisted dark denim jeans with no belt, I felt dumpy, like a freshly washed used car driving behind a garbage truck on the freeway, getting pelted by bits of trash skimming off the top.

I wasn't the only one who noticed the three of them: they caught the eyes of many science and engineering majors, their jaws hanging while they gawked in the most unsubtle of ways.

My stomach churned when I realized why the girls looked so familiar. They were the ones sitting in front of me on the first day of CS class. The students who were collectively hot for Jacob the TA. The ones who were now visiting said TA for office hours.

Maybe these three undergrads were seeking some guidance or academic assistance from Jake, and it was as simple as that. So what if all three of them had commented about his physical appearance . . . and didn't appreciate his desert-dry humor and his acts of kindness . . . and only saw a handsome face, powerful chest, muscular arms, and perfectly fitting tees. Who cared if these students weren't interested in the well-being of his cat?

Apparently, I did.

A sense of urgency jolted me into action. I threw away my trash and walked to the CS building. Pushing the elevator button, then rising slowly to the fourth floor, it occurred to me that I had no game plan. I'd already finished the week's lesson. And the following week's one as well. I had no questions about the assignments or grading. Was it even wise to be in Jake's office alone with him, given our history?

*DING!*

The doors opened and I stepped out into the grad student office wing. Even though the building was fairly new, the halls had an old-school smell to them, like polished wooden floors and the faint aroma of drip coffee wafting down the corridor. Cream-colored walls were lined with corkboards promoting events, seminars, and job opportunities for students with CS degrees. A few yards down, a long wooden bench in front of the grad students' and professors' offices was occupied by two female students I'd seen earlier.

They both startled at my presence when I approached.

One girl elbowed the other. "No one uses office hours but us. Weird to see someone else here."

I plunked down on the empty side of the bench and acknowledged the comment. "I have a few clarifying questions about the last lecture and it's probably easiest to just ask in person instead of email." I don't know why I bothered to say anything, even though what I said was true. It's not like they were the office hours gatekeepers.

The taller of the two commented, "We're usually here to get a better understanding of what was covered in class. A lot goes over my head and we need some individualized attention."

The other one snorted. "Yeah right, you're totally here for the sake of *learning.*"

"Hey." Taller girl shot her a look. "There's no crime in bettering our education while at the same time admiring our TA eye candy. Maybe we should come to office hours twice a week instead, so we can ask even *more* clarifying questions."

Shorter one nodded. "Sounds good." She looked at me. "Thanks for that idea."

*Yes, Lily, thanks for giving them that idea.*

The door creaked open and the third student came out, winking unsubtly at her friends. "Who's next?" she asked.

The pair on the bench stood at the same time and the taller one said to me, "We'll be quick. We both have to be somewhere soon and have the same questions and, um, mutual interests."

They walked into the office and the other member of their trio took a seat next to me. She pulled out her makeup bag from her purse and examined herself in her compact mirror. "Oh great, my mascara's smudged. I hope he didn't notice."

He, meaning Jake? The twinge in my stomach returned.

After a couple of minutes, I heard laughter erupt from the room. What was I even doing here? Jake needed to do his own thing, and I needed to do mine. We were playing nice now and there was no reason to complicate or confuse things.

I didn't need to be here. It was stupid of me to show up.

Stumbling to my feet, I unzipped my coat to provide relief to my rising body temperature and quickening heartbeat. Slowly breathing in and out, trying to maximize lung capacity, I gathered my belongings.

The office door creaked open and laughter rang down the hallway. Rather than stay, I marched to the elevator and hit the down button several times.

*Hurry up, hurry up!* The elevator grumbled as it rose a few floors, but then it stopped on a lower level.

"See you next week, Jacob. Huh, there was someone sitting here but she's gone now."

I couldn't wait any longer. Running down four flights of stairs, I burst through the main entrance double doors with a hard push and nearly tripped over my own feet as I followed the flow of students exiting the building. Breathing hard from the burst of cardio, I veered left to head back to my apartment to study. Once I got home and reread my notes, I'd email Jake any questions. A far better use of my time and energy.

I DROPPED MY backpack in the hallway and took off my running shoes, hardly noticing a pair of shiny silver pointy-toe flats that didn't belong to me or to Beth.

Mia popped her head out of my bedroom doorway. "Surprise! Did you see my fancy new footwear? I treated myself to new shoes because your girl just landed a new start-up client!"

"Congratulations!" I hugged her. "But why are you here and not celebrating?"

She laughed. "Are you kidding me? How could I not celebrate with my best friend? And you're going out with me tonight. Promise?"

"Of course! I'll put my studying aside for one night for you. Where are we going? Are you buying?"

A wicked grin and a glint in her eye . . . oh no, she was up to something.

"Where we're going, the drinks are free. The frat party!"

"What? No way. No!"

She pleaded with puppy-dog eyes. "C'mon. Think about it, you and me scoping out what Greek life is like now from a single woman in her thirties' perspective? I can sell this shit to Hollywood one day! Pleeeeease?"

I squinted my eyes at her. "You're telling me you want to celebrate landing a new publicity client by going to a Sigma Mu party tonight?"

I expected some level of hesitation but there was none. "Yes! Absolutely. It will be the story we tell our grandkids. Anyway, trust me, as a PR and publicity expert, I'm telling you this is worth doing because you'll never get this chance again."

Her confidence and enthusiasm were usually infectious, but no, this wasn't happening. While the words leaving her mouth were all true and it really would make a hilarious story one day, I wanted no part of any of this.

"I wasn't big on stranger-danger parties back then, so why would now be any different? Plus, we're in our thirties! Cougar much?"

I pursed my lips tight. Why was she pushing so hard for this?

She held up her index finger. "Hold on." Then Mia left my room and came back with my roommate.

"Even Beth here is coming with us to the party."

My roomie's eyebrows pulled into a deep V. "What? I was planning to bake a cobbler and watch *Hocus Pocus*. You said if I came in here, you'd help me bake."

"And I will, after we get back. The point is, Lily, that even your happy-go-lucky Mary Poppins roommate is going now."

"I am? And you think I'm like Mary Poppins? I love that movie! Julie Andrews is my idol!"

"Yeah, I figured." Mia looked straight into my eyes. "I'm not letting you become a solitudinarian. We didn't do anything fun back in undergrad because we were too busy studying and, I'll go ahead and say it, we were poor. Poor by Carlthorpe standards." She turned to Beth. "Our classmates back then weren't just Wall Street Manhattan wealthy, some of those kids got both sailboats and cars for their eighteenth birthdays."

Mia looked back at me and pleaded, "Now you're finally in a position where you have the means and you're not going to fail out of school this time or anything. No offense. So, let's have some fun. Let loose a little."

Admittedly, my time in college was not what I would call my "glory years." There was barely time for partying. But you know, I never reflected on that time in my life and thought, *My one deep regret in life is never doing keg stands and making out with someone in a frat house basement in the same night.*

Beth said, "Roomie, you're frowning. You being all sad right now hurts my soul. It's like watching Jerry Springer hip-hop dancing on TikTok. I don't wanna see that. Not ever. No, ma'am."

What was this, a staged intervention? Did I really need one? Maybe they were right about one thing . . . when I was out of my element, I routinely tried to control what I could and that usually led to a predictable, straight-and-narrow path. Was that why I'd stayed at my previous company for so long? Maybe it wasn't inertia. Had it been fear all along? I was never good at changing course or trying new things. Maybe this one time I could briefly steer myself into uncharted waters with this new force of wind in my sail.

"Fine," I muttered. "Only for a short while. Then we can bake and eat some celebration pie."

Mia's gaze flickered between Beth and me. "Yes! Thank you!"

Beth clapped. "I'm excited. All three of us hanging out for a night on the town!"

"One hour, tops," I said firmly.

Mia hugged me again, and then wrapped her arms around Beth and squeezed. "Thanks for helping me out. I owe you one. I'll go buy some vodka, it's on me."

Beth giggled. "Anytime! Just a quick question though. What party are we going to again?"

# Chapter Fourteen

Turns out there was one thing worse than showing up to a frat party in your thirties.

Showing up to a frat party in your thirties while intoxicated and wearing the *wrong-themed costume*.

Ethan had mentioned black and white, but I should have known better than to trust someone who frequently read Reddit on his phone during CS lectures instead of following along with the lesson.

Mia, Beth, and I discovered far too late that it was a stoplight-themed party as we approached the crowd of drunk guests.

Red. Yellow. Green. Everywhere.

No black. No white.

As we pushed through the sweaty dancing and swaying bodies near the entrance, we were barraged with questions about our all-black outfits.

It was Mia who came up with the best reply. "We're a stoplight when you lose power."

"Ohhh, like a blackout. Very cool!" Someone with sleepy eyes gave us high fives.

And this was why Mia was a think-on-her-feet PR super-star, even when she was plastered. With no smart retort of my own, and repeating what Mia had said to anyone who asked, this was also why I was a fourteenth-year student with no job prospects.

In the far back corner, a DJ was spinning actual vinyl re-cords rather than shuffling a playlist on his phone. He was wearing a Carlthorpe cap and a baggy Rastafarian-inspired shirt that covered all the color bases for the themed party. The bass thundered through the speakers, causing my chest to vibrate. No one else seemed to mind the humming and throbbing effect the music had on their bodies. It wasn't like I was imagining it: the guy next to me had a full cup of beer and it sloshed in his hand.

We got only as far as the front room before coming to a full stop. No one was moving at all, which wasn't only bad socially, but it also led to stagnant airflow. Not ideal for a house reeking of beer/cologne/perfume/BO. Were Greek parties always like this? I didn't have many data points from my past for comparison.

I turned to ask Mia if she'd had her fill of frat fun so we could abort this mission, and instead encountered a girl in a fitted green dress who shoved a red Solo cup full of frothy room-temperature beer into my hand. "Really clever cos-tume!" she admired.

"They say black is the new red-yellow-green!" Ethan shouted, sliding up behind me in his Elvis-esque white jumpsuit. "I'm so sorry I told you the wrong theme. Would it help if I told you I was color-blind?"

I cocked my head. "Are you?"

He shoved his hands into his pockets. "No, but I also don't want you to be mad at me."

I couldn't help but smile. "It could have been way worse. You could have said 'noblemen and wenches' and I would have believed you. Wearing black or white is no big deal." And if I was going to be honest with myself, wearing all black never failed me. Black was flattering. Black hid things. The last thing I needed was to dress like a walking high-lighter, bringing attention to my lumps, ridges, and squishy spots.

"Normally if you wore all black you'd be hard to find, but in this sea of greens, yellows, and reds, black actually stands out," he joked.

Standing out at a frat party was definitely *not* what I wanted. I needed to blend in—if anyone dared to tag me in photos online or dug into my past and exposed my current whereabouts, it could end my author career and any future job prospects. I'd be canceled in a heartbeat with the head-line "LILY LEE IS A LIAR AND A FRAUD, **AND** SHE GOES TO FRAT PARTIES." And they wouldn't be wrong.

He took a large step back and spun around. "I'm wear-ing the wrong thing too, so I didn't get the memo either. Or maybe I did, and I jumbled the message from PJ."

I smirked. "White is tricky and hard to pull off, but you wear it well."

Beth looked around, taking slow sips from her cup. "Whoa, it's so colorful here. Like the Lithuanian flag!"

"Like the *what*? Why do you even know that?" Mia cackled.

"Why do you not?" Beth said, dishing it right back with a laugh.

"Are you two friends with Lil? I'm Ethan."

"Beth. I'm her roommate." They shook hands and she turned to me. "Why does *he* get to call you Lil?"

Mia narrowed her eyes in my direction. "Yeah, I've never been able to call you *Lil*." She said to Ethan, "I'm Lily's friend from home, here for the weekend."

"Shoot, I forgot, she wants to be called Lily." He grinned. "Was she always a CS whiz? She's singlehandedly boosting our group grade."

"Single-handedly? Is she now?" Mia asked suspiciously, crossing her arms.

I took a sip of beer. "I'm not half-assing anything this time. I'm full-assing all the way."

Mia looked at Ethan and Beth. "Is full-assing a real thing? What the hell does 'half-ass' even mean? It makes you wonder where idioms and phrases are derived from. I was an English major, if you couldn't already tell. What are you two majoring in?"

Beth and Ethan said "Psychology" at the same time. Then they had a side conversation about their classes while I whispered to Mia, "Can we go now? We can't even get far inside the house. We've been in this doorway area for, like, ten minutes."

She lifted her chin. "You're right. But I have a plan."

"What?"

Mia shot me a wicked grin. "Follow me!"

Going around the outside to the back of the house was

far more challenging than any of us thought it would be. First, it involved moving single file while shimmying sideways, because the wooden fence alongside the property was maybe a foot and a half from the building at most . . . and it had splinters, which I found out the hard way. Second, there was something that resembled an air conditioner that was not only on, and blowing heat upward, but it was also blocking us so we each had to climb over it. And finally, because I was wearing a skirt and was too intoxicated for fine motor control, the whole crawling-over-the-blowing-device-while-air-shot-upward plan turned out to be a disastrous mistake. One that my friends could not unsee.

I tried to pull the fabric down while Mia and Beth helped me off the hot metal air box. Luckily the one person around who didn't see me was Ethan, who was too busy making his way straight toward the back patio, where snacks and drinks sat on top of a green Ping-Pong table. He ran toward them, arms outstretched, like he was reuniting with a long-lost relative at the airport.

"Wait, where's my beer?" I asked, looking over my shoulder to see if I'd left it behind me.

Mia said, "I have it. Or had it . . . I chugged the whole thing, hoping to flush out that image of you Marilyn Monroe–ing it, with your skirt flapping everywhere, but I think I need more alcohol."

Ethan erupted into a cheer. "We did it! There are chips! And a keg!" The relief in his voice made it sound like he had been stranded on an island and a crate of supplies had miraculously washed ashore. "I'm in heaven!" he swooned.

Grabbing two cups of beer filled to the brim, Ethan handed them over to Mia and Beth.

"What about mine?" I closed my eyes and the patio went spinning. "Never mind."

While the others drank, I pointed to the house next door. "Is that another Greek house? If not, they must haaaate all this." My hand flopped back and forth. "All this. Stuff."

Mia grabbed my shoulders. "Girl, it's only nine o'clock. We had only two drinks each! Get it together!"

Ethan handed me a cup of kettle chips. "This might help soak up the alcohol. Oh heyyyyy! PJ's here!"

He pointed back toward the house, where PJ emerged from the back door, wearing a Tribe Called Quest tee, red pants, and a wide drunken smile. "You came!" He ran up to Ethan and me and went in for a group hug, not realizing he had a cup in his hand and was pouring some of the liquid contents onto my shoes.

I frowned at my beer-tinged boots. "At least it isn't open-toe-sandal season."

Beth nodded. "Or real suede."

A few guys came over to ruffle PJ's hair. Two of them wore baseball caps and the other guy wore a terry-cloth sweatband with the Sigma Mu emblem. Within seconds, a large pack of partygoers made their way onto the patio. The instant swell triggered my rapid breathing as I looked for a quick exit. The house was farther away now that we had migrated toward the back corner of the deck.

"I . . . I need to leave," I whispered.

Mia took one look at my face and knew I wasn't joking. She asked PJ, "Can you get us out of here? Lily doesn't do well with crowds. Or enclosed areas. Or party people."

A few heat lamps were turned on, and the air on the covered patio became warm and ripe with sweat and beer stench. I swiveled my head to find a faster way to escape. Going through the house would be bad in terms of the number of bodies per square foot. Squeezing down the side of the house again was tricky, because it involved intoxicated climbing and, of course, flashing people. But of my two options, the flashing way out was the better one.

From behind, PJ grabbed my shoulders and steered me toward a nondescript section of the fence. "Push."

I pushed.

It opened.

A magic passage.

Within a matter of seconds, we were on the other side of the barrier, on an adjacent lot. Floodlights around the property all flicked on at once. A small dog barked at the window of a charming two-story Craftsman. When I waved at the pup and shouted, "Hi, puppy!" it quieted down and wagged its tail.

PJ laughed. "That dog hates everyone. I'm impressed."

Ethan groaned as he ran his hands along the fence. "Shit! Can we get back in? I left my chips and drink."

"It's hard to see the hidden opening, just keep pushing

and pulling. This property we're on used to be a sorority, and this secret entry between the two houses is well known among the Greek community."

While Ethan continued to feel up the wood slats to rescue his beer and snacks, I said to PJ, "Thank you for the quick exit. It was too much for me."

PJ nodded. "No problem. Thanks for showing up tonight. Grace had an orchestra performance, so she couldn't make it."

"Awww, look!" Beth pointed at the window. The dog was no longer there. In its place was an eerily familiar judgy cat. Furry face with a black masquerade-like mask. Piercing eyes.

"Hey, Lily."

I gasped as Jake walked down the driveway. "What are you doing here?" I demanded.

He pointed at the house. "That's where I live. And that's the guard cat, Bandit, who is a much happier kitty now after her oral surgery. And technically, you're trespassing, so I think the more important question is, why are *you* here? And why are you and your Charlie's Angels entourage dressed like you're going to burgle me?"

"Holy shit! Jake Cho." Mia threw her drunken arms around him. "Lily told me you were her TA, but seeing you in 3D makes it way more real for me." She jumped back. "Damn, you filled out. You been hitting the gym?"

Jake chuckled. "Mia, wow. I have been, actually, thanks for noticing. They have a great rock-climbing wall at the school fitness center now. I didn't know you were back at Carlthorpe too. Are you back on campus for Lily's book project?"

"What book project?" Mia asked, ignoring my telepathic pleas to keep quiet. "I'm just here for fun. *She's* the one who didn't graduate, not me."

Searing heat flushed my cheeks and neck, sobering me right up. *Shit.*

Jake's brows knitted together. "I see. So this means you're the chaperone? Are you the only graduate in this group?"

Mia shot me an apologetic look, realizing she'd disclosed too much. "Oh fuck. Sorry, Lily."

Ethan jumped into the conversation, if that was even what it was. It was more like a Lily roast. He looked over at the cup of beer in PJ's hand. "Heya, TA! Just for the record, I'm Gen Z but drinking age. So is PJ. We're twenty-one. Not like Lily and her friend." He held his hands up. "No offense to anyone here."

Beth chimed in, "Hey now, I'm young, I'm twenty-two." Her eyes darted back and forth between Mia and me, then she glanced over at Jake. "No offense."

Jake smirked. "No offense taken. Don't let my hair make you think I'm way older than everyone by fifty years. I'm the same age as Lily and Mia."

Beth's cheeks turned bright pink as she took a final sip from her red Solo cup. "Thank goodness you're not my TA, I'd be embarrassed by this entire encounter. Imagine seeing your teacher at a frat party." She shot a look at me. *Oops. Sorry, Roomie.*

I sat flatly, "Well, now that we've all acknowledged the ancient elephant in the room, and it's true that I still don't have my college degree, this would probably be a good time to get going. Sorry about barging onto your property, Jake . . . er . . . Jacob." I grabbed Mia and Beth by their elbows and tried to steer them in the direction of the street.

Beth wriggled out of my grip. "For the love of Taylor Swift. No more talking down on yourself like that, Roomie. No, ma'am!"

Mia nodded. "For once, I actually agree with Beth about something. But that ma'am thing stings a little."

We looked over at PJ and Ethan, who had abruptly left to figure out how to open the hidden door on the gate.

"You know we can just walk around the front now that we're on Jake's property, right?" Mia noted.

PJ nodded. "Yeah, but the drinks are just on the other side of this fence. If we go through the front, it's like you died in a video game, you lost a life, and have to start all over again. The final level is just"—he rammed his shoulders against the fence—"over. Here!" The door finally budged a few inches, which was all they needed for reentry. "Who wants to go back?"

Beth raised her hand. "Me!"

Mia looked at me. "Should I stay with you?"

I shook my head. "You go with them. Honestly, it's okay. I can get home."

"Okay, I'll report back any fun findings. And I promise not to bring anyone back to your room." Mia grinned and joined Beth just before they disappeared to the other side of the fence.

This left me alone with Jake, along with his voyeur dog and cat, both of whom were staring intently at us from the window.

The floodlights surrounding us clicked and the entire yard fell into darkness.

"I—I should get going." I positioned my feet toward the closest streetlamp, the only light source other than party fairy lights lining the top of the neighboring fence. "See you later." I shuffled my feet toward the road, moving carefully so I wouldn't trip or fall in the dark.

"Wait." Jake grabbed my arm. Electricity coursed throughout my body as his hand made contact. His touch was familiar, but also felt different, with a new firmness to it. As my eyes adjusted to a shadowy nightfall, I could see Jake stepping closer to me.

"So, you didn't graduate?"

Although I didn't owe him any answers, I did feel bad for misleading him before, especially since he'd been offering reconciliatory gestures over the last week. Now he knew why I was back on campus. I bowed my head and nodded.

"Who cares if you didn't get your degree? Plenty of people don't finish college and do just fine. Plus, you're an author now and have a consulting business. Who gives a shit, especially now?"

My shoulders slumped. "Well, *I* give a shit. I'm taking my STEM requirement for my degree, which is new by the way, and I'm auditing a stats class hoping to be let in eventually, and taking one other class elective just in case, to fulfill the rest of the coursework to complete my degree for real this time."

"You're being too hard on yourself." The softness in his voice relaxed me. "I respect you so much for doing this though. And I'm glad you're back. And they are too." He pointed at the window, where his pets stared down at us.

I smiled. "Thanks, Jake."

His hands hovered near my shoulders, like he was deciding whether it was okay to hug me. At that moment, I wanted to feel his touch again, to let him rest his strong hands on me and stroke my skin with his thumbs, like he did when we were together, just to see if the intimacy we shared all those years ago had any staying power.

Here, in the darkness, Jake and I had bent and twisted the principles of time to bring us back to our past selves, with the two of us alone, exploring each other. Even though it was hard to see, I tried to fix my gaze on his face and study it. I knew Jake so intimately back then. The angles of his face. The slight dimpling of his chin. The texture of his thick hair. Had so much time passed that we were basically strangers again?

I placed my hands on his chest, but then I wobbled and stumbled back a few steps, dragging him along with me as I clutched his shirt, bumping my backside into the driver's-side door of the black Mazda SUV parked in his driveway. Being pinned against a car by a hot guy on a beautiful night was never something I thought would actually happen to me, but here we were.

He whispered, "Lily."

Then, "Please don't go."

Those three words sent me free-falling backward to over

a decade earlier, teleporting me to a specific place, date, and time: the last moment I saw him, on the main walkway of campus, people swishing by and going about their day while we somehow moved in slow motion.

But it was me, not him, uttering the words "Please don't go."

Urging. Imploring. Pleading.

Please. Don't. Go.

Squeezing my eyes shut tight brought me spiraling back to the present. I peered through my lashes at Jake, who had chosen to leave me all those years ago. I remember how he looked that day: his skin flushed, his breathing rapid, unable to look me in the eyes. A typical physiological reaction to stress. And when he had to make a game-time decision, he went into fight-or-flight mode.

And he fled.

My gaze fell to the ground. Dropping my hands to my sides, I flicked my eyes over to the street. "I . . . I better go. This isn't a good idea." I added, "We can't do *this* again." I wasn't just referring to the present situation. I was taking into account our entire history together, because our past did, in fact, matter.

After I left Carlthorpe, it took years to fully overhaul my emotional well-being. It was a complete rebuild after being taken down to the bare studs. Was being with Jake now worth risking all of this progress? Because now that I was in my thirties, and aside from the whole setback of going back to college, I had rediscovered happiness. Was I better off in his company? Or was being self-partnered the best thing for me right now? Could I grow and flourish around him like I did on my own?

Maybe I wasn't emotionally equipped enough to get rejected all over again. Break my heart once, shame on you. Break my heart twice, well, I have only myself to blame, right? How could I possibly offer him my heart a second time . . . I was disillusioned to think he would choose me over everything else. It wasn't in his nature.

No. I wasn't brave enough for any of that. And adding the complication of Jake being my TA, any sort of relationship between us would be unprofessional and forbidden. What needed to happen next was clear.

I took a large step away from Jake. "I'm going to head home now."

The floodlights flicked back on, temporarily disorienting me and blinding both of us.

When my sight was restored, I could see Jake looking at me with regretful, soulful eyes. "Wait, I have my priorities straight now. Lately I've been—"

I cut him off. "I need to go. Goodbye, Jake." I turned my back to him and walked to the street.

He sighed. "Bye . . . Lily."

We bid our sad farewells again, like we had all those years ago.

# Chapter Fifteen

The knocking on my bedroom door grew louder and more impatient.

"Come in," I mumbled into my pillow.

It was Beth, wearing flannel pajamas with pink fluffy sheep on them. With her wide blue eyes and golden hair split into two long braids, she looked like she was twelve. "I was worried about you. Brought you warm milk and cookies." She paused and added, "I could hear you sniffling and I don't remember you being sick earlier."

My room was dark—a good thing because ugly crying in your thirties was exponentially uglier than in your twenties. Nowadays when I had a good emotional sobfest, my cheeks turned blotchy and my eyes swelled, like I'd been stung in the face by an angry swarm of bees. At my age, the subsequent de-puffing process took a full day.

She placed the plate and glass on my dresser, then plopped down on the foot of the bed. "You missed a fun party. Mia and PJ hit it off and were karaokeing by the end of the night. Ethan was wondering where you went."

When I didn't reply, she changed the subject. "Mia told me a little more about why you're back at Carlthorpe. I know this is incredibly cheesy, but I'm so glad you came back, because I'm having a better time my senior year because of you. I transferred in a couple years ago with a long-distance boyfriend and I'm pretty sure we're getting engaged after college, so I've been pretty nose-down in studying and not appreciating the social parts of college. You've already had a big impact on someone's life who hasn't actually read your book . . . yet. So chin up, lady! Time to take a big ol' bite out of a truth cookie—what you're going through isn't permanent, and even though it might feel like you lost something when you came here a second time, you've gained a loyal friend. And as a bonus, you get free, unlimited baked goods as long as you're under this roof! Some people might even be envious of that."

I lifted my head from my pillow and sat up, smiling weakly.

She handed me the plate of baked goods. "There's a theme of positivity here. I made these just for you."

The shortbread cookies were shaped like sheep and intricately decorated in icing. Beth had written "I believe in ewe" on all of them.

"Thank you. Or *ewe*. E-W-E." I smiled and bit off a sheep's woolly ass. It was delicious.

I CHANNELED ALL my energy the rest of the weekend into studying for midterms. Burying myself in the required

reading for my senior seminar and reviewing Python assignments were effective distractions, providing me with
mental and emotional distance from the last encounter
with Jake. By Monday morning, I felt confident about the
upcoming exams after so many hours of studying. I had a
quick breakfast and hopped into the shower before class.

My phone rang the second I turned off the water.

It was my editor. "Lily! Are you sitting down? I have some
great news!"

I was not sitting down. I was standing naked in a small
puddle of water from my dripping hair and body that had
pooled by my feet.

"You've been invited to speak to the London Business
School's U.S. alumni group in NYC in two weeks. It's part
of a debut book tour launch and they asked if you would be
the in-conversation partner."

This really was good news, and there were no signs of
a bait-and-switch "it's time to give back your advance for
your fraudulent credentials, actually" call. I sighed in relief.
I hadn't done too many in-person events and this seemed
like a good promotional opportunity. Towel-drying my hair,
I noticed she didn't outright mention the author.

"Who is the event with?" I finally asked.

She coughed. "Two authors actually. The O'Haras."

*No.* "Are you serious? Why me?" I cried out in frustration,
which my editor heard and took literally.

My editor replied, "Of course they'd want you! They specifically asked for your participation, actually; it was originally
supposed to just be the two of them. The topic was chosen

by the alumni group and will be 'Diversity, Inclusion, and Shattering Glass Ceilings Once and for All.'"

Now it all made sense.

Before I could say HELL NO, my editor added, "The O'Haras have arranged a signing opportunity after the Q and A with a local indie bookstore, and they're running ads in *The Wall Street Journal* to promote the event."

Okay, this was tempting. *The Wall Street Journal* audience wasn't exactly a perfect fit for me, but it was a way to broaden my reach.

"And it will be catered. Wine and fine finger foods."

Well, shit. She got me by dangling free food. "I'm in." My student-budget brain made me cave. Dining out was something I'd missed ever since I had returned to Carlthorpe.

"That's wonderful! If you're available, we would love for you to pop into our office this week so we can discuss your questions for this event, plus meet the O'Hara marketing team for some other promotional ideas they have for their book launch. They have a big marketing and publicity budget and we're thinking this is a good opportunity for you to ask for what you want. I suspect they're even putting in some of their own money and reaching out to their personal network, so we're hoping to maximize your exposure."

I looked around for a clean towel but settled for a terry-cloth bathrobe. "When's the meeting?"

She laughed nervously. "Could you come tomorrow afternoon or Wednesday late morning? I'm sorry if that's too short notice, but since you live close to our offices, we're hoping it's not a problem."

I cringed as she continued. "We're trying to move fast, especially if they're doing ads in newspapers." Knowing me all too well, she added, "I'll order in lunch and text you the menu. There will be desserts."

I laughed. "Sure, I can be there tomorrow."

With Mia offering her chauffeur services, we rolled into the city the next day after my 9 A.M. class ended.

As we headed into Midtown, I asked, "Do I look okay to meet with the O'Haras?"

"Yes. You can't even tell you've been slumming it with your dress code the last few weeks. You cleaned up nicely." Mia grinned as she pulled into a loading zone. "Meet me at my apartment when you're done. We can grab dinner and drinks before we head back."

"I was planning to take the train. I've already bugged you enough times for rides."

"Honestly, I don't mind the drive. And I love commuting to and from the city to Carlthorpe. It's like having a Hamptons or Fire Island timeshare, but rent-free and a full fridge."

A honk blasted from behind. "Drop off and pick up only, sistah!"

"Looks like you need to unload yourself ASAP," Mia said, looking into her rearview mirror. "Good luck today!"

"Thanks!" I hopped out of her car and waved goodbye.

Pushing the revolving door, I couldn't help but notice how my business clothes felt against my skin. In the glass reflection, everything looked familiar and put together, but I'd gotten so used to wearing jeans and sneakers around campus that my skirt, silk blouse, and heels were insanely uncomfortable, like I had borrowed someone else's costume for Halloween and it was unseasonably hot that day. When security asked for my ID and asked me to confirm my identity, I hesitated. Of course I was Lily Lee, the same Lily who had been in these offices several times before, but admittedly, something inside me felt a little different. On the ride up to the twenty-second floor, I tried to remember if this was how I'd felt when I started my first corporate job, wearing business clothes for the first time. Maybe the shift inside me I was feeling was just temporary, like someone forgetting to wear a retainer for a few days, letting their teeth move and then shift back to the right positions after reuse.

My editor, Katherine, greeted me at the elevator bank. "Thank you so much for coming on such short notice. When the O'Hara family contacted us out of the blue, it took us by surprise. Amanda can't make it, she was pulled away by HR for some kind of alumni outreach event planning." She smiled and swiped her badge to gain access to the floor. "They're here early, and now that you're here, we can just jump in and get started. Did you have any questions before we head into the meeting?"

*Yes. A few.*

*What's for lunch?*

*And am I just a random token non-white person to go on a tour with, or do they actually see me as their peer?*

*Is there compensation or reimbursement for expenses?*

*Maybe it's paranoia, but . . . is there an underlying motive for them?*

Offering my most gracious smile, I said, "No questions at

the moment. Let's start the meeting and I can get a feel for what they're thinking."

She opened the door to reveal the massive O'Hara publishing entourage. Other than Mary O'Hara, everyone else around the long, oblong table was male. Ten people in all, including the O'Hara twins. It was like an executive meeting at my last male-dominated corporate job all over again. Aside from below-market pay, I left there for a few reasons, and let's just say that dealing with this particular demographic in the highest ranks of the company was among them.

My marketing lead and publicity assistant lined up at the door behind me. We greeted the O'Hara team as we entered the room. My eyes widened as I looked past everyone and saw the lunch buffet against the far wall: some blessed saint had ordered a three-tiered dessert tray. My mouth watered as I shook hands with everyone.

We quickly took our seats so the meeting could begin. My team was not only outnumbered by the O'Hara party, we were out-everythinged. Out-marketed, out-publicized, out-budgeted, and even outclassed: they had partnered with all the finest spirits companies, fashion designers, and top business schools across the country, they announced. It appeared the O'Haras' *You Go, Girl!* book was going to be a hit no matter what, whether it was organic or devised that way, and by targeting so many aspirational brands, they were clearly going after a specific type of clientele who had probably never heard of me. And honestly, I'd never heard of half of them either.

So why was I here again? Especially compared to all the

name-dropped celebrities and influencers in their marketing presentation, I was a big ol' nobody.

After their publicity director covered event outreach,
they finally cut to the chase. "Lily, we would love to pitch
you with Mary and Cameron for some of the more urban
opportunities."

"Urban?" I had no idea what they meant by this. I'd never
considered anything about me urban. I wore clothes from
Urban Outfitters sometimes, that was it. And maybe listened to Keith Urban on occasion. I ate from dining establishments that were cash only, did that count? I wore J.Crew
flats and Madewell dresses for God's sake. What was this
urban nonsense?

Kylie, my publicist and fast friend, scribbled something
in her spiral notebook and pushed it over to me. "URBAN—
MAYBE SHE MEANS NOT RICH OR WHITE?"

Oh.

Silence took over the room. I bit back cutting words that
teetered on the tip of my tongue, knowing what I really
wanted to say about the O'Haras' perception of race and
class. It would certainly lead to the end of this so-called
partnership. But just as I opened my mouth and found the
courage to speak my mind, Mary O'Hara surprised me by
being the first to say something after the uncomfortably
silent stretch. "Lily, I adore your writing, and your book
inspired me to become an author myself. I've talked about
your book a lot in interviews because it's a must-buy for
anyone trying to make it in the business world, for anyone,
but especially women of color."

I took a deep, calming breath. "Thank you." I met her gaze without glancing down, because my therapist had worked with me a lot about accepting compliments and not dismissing them as being "no big deal," as I was always apt to do. It was a combination of being a modest people pleaser for so long, plus the humility stemming from my Korean heritage, with my parents instructing me to down-play all of my successes, while they were allowed to brag and talk them up.

She continued. "It was my idea to bring you into our mar-keting plans, but I didn't specify when or how." She turned to her brother. "Can't we just ask her to join wherever she's comfortable rather than dictate what type of events are best—"

Cameron interrupted. "We have more than adequate coverage in our core market, and the press releases are al-ready out. It's this larger, more urban reach I'm interested in pursuing. With her credentials and streetwise advice it seemed like, synergistically speaking—"

He'd said "urban" again, and anyone who used the term "synergistically speaking" was not worth my time. It was my turn to steer the conversation.

"Actually, I'm pretty busy today, so maybe we could wrap up sooner rather than later. I can look through the list of op-portunities in your appendix and let you know the ones that interest me once you've sorted out your targeting strategy. We can go from there."

Mary nodded. "Thank you, Lily. Any time you can offer is very much appreciated."

I responded, "And I'm still on board with the in-person event sponsored by LBS alumni. I'll email you the interview questions after the meeting. Shall we eat? This looks wonderful, thank you to the people who ordered it."

Kylie beamed and grabbed a plate. "I ordered too much, you all might need to take some home!"

My editor leaned over and whispered, "Thank you for being open-minded about this. We can just do the LBS alumni event for now and evaluate their other ideas. It's a great way to promote your book series."

I nodded. I hadn't agreed to much, but it was worth it to investigate opportunities open to me that I couldn't otherwise afford. One of the points in my book was about self-advocating and self-promoting, and how women need to do more of it. This was something I always had trouble with too.

Another thing I firmly believed in was for women to develop relationships and networks, even pushing outside of their comfort zone. I would need to run this O'Hara quasi-partnership by my personal board of directors—aka Mia, some former work friends, and Beth. They had my best interests at heart while the people in this room might have their own agenda. If the exposure and platform the O'Haras provided would be worthwhile, my trusted friends would help me see the true value and risk of this opportunity.

I took a turkey and Brie sandwich, Caesar salad, chips, and a weighty cupcake back to the table as the O'Haras' publicist confirmed that *The Wall Street Journal* ad would be running soon, and that the publisher would be promoting the event in social media leading up to that day as well.

Mary O'Hara said, "Thank you for that update!" just as
Cameron barked, "I hope you can do better than just *The
Wall Street Journal*. How much is it for *The New York Times*?
*The Washington Post*? Have you even thought about going
bigger with our brand?"

Cameron's handlers, all three of them, whispered among
themselves, and although it was too low to hear it, I caught
snippets of "too expensive" and "looking into it." Mary offered me an apologetic glance and forced a smile. She did
seem grounded and genuine, but I'd been burned in the past
by people who seemed one way and turned out to be another.
I wasn't going to let my guard down so easily. At least not
until I'd had lunch and my hangriness subsided so I could
think clearly.

Cameron eventually calmed down and the conversation
picked up again, going in an interesting and pleasant direction. We all talked more candidly about how hard it was to
release a book in a noisy, cluttered online world, and how
publishing was like being an entrepreneur because you had
to not only create a product but also promote, market, and
sell it. I chimed in and said one of my favorite perks was being able to read books by other authors before their release
dates, and both Mary and Cam couldn't wait for that time to
come. The room energy shifted from stilted to relaxed. So
we had a few things in common. Finding common ground
was good for relationship-building and gaining trust.

Mary asked, "I'd love to know what made you finally
write a book, Lily. It's so hard to not only get words on a

page but also have the guts to put your work out into the world. What inspired you to be so brave?"

It was a question I'd been asked before by business bloggers and podcast interviewers, but for people in this room, who already knew about publishing, my answer could go more in depth. "Honestly, I hadn't seen anyone write a book from a perspective like mine. I wanted it to be like a mini-mentorship for people just starting out, giving real-life, practical, actionable advice for those who needed to build their careers from the ground up."

Both Mary and Cameron nodded as I spoke, but what shocked me most was Cameron opening the spiral notebook in front of him and scribbling notes. I continued to talk about my mission to empower women and help them navigate the complexities of work-life balance, self-promotion, and performance evaluations, primarily in male-dominated environments.

Cameron placed his elbows on the table, put his hands together, and tapped his index fingers on his lips. "This is all very insightful." He made eye contact with me. "Thank you for sharing your perspective with us, I am so glad you came today."

While the words he spoke were extremely kind, something about his tone and demeanor was not entirely sincere. A nagging sensation pulled at my chest, but I couldn't pinpoint anything specific. This was different from the general feeling of angst and worry manifesting inside my chest every day, which was all too familiar for me. My internal alarm bells rang all the time for guys like him, and in response I always had my guard up. But I couldn't deny the niggling feeling that he was up to something. Or maybe this was just a vibe that guys like him radiated all the time and I happened to have an extra-sensitive douche-o-meter.

When the meeting ended, my editor, publicist, and marketing lead lingered in the room while Cameron and Mary walked with me to the door.

"Looking forward to our event next week," I said, shaking their hands.

Mary smiled. "Thanks for being part of our launch."

"See you soon," Cameron said with a megawatt grin. But for him, my douche detector wouldn't stop ringing.

# Chapter Sixteen

Looking out the window of the engineering library was a great way to alleviate screen fatigue. After working on problem sets for two straight hours, gazing at the oak and maple trees shedding their golden and blood-orange leaves onto the cobblestone provided a much-needed visual and mental reprieve.

A guy wearing a forest-green beanie chaining his bike to the metal railing caught my eye. After locking his wheel, he glanced toward the sky as snowflakes fluttered from the gray clouds. With his full face in view, I could see it was none other than Jake Cho, looking as handsome as ever in his knit beanie and down vest. Despite the near-freezing temperatures, he had on long olive-green shorts. To his defense though, snowfall wasn't typical this time of year. I would need to dig out my winter coat if drastic drops in temperature were going to be a regular occurrence.

As if Jake could sense me, he looked over at my window and I gasped. My body slithered down the back of my chair and I stared up at the ceiling. *Please God, don't let him know that was me.*

For a good minute, I studied the shape of the brown water stains on the textured ceiling panels above my head, then sat upright and looked out the window again. No Jake. His bike was still there. Which meant he was somewhere near—

"Hey."

I whipped around. Jake took a few steps forward and looked at my assortment of textbooks. "Studying for midterms?"

"Yes." I slammed my laptop closed so he couldn't peek at my job research and my sad attempts at writing the first chapter of my book. That meeting with the O'Haras had been a swift kick in the ass: a good reminder that I was here only to finish my degree, and that everything else was a distraction. Frat parties, office hours, socializing—all interferences. The biggest time waster? My stalking victim standing before me, who looked really adorable in his above-the-waist cold weather attire. *Go away, Jake.*

He bit his lip. "Could I be honest about something, and can you keep it just between us?" Jake pulled off his knit cap, revealing a staticky mess of black and silver hair. I wanted to smooth it out so badly but stayed put in my chair.

What did he want to tell me? We had so much history . . . it could be anything. Was it about our dating past? The weirdness between us the night of the frat party? My stomach clenched and my hands turned cold while my mind cycled through more possibilities.

He dragged a chair from a desk nearby. "I'm telling you this as someone who cares about you."

I gulped. Suddenly my ears began to ring, and the drumbeat of my heart made it hard to hear his next words.

"As your TA, I have to let you know that your overall grade dropped to an A minus because of the last few homework assignments. An A minus is great, don't get me wrong. But you won't be eligible for the internship consideration if you're not at least ranked in the top ten in the class." He hesitated before continuing. "And I know you could get there."

My lips parted with the intention of responding to him, but I didn't know what to say. Just a few minutes earlier I had been applying to dozens of high-level positions, and this internship opportunity at Solv was for college seniors. So why was I so disappointed in myself?

I had to admit, the last few homework assignments I'd submitted were not my best work, and judging by this conversation, we both knew it. If I wanted a shot at getting my foot in the door at Solv, a bona fide dream company that I would never have been considered for before, one that had high employee retention and always made the top of any "best company to work for" list, I had to try harder. Maybe my ideal job had been dangling in my peripheral vision all along.

There was still time to raise my overall grade. His warning was like lit kindling igniting an intense fire deep within me. "Okay, I'll take that into consideration when I turn in my homework and prepare for exams. Thanks for looking out for me."

"Would you like any help? I have some time before I have to go and I know the last lecture was a lot to take in, I could see it in everyone's faces." His doelike, earnest eyes got me every time. Bambi had nothing on this guy.

Ten-years-ago me would have said, "Hell no, I can do this myself," but I had literally written a book about how women in the workplace were always trying to do everything themselves, taking on too much, and were reluctant to ask for assistance, thinking it would show weakness. I couldn't fall into that trap, not again. It was against everything I stood for now.

Opening my laptop, I closed out the Word document of my book outline and pulled up the latest homework assignment and my notes from the last lecture. "Would you mind going over De Morgan's Laws with me? They're not as easy for me to grasp as I thought they would be."

Jake scooted his chair to my desk. His knees barely grazed mine and my skin tingled from making contact. "As your dedicated teaching assistant, I'd be honored to help you." He ran his fingers through the front of his hair, taming his magnificent mane in the process.

*Focus on the lesson, Lily. Stop dreaming about running your own fingers through his hair too.*

He went over short-circuit evaluations and Boolean expressions, and I focused intently on his words. Jake was a talented teacher, and he taught the material in a slightly different way than the professor had, with examples I could relate to better. But despite his excellent teaching, I found myself distracted when he took off his coat and rolled up his sleeves before typing on his keyboard. And holy . . . when he stuck his pen in his mouth while looking for a specific reference in the textbook, or leaned back in his chair to stretch, his shirt pulling up just enough to see—

"Anything else before we wrap up here?" he asked while putting his books and laptop into his backpack. "I'm packing up, but it's only because I managed to take over your entire table with all of my shit."

My cheeks lit on fire. "No. Thank you for, um . . . assisting with the teaching."

Jake chuckled. "Anytime. That's what I'm here for. My job is literally teaching assistant."

His departure allowed me to turn my attention back to writing the preface of my long-overdue book. The opening was the only part that didn't require any research, observations, or insights. I hadn't written much in weeks, but with the O'Haras' book out in the world, the pressure to release my next one increased exponentially.

An hour later, I wrote a few sentences, then quickly deleted them, over and over ad nauseam. Two hours passed and I was back to staring at a completely blank page.

This was going nowhere.

And it would continue going nowhere if I didn't do something about it.

I went into the draft folder of my email and found a note I'd written to my editor the last time I felt stuck, while in the middle of writing my last book. I was minutes away from sending it to Katherine, but thanks to her editor ESP, she called me just before I was at my wit's end, ready to call it quits. She worked with me to shape my book and I managed to finish the project a month after the deadline. I never sent the email, but I had saved it. Maybe to repurpose it one day. For a day like today.

*Katherine,*

*I owe it to you to let you know how things are progressing. So here's the truth. I'm in a rut. I honestly think I've deluded myself and others into thinking I have something unique or important to say, but as I continue writing, I'm feeling like maybe I don't. Or maybe someone else can do a much better job, and they should write this book instead of me.*

*Maybe I just don't know how to write at all, or I'm not expressing myself well in book form. How can I be a writer if I can't write any good words?*

*I've been able to draft only the first half of the book but it feels like a disjointed, blathering mess, kind of like this email. I'm too embarrassed to share anything with you because it's not in good shape. I'm sorry I wasted your time.*

*Sincerely,*
*Lily*

The difference between then and now was that at the time I'd written that email, half of the book had been drafted. For this new one, I had nothing. It was understandable, of course, since I'd focused so much of my time on my college classes. But now as we were approaching midterm season, the time trade-off was evident. Was it time to give my editor an update, a full disclosure of what I'd been up to the past weeks? Would she understand why the book proposal I'd turned in two years ago wasn't exactly clicking with me now? Or would she give up on me and ask me for the advance back?

How could someone like me write a book about career success? Maybe I needed to write about something I was an actual expert in.

Failure.

That idea made me laugh but it wasn't the worst I'd ever had. Maybe I could work with that. I opened a new file and jotted down a few new ideas, feeling my passion for writing return.

Perhaps I could do this after all, but it might need to be an entirely different book.

# Chapter Seventeen

*Twelve and a Half Years Ago*

*T*he Asian Student Association chartered a bus to Manhattan so members could visit NYU's and Columbia's
campuses, giving us an opportunity to watch the undergraduate Korean Student Association culture shows for each
school. The events took place on Friday night and Saturday
night on the same February weekend. It was my sophomore
year, and my very first time visiting the city.

Of course, as soon as the bus rolled into Midtown Manhattan, we went straight to Koreatown to eat Korean barbecue
on Thirty-Second Street.

"What does A-Y-C-E mean?" I asked, crossing and rubbing
my upper arms with my mittened hands.

Some of the Korean guys from my school laughed. The club
president joked, "All you can eat. Are you sure you're even
Korean?"

My face grew hot even though the temperature outside
was freezing. Presumably this Asian organization was for

students who wanted to connect with Asian culture, and for meeting other people who shared a common heritage, which was important to me. But oddly, the more I hung out with other Koreans, the less Asian I felt. To my friends growing up, I was very Korean. But to the other members of ASA, I was super Americanized. I'd been to Seoul only once. I wasn't fluent in Korean by any means and Carlthorpe didn't offer it as a language option. Mia was fluent, but she and I rarely spoke it. And maybe the worst tragedy of all, I hadn't actually been to any K-BBQ places in a big city, hence my ignorance of AYCE.

"There are all types of Koreans in the diaspora, as you should know," I argued.

Mia chimed in, "At least she's not obnoxiously overdoing the K-pop fandom like you." She gestured to his bleached floppy hair, which got a big laugh from everyone and ended the awkwardness.

The prices of meat on the menu in the window gave me sticker shock. But this was supposed to be a fun trip and I promised myself I would try to enjoy it. Rarely having opportunities to go on weekend trips, if there was any time to not stress about spending, this was it. We were in New York City!

The burning stomach pain in my mid-abdomen came roaring back, likely caused by my money-related worrying. I winced and squeezed my eyes shut, breathing through the agony. I popped an antacid and prayed the discomfort would subside for the rest of the trip.

Mia locked her arm into the crook of my elbow. "Sit with me and Andy. And Jake." She elbowed me in the ribs.

*Andrew Won was in a few of my classes. He was the smoker, stoner, drinker type that was as bad boy as guys at Carlthorpe got, the kind of guy Mia swore she would stop dating. He was the best friend of Jake Cho, the guy I'd had a heart-eye-emoji crush on since the day I joined ASA, but had done nothing about since I had a longtime, long-distance boyfriend at the time. There was no one specific thing that made him so attractive to me. He was lean, bordering on scrawny, and was always spending his time and energy on dozens of side hustles and hobbies, from making boba tea and selling it from his dorm window, to brewing beer in his closet, to selling cheaper, higher-quality Carlthorpe merch than the bookstore carried from his trunk. He was enterprising, and so busy that he never seemed to have time at all to, say, have a steady girlfriend.*

*At a table for four, Mia and I sat across from each other, and Andrew plopped down next to Mia, leaving the seat next to me open for Jake. Once we'd ordered and received our first round of drinks, it struck me that the way we were configured was almost like we were double-dating.*

*The food hadn't come by the time we finished off a second bottle of soju, and by then Mia was hanging on to every slurred word out of Andrew's mouth. Jake and I were enjoying each other's company too, but we weren't nearly as wasted as our tablemates.*

*Finally, the server brought out a large tray of assorted banchan, along with a large white platter covered with thin slices of uncooked beef. "Bulgogi imnida!" She turned on our grill and placed the little bowls of vegetables in front of* us. Rather than offer us duplicate sets of banchan for each side of the table, she instead plunked down fifteen unique side dishes. My favorites were cucumber kimchi, anchovies, and spinach. Mia handed those to me and swapped them for the spicier ones colored orange and flaming red from the hot pepper powder.

The server placed the individual strips of beef on the grill and the meat sizzled as soon as it made contact with the metal grate. The one fact I knew about eating meat from an indoor grill at a Korean restaurant: your hair and clothes would smell like burned meat until they were washed. The smoky, charred scent would infuse into hair strands as the night wore on, like a potent essential oil. I pulled my hair into a loose bun, hoping to minimize the surface area of the beef eau de cologne.

"Jal mogosimnida!" The server put the metal tongs next to me and then walked away.

Mia laughed. "She picked you to cook the rest."

Jake smirked at me. "As Obi-Wan said, 'You were the chosen one!'"

Nerdy Star Wars jokes always had a special place in my heart, and here he was, winning me over with one of the corniest ones.

"Well, if I have to cook this for everyone, you need to order me some soju." I smirked right back at him. Andrew was the only one who was old enough to buy alcohol, but he was also fluent in Korean and had a knack for charming older women, specifically Korean waitstaff ajummas. No one checked our IDs. Within seconds after ordering, the server brought over a new bottle of soju to our table.

*I worked on the meat while Andrew poured my next drink.*
*The fragrant smells of sesame oil and garlic wafted around*
*us as I flipped the crackling bulgogi. Jake took my plate and*
*passed it to Mia and Andrew, asking them for a sampling*
*of the side dishes from the other side of the table.* "Lily gets
first dibs. She's doing manual labor for us, the least we can
do is pay her in banchan units."

*Mia, now fully tipsy and leaning into Andrew's shoulder,*
*widened her eyes at me.*

Yes, I know, Mia. Jake is a cute, courteous, charming guy.

*Her eyes widened even more.* **You better hit that tonight.**
**He's single now.**

*Once the bulgogi was divvied up, we all raised our drinks*
*and toasted. Mia clinked cheers.* "To the city that never sleeps!"

*Lord, we ate so much. After we finished all the meat, An-*
*drew and Jake asked for a bowl of kimchi chigae to split, while*
*Mia and I each had a bowl of rice cake dumpling soup. Dduk*
*mandu guk was my all-time fave and once I decided that*
*loosening the purse strings on this trip wouldn't kill me, I*
*decided to get a bowl all to myself. Because why the hell not?*

*Jake asked everyone,* "Have you ever tried Korean food in
international cities? My family went to Paris and my God,
the banchan was so bad. It was a top-rated restaurant too."

*Mia joined in.* "I went to Athens with my high school Latin
class, and same thing, we tried the Korean food there once
because I missed eating it and it was so overpriced and mediocre." *She picked at the few remaining bean sprouts with*
*her chopsticks and devoured them.*

Andrew said, "The Korean food in London is okay, but you need to know where to go. It's also crazy expensive."

I had traveled to Korea only once, and that was the only time I needed a passport. "I've only had Korean food in Korea." I deadpanned, "The food was great."

They all laughed, and we all toasted to South Korea for absolutely no reason.

I sighed wistfully as I grabbed a toasted seaweed square. "One day I'd love to go to Spain though, even if the Korean food isn't good. It's one of the options for the study abroad program." It was something I had seriously considered and one of the few things keeping me at Carlthorpe. They had a world-renowned overseas program for college juniors and seniors.

Jake's eyes widened. "Really? It's something I've looked into too. Barcelona or Madrid. Time to use my rusty high school AP Spanish!"

I raised my glass of soju and toasted to us. If Jake went to Spain too, wow, even better. Knowing someone else there would be so much more fun.

"Well, I'm stuffed." Andrew fell back into the booth seat and rested his head on the padded wall. Mia leaned into his shoulder like the Tower of Pisa and closed her eyes. Andrew's face beamed. Mia sighed blissfully.

She seemed so happy. I wanted her to be happy.

Mia also looked asleep.

Jake whispered into my ear, "If these two call it a night, want to keep hanging out with me? I want to see more of the city."

He was so direct and it was exactly what I wanted to do. Of course I'd love to sightsee with Mia too, but she was snoring now, and definitely into Andrew.

"Let's head out!" Jake barked, jolting the three of us into an upright, startled position. We scooted out of the booth and put on our winter coats. As Andrew and Mia led the way, Jake rested his hands on my shoulders, playfully steering me out of the restaurant. My body shivered at his touch, but I tried to play it off like I was cold from the frigid gusts of wintry air let in from the open front door.

I'd be lying to myself if I didn't admit that I wanted something to happen between us on this trip. We had both gotten out of long-distance relationships, each of us dumped by our insignificant others. I'd been with my high school sweetheart for several years and was just getting used to the idea of being single. Was it too soon to date again? Or was the timing perfect?

It was hard to think of places to go after dinner: we were all so stuffed that dessert was out of the question. I looked up at the sky to see if it was a clear night, and the skyscraper to our left grabbed my attention. It was a place I'd always wanted to visit, and hordes of people streamed in and out of the main entrance. "Have any of you been to the Empire State Building?" I asked.

Everyone shook their heads. Jake searched his pockets for his gloves and knit cap while Andrew and Mia contemplated this sightseeing adventure. I tried to plead my case with Jake's help.

The Do-Over 187

*"Think about all the romantic movie moments you've seen or heard about featuring this historical, iconic building!" I boasted.*

Jake added, "Like Superman Two. The best superhero movie, by the way."

*I laughed. "I was thinking Sleepless in Seattle."*

"Zoolander?" Jake asked.

*"Stop it," I said.*

"King Kong."

*I sighed. "An Affair to Remember."*

"Independence Day," he teased.

*I crossed my arms and quirked a brow. "Why do you even know so many Empire State Building movies?"*

Andrew and Mia hugged and remained glued together. "I think we might call it a night," Mia said. "But it sounds like you two have a lot to talk about that I don't entirely understand."

*I smiled. "Okay, Jake and I will head back afterward."*

*The happy couple walked down the street toward the subway station while Jake and I headed northwest. The Empire State Building wasn't far away, but it sure felt like it was. The gusts of freezing air pushed against us, slowing our steps. The wind chill made it feel twenty degrees below zero as we gradually made our way to the entrance.*

*Hundreds of other tourists had the same idea as us, but luckily the line kept moving, not giving me time to balk at the price and bail when we reached the cashier and paid for tickets to the observatory. As I forked over my credit card, I whispered to myself, "This will be a once-in-a-lifetime experience.*

*It's worth it."* Signing the receipt and sending it back under the hole in the Plexiglas, we made our way to the elevator bank, where we waited with ten other people to be taken to eardrum-popping levels.

When the doors opened, Jake asked, "How are you with heights?"

I shrugged. I hadn't thought about it before. I'd been inside a few lookout towers in various cities I'd visited with my parents, but that wasn't the same.

"I'll be fine," I squeaked as the doors closed. The elevator whooshed upward. Maybe sensing my nervousness, Jake placed his hands on my shoulders again, and as he did that, I leaned back into his chest, shifting my body so my head tucked right under his chin. The elevator was only moderately full because of the limited capacity and everyone wearing big winter coats, so I didn't need to press against him, but did anyway. Jake didn't seem to mind. He didn't budge for the entire ride. Climbing to our destination, Jake's heart thumped against my back. His breathing sped up, matching mine.

We were the last two visitors to exit. I hesitated because the moment I took a step forward, this physical bond between us would break.

"Go straight ahead," the attendant said, as if I had no clue how elevator departures worked. Jake chuckled and then nudged me forward.

I followed the others ahead of me down the short walkway and through the glass doors leading to the open-air observation deck. Jake followed me so closely that he stepped on my right heel. If I hadn't been wearing boots, my shoe would have come off. "Sorry," he mumbled as the wind whipped our faces with subzero arctic chill.

"It's cold," I whimpered, stating the obvious. You think, Lily? Your teeth don't chatter like this usually?

Yes, I was baiting him. And luckily, he obliged. Jake immediately pulled me into a hug and we walked around the perimeter fused as one.

While he held me snug against his chest, I murmured, "Good thing we're bundled up. I couldn't help but notice you're appropriately dressed for the weather. No shorts?"

He looked down at my face and grinned. "Even I have my limits. Andrew said it would be ball-freezing weather." He pointed to various buildings near and far. "Look! That's the Chrysler Building. Thirty Rockefeller Plaza. The MetLife Building."

It was breathtaking. Taking in the panoramic view, it hit me all at once. I belonged here. In New York City. I examined all the historical marker signs, highlighting the locations of key landmarks and pointing at them with "EUREKA!"-level enthusiasm, as if I were an explorer discovering them for the first time. "And there's Central Park! Times Square! Statue of Liberty! The Brooklyn Bridge!"

On another night, this would have been the perfect romantic moment. But because of the blustery weather, this experience had less of a romantic comedy movie vibe than I would have liked.

Jake read my mind. He whispered into my ear, "You know what movie this reminds me of?"

I shuddered. Please tell me.

"Elf," he breathed heavily.

I tried to hold my laughter in, but I couldn't. I giggled and pulled his knit cap down over his nose. "Elf? Really?"

He lifted his hat with his thumbs and looked me in the eyes. "I happen to love Elf, it's the ultimate fish-out-of-water story. Don't you dare steal this joy away from me."

There was something about Jake that I found irresistible. He was funny. Smart. He pushed all the right buttons and appreciated me for who I was. He awakened all my senses . . . or maybe that was the freezing temperature and high altitude.

Without trying to overthink it, I decided that catching him off guard would be the way to combat his coyness. It would let me gauge if he liked me as much as I adored him.

Taking a deep breath in and out, I stood on the balls of my feet and pulled on his coat lapels. His eyes widened and he shut up about Elf while bringing his head down to my eye level. Closing my eyes, and without hesitation, I gently pressed my lips on his. Icy tingles ran through my body, clashing with the heat radiating from overactive nerves. My body was a complete mess, but I loved every icy-hot second of our very first kiss.

I released Jake's woolly collar from my clenched fists and took a small step back. Jake said, "You know there are actually a few great kissing scenes in Elf."

Oh God. Before I could declare this an epic fail, he pulled me in by the waist. "I'll stop with the jokes now, I'm just nervous," he whispered. Then leaning down, his mouth parted my lips, sending shivers down my spine. His kisses were *soft at first, and then each one burned with more intensity, making me dizzy.*

*Our teeth slightly chattered as we talked about traveling to Europe, seeing views like this from the Eiffel Tower and the London Eye. That was the night we began dating. Overlooking the magical, romantic Manhattan skyline, with a world of possibilities around us, we hugged each other tight.*

# Chapter Eighteen

A time-sensitive email from the registrar hit my in-box while my study group visited Jake during office hours.

*Dear Lily Lee,*

*You have been moved to the top of the Statistics 100 waitlist and there is an opening in the class. Please note that you must register online or come in person to the Office of the Registrar within 72 hours of the time this email was sent. Failure to register within this timeframe will result in you being dropped from the course. Should this happen, you will not retain your original spot if you re-add yourself to the waitlist.*

*If you are no longer interested in enrolling in this class, please respond immediately to allow another waitlisted student a more expedited opportunity.*

I reread the email a dozen times. One by one, Ethan, PJ, and then Grace eventually left Jake's office, leaving me alone with Jake.

"Lily? Earth to Lily! Are you okay?" He swat-waved his hand across my face like one of those black-and-white director clapboards.

Was I okay? Maybe? Maybe not? For weeks, I had tried very hard to get into the stats course, and now, facing the actual decision to take it or not, I was full-body paralyzed. My mouth, lips, and tongue couldn't even form words to tell Jake that I would be leaving his class.

Instead, I pointed to my screen. Jake wheeled his chair to me and read the email over my shoulder. I inhaled his clean, familiar scent and felt like a breathless college girl all over again.

"Oh. I see." His shoulders slumped. "This was what you wanted all along."

His words hit me one by one, seven slaps to the face, the melancholy in his voice making my heart hurt.

It was hard keeping my voice from wavering. "It's not personal; I wanted to take stats when I got here. And now a spot's finally opened up. It's that simple." I put my belongings in my messenger bag and stood from my chair.

Was it that simple though? Stats would probably be an easy A. I had a deep understanding of surveys and analytics from previous on-the-job training, I'd gone to all the lectures and understood them, and the class was structured so the grade was based on midterm and final exams. Taking this class had been the plan all along. I'd lost sight of my original goal, focusing way too much on an internship I was far too old for, and foolishly thinking I could live out this fantasy of whatever *this thing* was between Jake and me. Was it serendipity? Coincidence? Or the universe pushing us together . . . or maybe having a good laugh at our expense.

I couldn't deny that in the CS class, I learned something new with each lecture, knowledge I would have never gained. My entire life I'd thought it was impossible for someone like me to learn something new once I'd entered the workforce, but here I was, working my ass off and fighting hard for a top grade, hoping for a shot at the prestigious tech internship in a new field.

Jake looked up at me with his earnest brown eyes. "I guess I got used to seeing you a few times a week. Would it be embarrassing to admit that I looked forward to class and office hours because of you?" He used his heels to wheel his chair to the other side of his desk. "In fact, I've worked a lot harder lately and put in a ton of work on my dissertation because I was inspired by your being back on campus. You lit a fire under me. I pulled two all-nighters this week alone." He rubbed his chin and sighed. "And you've landed yourself back in one of the top spots in the class again. I really think you have a great shot at getting the interview for that coveted internship opening. You're the only woman in the running by the way, the other nine are dudes."

My chest tightened as my brain processed his praise. "I haven't decided anything yet."

He leaned closer. "This is me begging you to stay in CS." There was a hopeful glint in his eyes, holding me captive. "But if stats is really where you want to be, well then, I want to support you one hundred percent."

My mind swirled. "Yes," I whispered, trying to swallow the large lump in the back of my throat. "That was my plan from the start. For the easier grade, so I can get my degree, then get my dream job and write about it. But I appreciate all the time you spent with me. No hard feelings?" I scooted back my seat, came around the desk, opening my arms for a hug.

"I'm happy for you." He stood and folded me into a tender embrace. "If you've officially decided, I guess this means I'm not your TA anymore," he said in a surprisingly buoyant tone.

Synapses in my brain fired simultaneously. I tilted my head up, my heart thudding hard against my rib cage. "I'm not your student anymore." This artificial, invisible barrier between us had been lifted, along with the oppressive pressure to do well in class, knowing stats was in the bag. Instantly, my life shifted and settled into a better place.

He stared into my eyes with an intense gaze that sent a ripple of electricity down my spine. Jake tightened his arms around me as my hands shyly slid up his chest. He was much stronger, firmer, and bolder than he had been a decade ago, and my body responded to him, like muscle memory. I steadied my hands on his shoulders near his neck, then, without even thinking, walked my fingers up to bury them in his hair.

Jake leaned down and brushed a gentle, warm kiss on my lips. A shiver rippled through my body as I sighed softly, savoring it. Our second kiss was slow, intense, and demanding, hungrier and more urgent than sweet. It left my mouth flaring with heat, leaving me wanting more. Much more.

His lips continued to explore me, leaving a hot trail down my neck and to my shoulder. I took a step forward, forcing him to move back and bump into his desk.

Maybe Mia was right and it was time to seize the day. When would Jake and I ever get another chance at us? I looked over my shoulder at the door. "Does it lock? Even if I'm not in your class anymore, we need to be careful . . . the last thing I need is a scandal."

"Discretion is my middle name. Actually, it's Hyun-Joong, but you knew that." He arched an eyebrow and flashed a mischievous grin. "Hold on a sec." After sliding his hands to my hips, he offered me a quick peck on the forehead. "I'll be right back!"

Jake adjusted the front of his gray cargo shorts and opened the door. After scrubbing the whiteboard with the eraser, he wrote "OFFICE HOURS CANCELED" with a thick black marker. He shut the door and locked it.

Wiggling back to his original position between me and the desk, he asked, "All set. Now, where were we?"

"We were being careful . . . but having fun." I smiled and brought my hands to the center of his chest, slowly unbuttoning his flannel shirt one notch at a time, my grip growing steadier with each fastener release. He reached behind him and, with a large swipe, pushed notebooks off his desk onto the floor, the opposite of a magician pulling a tablecloth and keeping everything intact. Jake lifted me, turned us around, and sat me down on the wooden desktop.

Honestly, who wouldn't want the opportunity to have a sensual office rendezvous with a hot grad student? I eased back slowly and pulled his hard body into mine, breathing heavily as his chest gently pressed into me. Shivers of delight ran through me as his lips descended on mine again. Only minutes before, I'd had so much on my mind and important decisions to make, but at this very moment all my thoughts and worries were whisked away as my body shattered and melted into his.

# Chapter Nineteen

*Twelve and a Half Years Ago*

*L* ily?"

"Li-ly."

"LILY!"

My eyes snapped open. Jake's face peered down on mine. "You were dreaming. And it was the unpleasant, kicking-and-pushing-me-off-the-bed kind."

"Really?" I swam through the haze of recent memories, trying to piece them together. My stomach clenched tight as flashes, images, and sequences came flooding back. Me not going to class. Not doing any homework. Never studying. Then waking up the day of the final exam and realizing I was completely unprepared for it.

I'd had variations of this dream before—signing up for a course I never attended and forgetting I enrolled, walking into a classroom for the final exam only to find out I'd missed it, even showing up to a final exam naked—and they'd gotten more frequent the last few months. The knot in my gut tightened as the recollection of my latest nightmare grew more vivid and clear, like I had just put on a new pair of prescription glasses and my vision had started to settle.

The tenderness of his smile echoed in his gentle voice. "Wanna talk about it?"

Hell no, I didn't want to talk about it. The last thing I needed to do was scare him off by debriefing him on my achievement-related stress and the pressure my parents and I put on me. How could I tell him that I constantly thought about not measuring up and was always concerned about failure? The dream made me wonder if I was doing enough with my life. If I was prepared to my fullest capabilities. If I was even supposed to be here at Carlthorpe, or if it was an admissions mistake. Did rich and famous people ever feel this way, or was it just people like me who had to keep trying to prove themselves?

Jake's phone buzzed twice. He grabbed it from the side table, and I couldn't help but notice it was his ex-girlfriend. He'd entered the contact's name as "IT'S YOUR EX DON'T PICK UP."

A pang of jealousy hit me hard.

Jake read my face. "It's nothing. She's trying to raise money for a 10K pediatric leukemia fundraiser and it's the last day to donate. Gabby's hitting everyone up today. Going through her contact list."

Great, while I'm rolling around in bed, hungover, unshowered, looking like a human manatee . . . his ex was waking up early and sending text reminders of her selfless existence, helping out kids in need, all while staying physically fit.

"Forget about her, okay? Did you want to talk about your dream?"

I stared at his earnest face and shook my head. It was too personal. My anxiety avalanche wasn't something I had shared with anyone else, and what my parents did know of my struggles they saw as a weakness, and an excuse for poor performance. Maybe I would talk about all of this openly someday, but not now. Especially not with Jake half naked in my bed.

"Or want me to help you think about something else?" His longing gaze muddled my mind again, but in a good way. All I could think about was his thick wavy hair and those brown, playful eyes. Jake slid under the covers and wrapped his arm around me, pulling me into him. My skin tingled at his touch as he ran his hand down my soft curves.

"Yes, please," I whispered. "Help me forget."

His lips brushed against mine as he spoke. "Is it working?"

I giggled. "I think so."

"Well"—he kissed me lightly on the mouth—"the best way to move on from this dream is to focus on the present. On me. You. In this bed."

His lips forged a path down my neck. I trembled, even though his kisses were warm and soft. I loved being with Jake. He was so different from me: I was so much more of a type A personality, possibly fated to have the same exam anxiety–ridden dreams for the rest of eternity. I didn't want to ask if he'd had similar dreams and worries in life, because he was right about one thing: to focus on us now. Him. Me. In bed.

*Jake eased the loose strap of my camisole off my shoulder. My hands worked their way down his chest, past his abs, to his boxers. He undressed me slowly, and as he lowered himself over me, every inch of my body flooded with desire. There were no words to describe what I felt for Jake in that moment, because how could I capture the hope, promise, and joy of someone who helped me escape the trappings of my mind?*

*I couldn't. And that was when I knew my entire heart belonged to Jake Cho.*

## Chapter Twenty

T his is an intervention," Mia said on the phone while I
pulled on a bathrobe I'd found draped on a chair. Luckily Jake was in the shower and not within earshot of my best
friend trying to discourage bed frolicking with my TA.

"Did you drop the class yet?" she asked with an edge to
her voice. "Aren't midterms in a few days?"

Busted.

I had spent so much time studying for exams and hanging
out at Jake's that I had put off the enrollment and dropping
of classes till the last possible moment. And it wasn't like I
would dare to try to take these classes pass/fail this time.

"I'll do it tomorrow. It's the last day to get into stats, so I
don't have a choice. It's on my calendar and I set an alarm,
so don't worry."

A loud groan came through the phone speaker. "Not that
you asked me for my opinion, but I think you should stay in
the CS class. Think about it. You're learning new things, it's
challenging for you, and you were enjoying it." She snorted.
"And honestly, I'm pretty worried because you haven't been

home two nights in a row. Beth told me you've been bunking elsewhere with your TA."

*Mental note, remind Beth not to rat me out to my BFF. That was roommate code, right? Thou shalt not disclose personal details of rent-paying roomie to non-rent-paying freeloader.*

"Soon to be *ex*-TA," I corrected. "And weren't you the one encouraging me to have fun this semester?"

"Yes, but Jake Cho's gotten all into your head and you need to focus on *yourself.*" She cleared her throat and deadpanned in a voice imitating my very own mother, "Ji-Yeon! You need work hard in college, date later!"

"Thanks, *Umma,*" I quipped. It was exactly my parents' philosophy in high school and college: make good grades, don't get distracted by boys. And then when I left Carlthorpe, bam! A complete 180. *You need a boyfriend, Lily. You need to get married, Lily. Why are you not dating anyone, Lily? Where are my grandchildren, Lily? Ai-ish!*

It was too much pressure. And they always used my older sister as a point of comparison: she graduated from Tufts University's MD/PhD program and met her MD/PhD husband there. It was like my sister, Sara, had won Olympic golds in both individual and team events. Two doctors both with dual degrees? Four doctorates in the family? Overkill much?

And it never ended. I'd learned a lot about myself the last few years from numerous therapy sessions and conversations with my Korean friends, and now that I could recognize that the pressures my parents placed on me throughout

my childhood and early adulthood were unfair and unten-
able, I could see how my mental and physical health suf-
fered because of it. Cultural stigmas prevalent in the Asian
community—and the shame associated with seeking mental health support in my family—prevented me from getting help earlier. With the burden of generational success
my immigrant parents put on me over the years, and the
goalpost of high expectations they were always shifting to
out-of-reach positions, minimizing my exposure to them
and setting conversation boundaries were the only ways I
could keep my anxiety in check.

It helped so much that Mia and I both came from similar
cultural backgrounds, and even if it meant using humor as
a means of coping with our shared traumas, the open and
honest conversations we could have with each other were
invaluable to our overall mutual well-being.

"Don't worry about me. Jake and I have boundaries. I
hang out at his place so we're not seen, we order pizza and
Chinese food delivery, and keep things low-key. Basically,
it's like college again. The first time."

Mia clucked her tongue. "If you say so. Did you snoop
around his place? Does he have, like, a secret gun vault or a
drawer of sex toys?"

"That's not going to happen—he's almost done with his
shower," I whispered. "And there's nothing freaky about him
that I could see."

"Maybe you could lock him in the bathroom somehow.
Don't you want to know what he's been up to this whole
time?"

She did have a point. I knew professionally what he had done, and we'd caught up on how our families were doing. We talked a little about our parents: his were retired in Connecticut, my parents were mostly preoccupied with my sister and her family. She had two rambunctious toddler boys and my parents were helping out every other weekend. But ten years was a long time. That was 120 months of collecting emotional baggage. And pets.

The phone beeped. It was Mia requesting a video call, and she grinned as soon as she saw my face. "Oh man, you look so happy. I want to say I'm elated you've been relieving your stress through *vigorous physical activity,* but you NEED to show me around his place *right now* so I can flag any suspicious, serial-killer, freaky-deaky shit."

"And what if I don't give you the virtual tour?" I prodded.

She rolled her eyes. "For you, I would break into a dude's house and look around myself."

Mia laughed when she said it, but she was the kind of person who would do something like that just to protect me. It was admirable and a little bit frightening. It made me happy she was a friend and not a foe.

I sighed and reversed the camera so I could pan the room. "Bed, dresser, window, chair on one side. Closet . . . a few Grand Canyon and mountain range pictures on the wall, a nightstand—"

"Can you go back and turn on the light in the closet? I want to see if he's messy or organizes his shit all neat in a fucked-up, controlling way."

I flicked on the light. Disorganized piles of sweaters and

winter clothes on dry cleaning hangers crowded the entire space. "Does this scream serial killer to you?"

She shrugged. "He needs to get some real hangers. Seriously, they're not that expensive."

I popped my head into the hallway briefly, relieved Jake was still showering. "Only another minute," I said. "He'll be out soon."

"Show me the books next," she said.

I moved the phone across the tall white bookshelf. Mia yelled, "Hey, stop right there. Who's in those photos?"

"Just his high school graduation." He was standing with his cap and diploma with his parents and a few other young people. One was a girl, and his arm was around her. "I don't see anything that's life-threatening here. He's just plain ol' Jake with his high school girlfriend. It's a sweet photo."

She crinkled her brow. "Can you zoom in on the picture next to that high school one?"

"Why? It's Jake's college graduation photos with his parents." I sighed. "I guess he likes how he looks in caps and gowns. Maybe that's why he's going for a PhD, just for the photo op."

A pang of sadness hit me, not only because I was looking at a college graduation picture and that obviously hit me where it hurt, but ten years ago, at my fake commencement, was also one of the last times my umma, appa, and I were together to celebrate something. And it wasn't even for something real. My old diploma, if I still had it, was bogus. I'd achieved one less milestone in my life this whole time, and knowing I had messed up something so simple really screwed with my head.

"It's a little weird he doesn't have photos that are more recent, I'll admit that. But like I said, maybe he's got a thing for graduation gear. Anyway, are we done here?" I asked.

"Not yet. Give me a close-up view." Her eyes narrowed as she examined the bookshelf one last time. "There's a frame pushed to the back, way behind the high school grad one. What's up with that?"

The small 4 x 6 frame was in the shadows but still not completely hidden from view. I pulled it forward while keeping my phone positioned on the shelf so Mia could get a good look too.

It was a photo of present-day Jake, with a gorgeous Asian woman. Fingers intertwined, smiling at the camera. Her left hand was slightly lifted to show off a simple solitaire engagement ring. He wore a dress shirt, black striped tie, and, of course, shorts. Awful, black pleated ones.

Mia said it before I did. "Holy shit! That woman is the same girl in the high school photo."

Thoughts and memories from the past flooded my brain. The girl in the high school photo was his high school sweetheart. He had broken up with her in college a few months before we started dating. Mia and I had joked about me being a rebound. But this woman in the engagement photo . . . it was her.

Jake had gotten back with his ex.

When?

How long ago? And for how long?

Obviously long enough to be almost married to her.

I gulped hard and tried to calm my breathing. Mia yelped as she pieced it together too. "Ohhhh shit! That's his re-ex! Wait, what does that make you?"

*Also* a re-ex? My mind spun to the point of dizziness. Was this a pattern of his? Do-over relationships with ex-girlfriends? And did he go running back to his ex because he realized what *they* had was better than what *we* had?

Jake came into the bedroom and caught me with his engagement picture in my hand.

"Oh shit." He grimaced.

I dropped my phone as Mia yelled on its way down, "Oh shit is right." From the floor, she yelled, "Jake Cho! You have some explaining to do!"

# Chapter Twenty-One

I can explain," he pleaded while securing his towel around his waist. "It's not as bad as it looks—although, it looks pretty bad."

"Well, that certainly doesn't sound good," Mia's muffled voice cried out from the carpet. For a brief moment I'd forgotten she was still there.

I picked up the phone. "Sorry, Mia, I have to go."

"But—"

I ended the call. Still simmering with anger, I haphazardly put on my clothes and threw my phone and charger into my bag. The last thing I needed right now was to be emotionally tied up with a guy who was still hung up on his ex. His re-ex. Or ex-ex. Specifically the person who he was dating before me, and then had gone back to sometime after we'd broken up, to date again. He was going to marry her, dating me back then only as a rebound. I don't know why this had me worked up so much given our time together in college was so far in the past, but it did. My stomach turned sour thinking about how he'd given me hope that maybe we were meant to be together this second time. He'd probably made her think the same thing.

A fresh wound to the heart during a critical midterm season. Fantastic.

"We're over, her and me. We broke up a few months ago."

So this was a fresh breakup? Even worse. That did not bode well for us, especially given his history of repeat dating.

Crossing my arms, I said, "You probably thought you two were over in college too. But then later you put a ring on her finger."

He pursed his lips. "We were over, and yes, we started dating again years later, because we saw each other at our ten-year high school reunion and had a fun time together. She pursued me hard and it was flattering, to be honest, because I hadn't really dated much since college. But as we spent more time with each other, it was clear we'd both changed, and not in ways that were compatible." He retucked his towel to tighten it. "I'd finally gotten my act together professionally by going back to school for my PhD, and she was high on the corporate ladder at an insurance company, being groomed for an executive position. She nagged me all the time about finishing my PhD quickly so I could get a *real* job, and called me lazy pretty much every day. Our adult lives diverged, and we were more different than ever before."

He continued. "I ended it officially a few months ago. We hooked up a few times while we were broken up though." Jake bit his lower lip, then ran his fingers through his damp hair. "Maybe I shouldn't have said that last part. I don't suppose it would make it better if I told you that she was the one who bought the framed photo and put it on my shelf?"

Um, no. "That might actually be worse." I shook my head. I didn't want to use the term "lazy," especially after he mentioned how it hurt his feelings, but was it really that hard to get rid of a framed photo from your shelf?

There was something else about what he said that bugged me. "So, she pursued you after your reunion? And in high school she pursued you then too?"

He nodded. "Yeah. Why?"

"Have *you* ever pursued someone romantically, or have you always just gone with the flow? Were all of your relationships out of convenience?" If his ex made the first moves, and in college if we got together only because we'd both broken up with our significant others and it was super convenient for both of us, what did that mean for us now? I'd found myself in his class by chance and—oh God, was this *only* dating of convenience? Did he even know how to passionately pursue anything?

I was not going to be part of this . . . whatever this was. A game? An unhealthy psychological pattern? No way. Not me.

My heart constricted inside my chest. "I'm sorry, this thing between us has to end. It's not working for me," I blurted. "I have midterms to study for and an author event coming up. I need to go."

"Wait!" Jake was still in his towel, salt-and-pepper hair glistening, with water droplets trickling down his chest. Damn, I needed to get out of here before I outright lost my mind.

I grabbed my bag and headed toward the door. "I'll see you around." *Platonically*.

Jake took hold of my arm and tugged gently. "Okay, please don't forget to drop the class. They're strict about that and appeals after the final drop date rarely get approved. I don't want you to get penalized again."

Right. The CS class. I'd almost forgotten. All the points Mia had made about why I should keep the class migrated from the back of my mind to the front. She was right. In Fundamentals of Code I was learning something new. The coursework and lectures were interesting, challenging, and rewarding. And getting an interview for that coveted internship at a company rated "Best Place to Work" by *Forbes* and *Time*, that would be a solid bonus. If Jake and I were finished with . . . whatever this was between us . . . maybe this college do-over would prove to be worth the time and effort if I stuck with computer science.

My mind was made up. And the looming deadline helped propel me into action.

"I'm keeping the CS class."

Jake's eyes opened wide. "You what?"

My chest swelled with conviction. "I'm keeping the class. I'm going to do my best, study hard, try to ace the exam, and then see what happens with that internship."

He frowned. "And what about us?" His downturned lips looked sadder than I'd ever seen them before.

Well, that really was the million-dollar question. Did I wish things were less complicated and I could ravage him right now, with no strings attached, yanking off his towel

and pretending I was a sexy matador? Yes. But that wasn't
how the real world worked, and I had to think about what
was best for me. "Truthfully, I don't know. But for now, we're
back to the way it was just a few days ago, TA and student.
Back to boundaries." I took a step back to symbolically show
that I would practice what I preached. No more special
closed-door office hours. No more spending the night. None
of that anymore.

Jake walked me to the front door, and spoke once he'd
unlocked the dead bolts. "Good luck with exams. And let me
know if you need anything. I've been pretty busy lately so
you might not see me around as much, but maybe it's for the
better, so we can focus on what's important."

I nodded. It hurt my heart to say goodbye after we'd had
a few days of carefree fun, but it was time to get back to reality. "Bye, Jake."

He looked at the floor. "I hope to see you around. And I
hope you get the internship."

The porch lights flicked on as he closed the door, and
a movement at the window caused me to turn my head.
It was Jake's dog and cat, peering at me through the long
cream-colored drapes. I waved at them, offering them a sad
smile, then scampered down the steps.

## Chapter Twenty-Two

The CS midterm and the O'Hara author event fell on the same day. As soon as I finished my exam in the morning, I jumped into Mia's car so we could book it straight to New York City to make it to the evening book launch. To add literal sprinkles to my shit sundae, it started raining, which made visibility nearly impossible thanks to the half-speed windshield wipers on Mia's million-year-old Mazda. Our total drive time shot up an entire hour.

"I have to pee," she exclaimed as I threw my belongings into the back seat.

"Are you serious? You didn't go when you were in our apartment?" Mia had spent a lot of time at our place lately, so much in fact that she was now practically living with Beth and me. It was weird going back to the city now: I'd gotten used to a slower-paced, sheltered college-town life. And Mia had gotten used to living with us rent-free and eating Beth's unlimited pecan bars.

She shook her head. "It just hit me on the drive here. Stay in the car and keep the engine running if you're cold. I'll go in one of the engineering buildings, where there will be plenty of ladies' room stalls open."

I pulled down the sun visor to see the damage I'd caused from pulling an all-nighter. On most days, I looked and felt youthful enough to blend reasonably well into the university population, but not at that moment. A hollow-eyed, sallow-skinned, baggy-eyed version of me stared back, the natural light enhancing and highlighting my poor makeup concealment. For me to look fresh and at the top of my game for the evening event, I would need to take a nap in the car and pray that the restorative power of sleep could help repair my fixer-upper face.

Mia jumped back into the driver's seat and threw a bag of chips at me. "Found a vending machine. I assumed you had water already since you carry around that two-liter bottle of yours all the time."

I looked down at my XL Hydro Flask. "First of all, it was on sale at the bookstore. And second, I save money by not buying bottled water anymore."

She harrumphed and put her Diet Coke in the circular drink console. While fiddling with the sound system she asked, "How was the exam? Did you ace it?"

I answered her with what my therapist had helped me to say. "I did the best I could do within my abilities and within my control," adding, "My nerves hit pretty hard when I read exam problems about interfaces in Java. But then I really hit my groove."

She looked at me. "That's the nerdiest thing I've ever heard you say. But it sounds awesome." Mia turned her attention back to the road, thumping her fingers on the steering wheel as she set the cruise control. "I'm proud of you, girl."

"Thanks! If it's okay with you, I might need to conk out for the rest of the trip. I'm exhausted."

"No problem. I have just the thing to put you to sleep." She switched the media mode to audiobook and hit play. As I reclined to a better resting position, I heard an annoying, haughty voice come over the speakers.

"Chapter One. Being Born into the O'Hara Legacy." It was Cameron O'Hara, narrating the *You Go, Girl!* book. I bolted up from my seat and Mia burst into laughter.

"I downloaded a sample chapter from the publisher's website kinda as a joke, but shit, I didn't know he narrated it. Isn't it a *female* empowerment book? Why isn't Mary narrating if they wanted an O'Hara? It's such a bad look."

It was. And an interesting potential question for the event, especially if Cam pissed me off and I was feeling punchy. I had skimmed the advance copy of *You Go, Girl!*, and it was clear that there wasn't anything insightful or groundbreaking that made the book stand out from the other preceding female-focused business books on the shelves. Many of the points in the book were also in *Lean In, How Women Rise*, and even in my *How to Be a Work Supernova*. Men already dominated the nonfiction business book market—did we really need them narrating women empowerment business books too?

I dozed off instantly and when I awoke, Mia was paying a toll booth worker. "Hey, Sleeping Beauty. You were out like a light the entire trip. And you missed a drive-through stop. Your loss."

My eyes focused on the dashboard clock. We were entering Manhattan with a decent amount of time to spare. She must've driven fifteen to twenty miles over the speed limit the whole way.

I sat up. "Thanks for giving me time to get ready. Are we headed to your place?" My voice croaked out those words. I must've been sleeping with my mouth open. Wonderful.

She pointed to a bag on the floor. "I bought you a Happy Meal. I didn't know how hungry you'd be."

Mia loved her fast food. Her consumption mantra was "organic = worms enclosed," and honestly, she was kind of right. As roommates, anytime we went on a health food kick and bought organic veggies or fruit from the store or farmers' markets, we almost always found creepy-crawly things lurking in the leaves. I'd gotten used to washing and de-verminizing my food, but Mia enthusiastically took the opposite approach by deliberately seeking out GMOs and conventionally farmed produce, and finding joy in drive-throughs.

The sun had just descended behind the tallest Midtown skyscrapers ahead of us, giving the city skyline a literal glow-up. A yellow taxi behind us honked as Mia tried to pull into a spot that a black Lincoln Town Car had just left open. She pulled in with expert-level parallel parking, and the taxi driver rolled his window down and screamed profanities at us as he sped away, using phrases that didn't necessarily make sense strung together, like "punk bitch ass son of a bitch."

Mia shifted the gear into park and relaxed her shoulders. "Home sweet home."

"Thanks so much for driving. I'm sorry I didn't even switch off with you and do my share."

She popped open the trunk. "No worries. You can drive back home."

My notifications alerted me that the event was in two hours. With our roller bags in hand, we ascended the staircase to the top floor of the five-story walkup. It had been a while since I'd made the trek to her apartment, and I had to pause a few times to catch my breath.

"College has made you too soft," Mia teased as she sprinted up the last flight with her Samsonite roller bag in tow. By the time I made it through her front door, she had already pulled two cans of beer from her fridge.

I shook my head. "No thanks, I don't like to drink before events. Dulls my brain and the fizz makes me burp."

The IPA hissed as she pushed in the tab. "These are actually both for me. You can get your own. I'm not your butler." We both burst into a fit of giggles. It was nice to be back, but it felt a little weird now, having fun without Beth in the mix.

I drank the last remaining sips from my water bottle, then headed to the bathroom to change. The lighting was soft and muted, which made it hard to apply my makeup. A more harshly lit environment meant there were no surprises, and nothing was hidden. In this mirror, I looked too well rested, energized, and even kind of pretty, in a photo airbrush filter sort of way, so I relocated to Mia's high-wattage bedroom to get a dose of reality. Turning on her overhead lights, the floor lamp, and the ring light on her desk would let the true Lily emerge so I could conceal, pat, and paint on the image of a successful career woman.

After trying on three different outfits, I settled on a sheath dress with a chevron pattern and a fitted black blazer. I found Mia lounging in the living room and spun in a circle so she could give appropriate feedback. "What do you think?" I asked.

"You look like a smart, sexy newscaster. It's a good look. Do you still have your black librarian glasses?"

I fished them out of my purse and perched them on my nose.

"Yes," she agreed. "That's perfect. You are smart, sexy, and a little intimidating. You'd hardly guess you were but a mere college student taking an exam earlier today!" Mia raised the two beers in her hands. "Cheers!"

I grabbed my bag and the spare set of keys, then headed to the event at Gramercy Bookstore, eight blocks away. It was my choice for venue, and I'd picked it because it was woman-owned and near Mia's apartment. A crowd had already formed outside when I arrived. If I had to guess, it was mostly friends of the O'Haras. Lots of pearl necklaces, Hermès ties, and Chanel purses. An opening in the doorway allowed me to slip through to the event area to find a bookstore employee or publicity manager hosting the event.

"You're here!" To my surprise, Mary O'Hara ran up to me and offered a handshake. "I'm so glad you made it. Thanks for doing this event with us. I'm a huge fan, as you already know."

As she energetically pumped my hand up and down, I studied her face to see if she was being genuine. She wore an earnest grin across her face, which made me believe her. Maybe Mary actually wanted me to be there, and that's why she'd pushed the publicity team for this launch event. It seemed much more plausible than Cameron being the thought leader when it came to finding an in-conversation partner who didn't look like himself.

Cameron emerged from the employee back room, as if my inner thoughts conjured evil spirits. He whispered to his sister, "I can't believe they didn't offer us craft services. We have to eat and drink out here with the regular people." He waved toward the patrons of the bookstore, and I could not help but notice that I, too, was included in the area within his dismissive hand swing.

"Cam, Lily's here, our conversation partner today."

I reached out my hand, only to have him mutter, "Good to see you again," as he offered a quick handshake, then beelined past me to a couple who had just claimed seats in the audience. I knew who they were. The Van Sant power couple, angel investors who were on MSNBC, Bloomberg, and CNN Business around the clock.

I offered Mary a tight smile. "Well, I'm sure they're more interesting than me. Did you get the questions I sent a few days ago? Wanted to give you the opportunity to prepare, and depending on your answers, I might add a few off-the-cuff questions into the mix, to keep the conversation flowing organically."

"Thanks for sending those early. And your plan sounds great."

The event drew a predominantly white crowd, but among the more diverse attendees was a healthy representation of Asian American women, many of whom had my book in their hands, on their laps, or sticking out of their tote bags. My heart burst into confetti and mini streamers as the events manager from the bookstore introduced us.

While smiling for forty-five minutes straight, I asked the O'Haras all of my prepared questions, alternating between them. What was it like to write a book together, Cam? How long did it take you to write it, Mary? Cam, did you outline first? Last one, Mary . . . did you write together or divide and conquer?

The remaining fifteen minutes was an open Q&A for the live audience and for the virtual participants streaming the event on the bookstore's website. The first question was from a guest in the front row: What are you all working on now?

I let the O'Haras speak first and used that time to rack my brain for an answer. Word would definitely get back to my editor, and since I'd been giving Katherine and the editorial assistant, Amanda, vague non-updates the last couple of months while I was studying at Carlthorpe, my publishing team was probably just as eager to hear how close I was to turning in my next project as everyone else in the audience. Mary O'Hara said she wanted to write a new book about philanthropy and was researching foundations. Cameron said he was going to set up meetings with some "buddies of his in Hollywood" to see if his book had movie potential. The audience didn't sound surprised by either of their answers.

My turn. "I don't want to give away too much, but I've been spending a lot of time researching the pursuit of dream jobs. It's taken me longer than I'd hoped to write this next one, and I've been distracted with personal matters lately, but I'm hoping to have time in the next few weeks to hunker down and get it all down on paper." Mia had been updating my social media accounts with generic posts about finding inspiration, replenishing your creative well, and getting out of career ruts. If anyone was following me, they would see those messages aligning with what I'd just shared with the crowd.

The next question was from a former teacher of the O'Haras. "Where's your favorite place to write?"

Mary offered my typical answer: in coffee shops. Cameron said, not even joking, on his yacht.

I responded, "I love a good coffee shop too. It really awakens all of my senses, and I can't get enough of that ground coffee aroma. I wish someone could sell this scent as a candle. But I also love libraries, I've been spending a lot of time in them lately."

"The New York Public Library?" Cameron's thick caterpillar brow quirked up.

I sidestepped his question. "It's one of my favorites."

"I'll have to try it sometime, I guess." I couldn't picture that at all. I could, however, picture Cameron building a fancy library, each shelf filled with his own coauthored books, on his yacht.

The event manager chirped, "We have time for one more question from the in-person audience, and then we'll see if we have time to take a few from the virtual viewers. Feel free to add comments or questions in the chat." She pointed to an Asian woman in the front row.

"Hi, thank you so much. I'm Haley Cha." She cleared her throat. "What inspired you to write your book? Or in Ms. Lee's case, the first book in her series?"

Mary gestured for me to go first, but not surprisingly, Cameron started speaking. "I hadn't seen anyone write a book from a perspective like ours. Mary and I wanted this to be like a 'mentorship in a book' for people just started out in their careers, giving real-life, practical, actionable advice that works, as well as offering perspectives of others who also had to build their careers from the ground up."

His words hit me like uppercut jabs to the chin. He had said nearly verbatim what I'd expressed to Mary and him in confidence when we met in person. It was low, not only to take words from other people's mouths and pretend they were your own, but to not give me credit either? This was absolute bullshit. And he wasn't going to get away with it.

Mary jumped in, her voice wavering. "Just wanted to add that these views were originally shared by Lily, who really is our beacon of light. We're following the path she already forged with hard work, sweat, and tears, so we really appreciate that."

"Thank you, Mary. Cameron took the words right out of my mouth. Literally." I shot a look at Cameron, who didn't even blink an eye after plagiarizing a sound bite from my previous conversation with him, pretending it was his own unique insight. "I think we're nearly out of time, but if anyone would like to ask me follow-up questions, I'd be happy to stay a few minutes after the event to answer them." My fists shook with anger as I tried to calm my erratic, slightly panicked breathing.

I glanced at my purse. There were prescription pills in the zippered side pocket for emergency use only. Hopefully I wouldn't need them.

The events manager chirped, "Unfortunately, it looks like we are over time actually. But we have a few quick comments from the virtual event-goers. 'Good luck with your launch, Cam and Mary,' that's from Mrs. Murphy, the chief people officer at the O'Hara Holding Company. Lots of people are saying hi and thank you to Lily, for being an inspiration to women everywhere."

I blushed. "Thank you!" I responded cheerily.

"One more comment, from Lily's mom."

My stomach lurched. *Oh no.*

"She says 'Daebak! Lily, please call home soon.'"

Chuckles rippled across the live audience. I laughed too.

"She also says, 'Good luck with your studying.' I'm not sure what she means by that."

*Oh shit.*

The crowd noticeably quieted, giving me very little time to think on my feet with an explanation. "Thanks for watching, Mom." I smiled at the audience. "As usual, she's trying to keep me on task. I'm sure she's referring to all the research and writing for my new book. It feels very academic." My body temperature rose as I spoke. My skin was burning with discomfort.

The audience clapped as we stood and made our way off the stage. Cameron approached a group of women from London Business School, and as I walked to the buffet table to grab a bottle of water, I heard Cam say out loud to all of them, "I agree, Lily's latest book is primarily geared toward women of color, but I'd argue that our book could be too. I mean, who better to provide advice on how to make it in a white man's world than a successful white man?"

Did he seriously just say that to a group of professional women? Cam was like a caricature of a cocky, privileged stock character in a mainstream sitcom, but I knew as well as anyone that these guys really did exist in the real world. I'd encountered plenty of them, and they really did get their way most of the time, both in academia and in the corporate world, resting on their laurels of mediocrity. They delegated work and took credit. They rephrased ideas in meetings and were touted as the smartest ones in the room. Senior-level executives, both men and women alike, in most industries routinely offered the Camerons of the world unlimited chances to shine, but were more rigid and scrutinizing of others who didn't fit that demographic.

It reminded me of a *New Yorker* cartoon of a man and woman on a date. She stares blankly at him as he enthusiastically says, "Let me interrupt your expertise with my confidence." That was the personification of Cameron.

The group of young women migrated away from him and gathered around me. One of them tucked a brown, curly lock behind her ear and spoke. "I am so happy you're here. I took the train in from Connecticut! I loved your career guide and can't wait to read the entire series. Are you signing books today?"

My chest swelled with pride. I hadn't had many signing events, so this was a rare opportunity for me. "Yes, I am! Let me find a table and a Sharpie."

She smirked. "Can you personalize mine? I'd love for you to write something like 'Cameron O'Hara is a loser and has no business writing a book about career adversity.'"

I laughed hard. A kindred spirit. "I might need to paraphrase it a little, but I'd be happy to sign your copy."

A long line formed behind her, and each reader let me know how I'd helped her professional career. One woman asked, "Is your new book coming out soon?"

One of the women in line nodded. "The world needs to hear what you have to say."

My heart squeezed. "Thank you. I'm working on it."

# Chapter Twenty-Three

**M**y midterm exam results came in while we were driving back from NYC the next morning. I slapped Mia on the arm, waking her up from her drooly slumber.

She squinted at me. "Shit, I was having a good dream too! What? Is it time to eat?"

I pointed to my phone perched on the car mount. "You need to click on the link. My grades came in and I can't pull over right now to check. Sorry about waking you up, but you know, it's urgent."

Mia sighed and shifted her seat into an upright position. After grabbing my phone and clicking around, she squealed. "Well, hot damn! You got an A. TWO As. Wait, you didn't tell me you took stats AND computer science! I thought you were dropping one and adding the other?"

I beamed. "And I have my influencer culture class paper due at the end of the term, but I've gotten high marks so far. I added stats because it was an easier class for me, but didn't drop CS. I figured I had the time and wanted to prove to myself that I could still learn something after all."

She tapped her head twice with her index finger. "That's smart. Was it more expensive to add extra classes?"

I shrugged. "I worked out the finances, but I figured if stats is more of a sure thing grade-wise, it would help me hedge if my CS grade is terrible. And in the Global Audience and Influencer Culture class I'm actually learning a lot that might help me build an audience for my books."

Mia said, "It's exciting news. Two As! Too bad there aren't a lot of people you can tell right now."

*Tap. Tap. Tap. Tap.* My fingers rolled in a 1-2-3-4 count on the steering wheel.

Mia put the phone back on the cradle. "You want to text Jake, don't you?"

"No." *Maybe.* "Of course not." *Okay, yes. I wanted to see if I was still at the top of the class.*

She paused when she noticed my phone light up. "Well, well, well, Jakey just sent you a message saying he was proud of you. Where are you guys at right now? Fighting? Having I-hate-you-but-DAMN-you're-hot sex? Should I send him a middle finger emoji, or the eggplant one?"

I narrowed my eyes and shot her an exasperated look, which she ignored because she was busy swirling her index finger next to my cheek and laughing. "You're blushing! Anyway, the good news is he texted first, so he's thinking about you. When you told me he was back at Carlthorpe, I was rooting for a Ben Affleck and Jennifer Lopez second chance, happy, healthy reunion. And now with him texting you, I'm feeling it. Instead of Bennifer, you can be Jily . . . or Lacob."

"You can go back to sleep now," I deadpanned. "In fact, I insist."

After some more teasing, she shifted her seat upright and switched the conversation to more serious matters. "I've been uploading photos to your social media account and asked your in-house publicist to send photos from your event, which I just shared publicly. You had a great turnout. Can you believe your mom showed up to the virtual part of the event? And lots of people are commenting about how you revealed more about your next project and they can't wait to see what your next book is about!"

"I can't wait to see what my next book is about," I scoffed.

Mia shot me a WTF look that I could see in my peripheral view. "You *still* don't know what your book is going to be about? I thought you got an extension and it was due in a few weeks."

I stared hard at the road. "It was supposed to be about getting your dream job, but c'mon, look at me now. I've regressed so much the last few months and one of my only job prospects right now is an internship, and it's a long shot. Who wants to hear about a loser thirty-something going back to college to finish her degree?"

"Oh my God, are you kidding? This is what people LOVE to hear about! Trust me, I'm a PR person. This is exactly the kind of story everyone loves. No one gives a shit about the O'Haras. Okay, well, certain people do, I'll give you that, there will always be people obsessed with the rich and famous. But you have a unique story that rarely happens to people but is oddly relatable, and you are absolutely killing it.

It's about resilience and perseverance. Humility and grace. You have two As on your midterms in math and CS classes at Carlthorpe, which was recently ranked number one in most studious universities, beating out all the Ivies and engineering programs. It's a nerdy school, Lily, and you're doing great . . . maybe even better than you did ten years ago. That's something."

I pursed my lips, fighting a smile. "Wow, the way you're talking me up, you almost make me want to believe in myself too." We both laughed. "I had to clear my calendar of virtual book events, podcasts, and guest blogs so I could study, and felt a ton of guilt for saying no to things, but I'm glad it's paying off."

She clapped her hands together. "I think we should go out and celebrate. You're a STEMINATOR now."

"Stop."

"STEMINIST?" she asked.

"No."

"STEM-ALICIOUS?"

"Oh my God, quit it!" I smirked. "Fine, let's go celebrate, but no frat parties please."

"Great! I'll text Beth. Should I invite . . . Jake? I bet your mom would want to come."

*Hell no.* "I want this celebration to be easy. Like French fries, nachos, and sangria at home easy. Not ex-boyfriend-turned-teaching-assistant, turned-friend-with-benefits, turned-back-to-TA messy. I'm discovering this thing Jake and I have is the opposite of no strings attached. It's littered with booby traps, landmines, tripwires, hand grenades, and even those hidden snares that string people up by the ankle and hang them upside down from tall trees."

"Now you're just being dramatic," Mia said.

I shot back, "No, dramatic would be including an elaborate trapping pit, the kind that's camouflaged with branches and leaves."

She muttered, "Okay, so no Jake. And obviously no parents. How about your other friends, the ones from the frat party?"

I took the Hill Avenue exit, the main drag leading to Carlthorpe. After four hours of driving, we would be back to our idyllic campus life in a matter of minutes. "I like them, but let's just keep it simple and low-key, I don't want to celebrate if my friends didn't get good grades on their exams."

She nodded, agreeing with me for once. "I have some downtime, just wrapped up two big projects and am ramping up on another one soon. I'll go grocery shopping and we can make a feast."

"As long as there's wine, I'm in."

She reclined her chair. "With me, there will always be wine, you know that."

I smiled. "And that's why I love you."

BECAUSE IT WAS my celebration night, Mia and Beth kept me out of the kitchen while they prepared dinner. It was a good thing too, because when I peeked in, every single pot and pan was either being used or in the sink. They refused any help when I offered to cook or clean, so I took a seat in front of the TV and asked Siri on my phone to flip a coin. Heads was baking shows. Tails was true crime.

"It's tails," Siri confirmed.

I picked a new-release, small-town serial-killer documentary and yelled, "I'm pressing play on the latest murder show!" but then hit the pause button when the title *Slaughtertown, USA* appeared and my friends still hadn't made an appearance. But whatever they were doing in there, it was making our cozy apartment smell like heaven, with savory aromas of onion, garlic, and sesame oil, accompanied by notes of confectionary sweetness from vanilla, brown butter, and chocolate. Feeling guilty when I heard all the banging and clanking of metal, I patiently waited for them while sipping Syrah and researching the internship program offered by Solv Technologies. I discovered that the cofounder, an anthro major, graduated from Carlthorpe a few years behind me. Well, I guess technically I was a few years behind *him* now.

Was it depressing that my very best job prospect at the moment was for an internship at a company where the CEO was three years younger? Maybe more than a little. And the fact that it was currently my *only* job prospect made me chug my remaining half glass of wine. I examined the bottle. Two-thirds left. I'd need to pace myself.

Before I returned to Carlthorpe, Solv Technologies was a company I never had on my radar, because it was rumored that they allowed only a certain caliber of candidates to interview. Ones who had all the checkboxes ticked and the right pedigree. Without any tech industry experience, my candidacy would have been an immediate "no" without so much as a phone screen. The CS course I was taking wasn't a weeder class for hard-core engineering students, but with a professor on their board who was well known for working with large tech companies and teaching coding curricula designed for real-world experiences, it was a great way to find graduates who shared the same programming philosophy to place in roles throughout the company. It was revolutionary really, and pretty cool that I was one of the students vying for a position.

I looked at my glass and swirled the burgundy elixir. When did I pour more wine?

"Whoooooo's ready for a feast?" Mia popped her head into the room and waved for me to come into the kitchen.

Carrying the wineglass in one hand and the bottle in the other, I migrated over to my friends, where a multicourse banquet awaited me. On the center island was a wide array of my favorite Korean foods, including my favorite banchan. Mia always laughed at how simple my tastes were when it came to the side dishes: most of them needed only sesame oil, garlic, and salt. So what if I was a proud Basic Banchan Bitch?

"I went shopping this morning and bought a bunch of ingredients and marinated meat from the new Asian market an hour away. I made only the bean sprouts, spinach, anchovies, and sesame leaves. Oh, and the rice. I made that too." With potholder mittens, Mia pulled a pot off the stove and placed it on a trivet next to the sink. Steam spilled out as she lifted the heavy top. It was galbi-jjim! "I bought it from the Galleria Market, the marinade was a little too sweet so I added soy sauce, sesame oil, and a dash of garlic powder to balance it more."

It smelled like heaven. Everything did.

Beth pointed to the oven. "The chocolate gooey cake is almost done. I still need to wait a few minutes before I frost it."

Mia handed me a paper plate. "Let's pretend we're at Old Country Buffet, but Asian style, with homemade Korean food and fewer senior citizens."

"Ain't nothing wrong with older folks." Beth put her hands on her hips. "Especially ones like my nana, who still sends me twenty-dollar bills inside a birthday card every year."

"Bless the nanas who give us crisp bills from the bank," I said, holding up my wineglass.

The timer dinged and Beth rushed to the oven. Even when she made something simple, like sugar cookies or a vanilla sheet cake, there was artistry and finesse in the final execution, so you knew she had a culinary gift. It wasn't just someone reading recipes off the side of a box. Beth made everything her own, whereas I, on the other hand, made lumpy, nonuniform desserts that looked like a toddler using brown Play-Doh had decided to create something ambitious. I admired Beth. She had developed and refined her culinary skills by the tender age of twenty-two.

"I made a ganache that will pair nicely with chocolate hazelnut mousse," Beth said.

My jaw hung open. "So you're telling me that you took everything good about Nutella and put it into a cake? Thank you!"

Mia smacked her lips. "I can't wait!"

We started with the savory part of the Korean bacchanalian feast. I walked alongside the kitchen counter and island, taking heaping spoonfuls of beef, glass noodles, and marinated vegetables, leaving some space for the stir-fried anchovies. One thing I missed about living in NYC was easy access to ethnic food. One noticeable shortcoming about the Carlthorpe neighborhood was that, even though the population had become more diverse over ten years, there was only one Korean restaurant. It was open for lunch but closed for dinner and was currently shuttered for minor renovation. But honestly, the food wasn't even that good, so I hardly ever went there, even when I was desperate for a comfort meal.

Mia handed me a gift bag once I took a seat at the table. "Beth and I never agree on shirt slogans, but this is one we both liked."

It was a black fitted ladies T-shirt with the words HOT GIRLS CODE in white letters. I put it on over my long-sleeve waffle Henley and modeled it for them, twirling and then stumbling, losing my balance.

Beth, who rarely said anything mean, petty, or catty, mumbled into her wineglass, "Clumsy girls code too, I guess," and we all laughed.

I tried the beef short ribs first. "Mia! They're so tender."

She smiled. "Right? It took a while but they finally got to that falling-off-the-bone texture."

Beth disappeared into the kitchen a few minutes later. I thought she'd gone to get seconds, but she came out with a shiny, chocolatey square cake and put it down in the center of the table.

"It's too pretty to eat," I said. "The ganache came out perfect."

She beamed. "I have some good news too. Not as exciting as acing CS and stats exams, but I have some job interviews lined up, in case I don't get into grad school. Two consulting, one paralegal, and one nonprofit."

"Congratulations!" Mia and I cheered in unison.

I'd nearly forgotten what it was like to be a senior who wasn't on a premed, pre-law, or academia track. None of my friends my senior year had known what job they wanted after college, especially those like me who had a hard time choosing a major. Some people glamorize the transition from college and adulthood, like it's a milestone where people can't wait to rip their training wheels off and go riding on their own. Yes, adulthood can be a beautiful thing. But for some people, it's less about choices and more about circumstances. They settle. They take the only job they were offered. They take a less exciting job because the coveted positions were too competitive or the pay and benefits were worse. Sometimes the training wheels accidentally pop off too early and the person pedaling can't break or steer straight. Cars honk. People yell. And the bike ends up in a ditch.

The whiff of fragrant hazelnut cream brought my wandering mind back into focus. Beth had cut a few slices of cake and placed the corner piece in front of me.

Mia moaned, "Oh my God, this cake is better than sex."

I was going to say, "Way to ruin it for me, Mia," but was it really ruining anything with a comment like that? I loaded the tip of my fork with fluffy hazelnut and chocolate goodness, then opened my mouth and took a bite.

Wow. "Mia's right. This is maybe even better than my midterm news," I marveled.

Beth's eyes rounded when she took a bite. "This is my best attempt yet. Go me!"

After we finished our desserts, I asked, "Do either of you think there's any downside to applying for the internship at Solv? The professor sent me a link to set up the phone screen for a recruiter!"

Mia took a swig of wine. "What does Jakey say?"

"I haven't talked to him for a while."

She narrowed her eyes suspiciously at me. "Hmmmmm. He would be the perfect one to ask."

I nodded. "He would be, but I don't want any special treatment now that he's my TA again." No need to cause more messiness between us. Once I'd discovered that he'd gotten back with his high school sweetheart, I couldn't shake the nagging feeling that he was keeping me around on the sidelines as someone he could date until someone better came around.

Mia said, "I texted with him. He was polite but super short. Maybe he's moved on to something else."

*Or someone else. Like his re-ex girlfriend.* I sipped the remaining wine from my glass. Maybe it was time to move past this, to finally close the book on the Jake and Lily saga. For both of our sakes.

Beth said, "Well, I think you should interview. There's no harm in trying something new. Maybe you'll be pleasantly surprised."

Mia tipped her glass at me. "Your peppy roommate makes a good point. I heard this quote the other day: 'The most difficult decisions are those that shape your future.'"

I nodded. "That's true. Where'd you get that from?"

"A Panda Express fortune cookie. But it's relevant. If you got the job, I hear they have really good free lunch offerings at Solv."

I'd made worse decisions for reasons dumber than free lunch. "Great! I'll apply tomorrow, when I'm not drunk."

Mia laughed. "You always were my smart friend." She stood from her chair and brought over another bottle of wine. "We're switching to Pinot. I like it better and it's a screw-top." Within seconds, we all had full wineglasses again, and we migrated over to the TV to unpause the serial-killer show.

Great food. Caring friends. Interesting conversation. And murder documentaries.

What more could I want in life?

# Chapter Twenty-Four

L oud knocking at the door interrupted my slow, pains-
taking process of editing my cover letter for the Solv
Technologies internship.

In popped Beth's head. "Do you have a swimsuit I can
borrow? I'll wash it and give it back today."

I arched an eyebrow. "You're going swimming in Novem-
ber? It's freezing outside."

"It's not like I *want* to go swimming now." She pulled her
hair into a tight ponytail. "It's one of the open days for the
swim test at the fitness center."

My stomach lurched and all that wine from the previous
night threatened to pay a visit. "What swim test?"

"Are you serious? It's the one we need to pass to graduate."

I furiously typed search word combinations of "swim
test," "Carlthorpe," and "graduation requirement," and sure
enough, online articles from the campus paper and student
handbook came up as search results. Seniors needed to
pass a swim test to graduate or waive out of it by taking
an introductory swim class for the PE requirement. The

old swim test requirement was abolished at the turn of the century, but after the school recently received a large conditional endowment, they reinstituted it a few years after I left Carlthorpe.

I folded my arms on my keyboard and pressed my forehead into them. "Oh God, why me? I can't swim."

Her eyes widened in horror. "Like you can't swim at all? Or do you mean it like, 'Oh God, I haven't swum in, like, five years'?"

I lifted my head. "I haven't swum since high school. And *swim* is an exaggeration. I sink. You'd think that going from a C cup in college to a D cup now would mean I'm more buoyant, but it's actually exactly the opposite. It's like my body is sixty percent sand instead of water. I can kind of doggy-paddle. Floating on my back is iffy. I know some basic strokes but I can go maybe one lap." I needed three. Three whole Olympic pool laps.

"High school was only four years ago . . . oh shit. I keep forgetting." Beth winced. "Maybe it's like riding a bike and it will all come back to you."

Clearly this girl had never seen me ride a bike.

It was too late to add the Intro to Swimming PE class to my course load, and I couldn't graduate without passing the test before the end of the semester. All these years of summer vacations, tanning poolside, going down lazy rivers, and I never once tried to swim. The last time I got into the water was to order a round of drinks at a swim-up bar.

Beth changed her tone and spoke to me like she was coaxing a preschooler. "Hey, maybe I can help. I was a lifeguard in high school and taught lots of kids how to swim. We can go to the pool a few times a week to work on your strokes and build your stamina."

Oh God, my stamina. Earlier that morning I dropped a Q-tip on the bathroom floor and got winded squatting and crawling around the floor, trying to reach for it in a crevice next to the sink. How could I possibly go from Q-tip crouch-n-crawl fatigue to seventy-five yards of swimming in a few weeks?

I opened the top drawer of my dresser and pulled out a swimsuit. "It's a two-piece, and it's meant more for lounging than exercising. It'll be big on you." The black-and-white swimsuit had cute detailing and was expensive, even on sale. I'd worn it only a handful of times. I thought it was dumb to pack it with my boxes headed to college, but I guess I was wrong.

"I'll wash it and give it back to you when I'm done." She took the suit from my hands. "And I mean it, let's go to the pool soon to get you used to being in the water."

My breath quickened and I tried to slow it down with slow exhales. It almost felt like I had low blood sugar because my knees weakened, my head got lighter, and the room came in and out of focus even with calm breathing.

"Lily? Are you okay? Is it something I said?" When I didn't answer, she grabbed my chair and rolled it over to me, then helped me sit.

It took some time for this bout to pass. I explained what was going on so she wouldn't get freaked out. "I'm sorry, I should have told you earlier when I first moved in." I swallowed hard and took a deep breath in and out. "I have high-functioning

anxiety. I've dealt with it since college, though I suspect it
started much earlier than that." I took another deep breath
and divulged something only a few people knew about, not
even my parents. *Especially* not my parents.

"It started with insomnia in high school. Then, after
weeks of terrible sleep, I woke up one morning during exam
week and it felt like I had something stuck in my throat, like
a ball of sadness and worry, and I couldn't swallow it away.
Then, in college, the ulcers and stomach pain came. After
years of hiding it from family and friends, I finally went to
seek help, thanks to Mia putting me in touch with a friend in
the medical field. I've been able to manage it over the years
with medication and therapy, but it resurfaces. I can't go to
concerts anymore—too scared of mob mentality and crowd
surges—and one of the reasons I left corporate America was
because it became clear that no amount of self-care and PTO
days was helping with my job-related stress. Since then, I've
made life, work, and family adjustments for my mental and
physical well-being, trying to minimize my anxiety when I
can." I smiled weakly. "Apparently swim tests are a stress
maximizer."

I expected Beth to give me a full-on "rah-rah-you-can-
do-it!" pep talk, saying something motivational or responding with a semi-relevant, Midwestern-funny anecdote.
Instead, she bent down and tackle-hugged me, pinning my
arms against my torso, squeezing air from my lungs. She
nearly caused me to lose my balance in the chair.

"You inspire me so much!" Beth eventually loosened her

arms, allowing me the luxury of reinflating my lungs and chest. "I mean it."

"Thank you," I said while gulping air. "Wow, you're really strong."

"It's the kettlebells." She smiled. "Thank you for telling me about your anxiety. I'll do my part to help. And I'll make your swim test preparation as low-hassle as possible. It'll be great."

"Thanks." Once she had unsqueezed my upper body, I hugged her back. "And thank you for being a good friend."

Our hug fest was interrupted by an urgent email notification, which meant the message had come from someone on my VIP list.

It was a note from Jake. But it wasn't personalized to only me, it was a mass email.

*Dear CS class,*

*Congratulations on finishing midterms! As we ease into the final weeks of the semester and prepare for finals, I wanted to introduce you to Sudhir Misra, who will be sharing the remainder of my TA duties this semester. He attended Wake Forest for undergrad and is in his third year in the CS PhD program, specializing in machine learning approaches to predicting Parkinson's disease using gene expression. I've linked to his bio below.*

*Our new office hours are as follows: M and F, 1–3pm Office 1001011 for Sudhir, and Th 1–3pm Office 1001011 for Jacob.*

*If you have any questions for either Sudhir or me,*
*please let us know. And as always, see you in class!*

Jake hadn't been to the lectures that week. I assumed that he was sick, or vainly assumed that he was avoiding me at all costs. With this new TA development, it seemed like there was something bigger going on than just us.

"Anything important?" Beth asked, studying my reaction.

"Not really. Jacob seems to be transitioning out of his TA duties and he sent an email to the class about it." I tucked my phone into my jacket pocket.

Worry flashed across her face. "Is he okay? Like what if he's on the one-way escalator to heaven?"

Nothing like that had even occurred to me. Leave it to Beth to show me a new, albeit morbid, way of looking at this situation. "I'll reach out to him to make sure he's okay."

She hugged me again, but this time with less strangulation. "After you message Jake, let's go sign you up for a swim test."

I couldn't think of two things I dreaded more. But with Beth's encouragement, I reluctantly agreed to do both, and she rewarded me with a half sheet of apple strudel. Rather than text Jake informally, I replied to his email and vaguely asked how he was doing. I received an out-of-the-office reply, implying he was busy and it would take a few business days to get back to me. Jake being busy and possibly overextended wasn't a surprise.

After registering for a swim evaluation, I immediately received confirmation from the Department of Athletics that my swim test had been confirmed during finals week, the very last date available this semester. I prayed Beth could whip me into shape in the few remaining weeks. The rest of the night, I googled variations of "easiest swim stroke for beginners" and stress-ate all the strudel for dinner. Was this dumb swim test the final thing between me and my degree?

I knocked on my wooden desk for luck.

Hopefully. Fingers crossed for no more surprises.

# Chapter Twenty-Five

O n the phone, the Solv Technologies recruiter explained that the hiring process for interns was lengthy, and this was the first step of three.

"Once you pass the first phone screen, you move on to a phone interview or in-person meeting, depending on availability, with one of our hiring managers, who will assess you for several types of roles at the company. We currently have openings in product management, programming, and UX. If that goes well, we might fly you out to our headquarters for a full day of in-person interviews or have you go to the closest office location to you, which in your case would be our Chelsea office in Manhattan. How does that sound?"

How did it sound? Exhausting. Exhilarating. Definitely something I wanted to do. She put me on hold as she looked through her calendar, checking for available dates.

I had an advantage over the other internship candidates: I was a part-time student, so I had more time to prep for an interview. Plus, according to my author bio, I was literally an interviewing expert. If I couldn't get past the phone screen, what would I even do with myself? The longer I waited for the recruiter to get back to me with available dates, the more pressure I felt mounting: fear, anxiety, self-doubt, all rearing their ugly heads, trying to convince me I shouldn't go through with it. That this was all just a waste of time for the company and for me.

*You've earned this, Lily,* a tiny voice inside me said, one that sounded a lot like George Takei, aka Sulu of the OG *Star Trek. Don't diminish your accomplishments,* the voice said louder. *Stop underselling yourself!*

"There's an opening next Wednesday at noon. How does that sound?" the recruiter asked, unmuting her phone.

"That's perfect," I replied confidently.

THE RECRUITER INTERVIEW the following week went so well that she actually bought my latest book while we were on the video chat. The meeting was only thirty minutes, and it was mostly a screener for company fit, although she did ask a couple of quasi-technical questions.

At the end of the call, she said, "Professor Stevenson is on our board of advisors, and we absolutely love recruiting students from his classes. Unlike other CS experts, he really focuses on practical techniques and principles that help developers write code that is easy to understand instead of teaching mostly programmatic theory and postulations." She held up her phone to show me a receipt. "But you know all of this. By the way, your book will be delivered to me next week. I'm excited!"

"Thanks for buying it!" Even if the interview didn't go well, at least I'd made a book sale.

She smiled. "If it's okay with you, we can go ahead and set up your next meeting in our Manhattan office. Would it be possible for you to get to the city in a couple of weeks? We would reimburse for train fare and related travel expenses, of course." After a few clicks of the keyboard, she said, "Oh. This is a highly unusual situation, but it looks like the hiring manager might be going on paternity leave soon; his calendar is blocked out starting next week. Is there any chance you could meet him this Friday instead?"

Friday was only two days away! Logistically, yes, I could make the meeting happen with a precisely timed train ride and an Uber once I arrived in the city. Or maybe I could go a day early and crash with Mia. But that would leave little time to prepare for the interview. On the other hand, maybe it was prudent to interview earlier rather than later. I heard that Solv interviewers simply voted "yes" or "no" for potential hires based on specific criteria, kind of like how the early decision process worked for colleges, but without the deferment option.

*You can do it, just try,* my George Takei inner voice encouraged.

The recruiter's eager virtual face awaited my answer.

"Friday works for me," I replied. "I can't wait."

The next day I arrived at Mia's at midnight. Letting myself in, I crashed on her futon after brushing my teeth and washing my face. Waking up to my 8 A.M. alarm, I was greeted by half a bagel with cream cheese on the coffee table along with a milky, chocolatey iced coffee. I hadn't even heard Mia leave. I must've needed that sleep.

Under the peephole of the door, she'd taped a note at eye-level so I'd see it on my way out. "Bitch, go do your thing!"

I couldn't help but smile as I locked the dead bolt when I left.

The interview was at ten and I left the apartment just after nine to take the subway to Solv, which was less than a block away from Chelsea Market, one of my favorite places in the city. If it had been any other day, I would have taken the time to stroll the food hall, sampling various treats and buying an assortment of groceries and freshly made baked goods. Instead, I scurried past the main entryway on Ninth Avenue and passed through the revolving glass door in Solv's building.

One other person was at the front desk getting cleared by security. When he turned around and put his sticker badge on his suit jacket lapel, I could hardly believe it was Ethan. Clean-shaven, combed-haired Ethan, wearing a sharp, fitted, expensive suit. He had transformed into a go-getter, sophisticated hottie.

"Hey, you," I said, stepping up to the desk, handing my license to the security guard. "I didn't know you were interviewing today. Congratulations!"

A wide grin spread across Ethan's face. "I wasn't sure who else was applying. Glad to see you here too. I figured you would be interviewing, but I didn't want to ask just in case. You look great, as always."

I blushed and smiled back. "You do too."

"I think what you mean is I cleaned up really well for this. You can say it," he said with a bashful glow in his cheeks. "I posted a photo on my Instagram account and people won't shut up about how I look now. So flattering, yet so offensive!"

Since the start of the semester, Ethan and I had maintained a playful noona-donsaeng relationship, where he deferred to me as his elder sister. If we hadn't had that history, I might have eventually given Ethan a second glance or two. Or three.

He added, "I studied my ass off for that exam, but I still can't believe it got me into the top ten. I think they're taking two interns from Carlthorpe. I hope it's both of us."

It would be fun to work with Ethan. He was easygoing and smart, and he did his share of the group project work without slacking off. In fact, all my group project teammates were reliable, helpful, and intelligent. I'd lucked out.

I received my badge from the guard, peeled the backing, and put the sticker on my blazer.

"After you," Ethan said, gesturing me to lead the way to the second elevator bank, which took passengers to floors 25 to 49. The elevator dinged as soon as I pushed the button, suggesting that luck would be in my favor that day. I took an eager step forward when the doors opened, then remembered to let everyone out before entering. I'd almost forgotten my elevator etiquette.

I backed up into Ethan, who yelped when I stepped on his foot.

"I'm so sorry!" I yelped back, turning my head to offer him an apologetic smile.

"If I didn't know you were a nice person, I'd say you were trying to literally stamp out the competition, Noona."

I laughed. There was that noona thing again. But it was fine with me: he was ten years younger, and as handsome as he was, he just wasn't my type somehow. Did I mention he was ten years younger?

Just when I thought the elevator was clear for entry, two more people stepped out. To my dismay, I knew one of them.

"Oh, hello, Lorrie. What a surprise." It was Cameron O'Hara, walking up to me with an extended hand. "How's the book coming along? Is the next bestseller releasing soon?"

Although he got my name wrong, which wasn't so bad given that I myself was terrible at names, the thing that set me off was that he knew the writing wasn't going well from our last event together, and I couldn't tell if it was just conversation fodder or he was trying to get under my skin. Either way, I didn't appreciate it.

With a stoic face, I managed to say, "Nice to see you again, *Chad*. But I'm off to a meeting. Let's catch up another time." *Or rather, let's not.*

"It's Cameron." He glanced at my name badge as he held the door open for Ethan and me to enter. "Oh, you're Lily. That's right. You're off to Solv? I was just there, discussing an enterprise cloud project with the head of development. Who are you going to see?" His voice spiked with more intensity and one-upmanship than genuine curiosity, like he was demanding to know information that was none of his business.

My mouth went dry. I was here for an internship interview,

and if he found out . . . shit. He would have the power to instantly turn my world upside down.

Ethan glared at Cameron. "I'm sorry to interrupt, but I have an urgent meeting to attend and you're holding up my ride." He pressed the door close button, and the elevator shut in Cam's face. I heard him mutter "Asshole" through the steel doors.

My heart pounded a million beats per minute. While I caught my breath, Ethan said to me, "That guy gave me serious dick vibes. And last thing I needed was for that dick to dick around while we should be checking into Solv. The earlier we are, the better. We show initiative and make Carlthorpe look good when we're both here early." He smirked and repositioned the sliding shoulder strap of his leather laptop bag. "I got your back, Noona."

"Thank you," I said, finally getting my voice back. I couldn't stop replaying how unlucky I was to see Cameron here, but at the same time, I had to thank the stars I hadn't seen him earlier in the lobby: he would have heard Ethan or me check in, asking for the intern hiring manager. He would have known everything, or figured it out eventually. And thank God Ethan had been able to read the situation to know that Cam was bad news.

Ethan and I exited the elevator, checked in at reception, and took seats in the waiting area.

"Are you nervous?" he asked.

I nodded. "Did she tell you what type of roles they were interviewing you for?"

"She said they'd consider me for development too, but I needed to sharpen my coding skills."

We learned light programming in our class, but because the course emphasis was more on spotting, identifying, and editing efficient and smart code rather than advanced code development, passing a programming interview would take a ton of extra practice and training since our class barely scratched the surface. But I could see Ethan doing this in his spare time, especially if it meant opening opportunities for working at Solv or similar companies.

The door next to the reception desk opened and a young man wearing clear plastic glasses that looked like hipster safety goggles emerged. "We're ready for you two. If you could follow me, I'll take each of you to your first meetings."

I passed through the door and held it open for Ethan.

Ethan was dropped off first. "Ready, Lily? You got this. But wish me luck."

I offered a reassuring smile. "Luck is just a mix of preparedness, timing, and opportunity. You have the holy trinity. You'll do great."

"Thanks. I know you will too."

We waved at each other as we headed to our separate interview rooms.

# Chapter Twenty-Six

The pool was freezing. The icy temperature was enough of a shock to my system to prevent me from constantly thinking about whether I'd get the internship or not.

A week had passed. Still no word.

According to the sign posted on the doors of the gym, the heater had malfunctioned overnight but maintenance had fixed it an hour ago. Allegedly. So the good news was no one else was in the water with me and it was warming up. The bad news was my teeth were chattering, and Beth was full of hyped coach energy.

"The heater's working, it'll take a while though." Beth blew her whistle. "Kickboard time, Lee!"

"D-d-d-do you really need that whistle? We're the only ones here."

She blew it again. "You asked me to help, and this is how I help. Now go kick!"

Sergeant Beth scared me, so I did as she requested. I kicked to the other side, then grabbed the edge.

The shrill whistle echoed as Beth blew it while walking

around the pool. "Go two more laps back-to-back and then you can rest. You need to be able to do a full seventy-five yards without any breaks."

I groaned and kicked. After finishing my laps, I grabbed the edge and threw the kickboard over to Beth's feet. "Done. Can I get out now?"

She crouched down next to me. "Not yet."

"Please, no more whistling."

"Look, I don't expect you to be Michael Phelps, but you need some endurance if you're going to pass." She stood and flipped through pages on her clipboard. "We can move on to your assessment if you'd like."

"My assessment?" My jaw dropped.

"Yes. Assessment. Let's see all the strokes you can do. I'll pick your two best ones and we will work on improving those in our next session. There's not a lot of time till your swim test, so we need to be efficient."

More groaning. More kicking. I paddled, stroked, and splashed while rotating through my swim stroke greatest hits. There were only five. Actually, maybe four—ish. Fine. Just three. Slim pickings, but it made Beth's job easier.

She paced back and forth a while, then scratched her temple. "Your best strokes are the dog paddle and that weird frog kick thing, which I don't know if it even has a name. But those use so much energy. I'm going to have to teach you a new stroke or two instead. Are you good with that?"

Before I could answer, she added, "You know I believe in you, right?" Without warning, she bellowed, "All right, Lily!

Let's GOOOOOO! Get moving! Grab the kickboard, hold it to your chest, and let's swim to the other side on your back."

Then she blew the whistle.

THE NICE THING about being at the pool was the untethering from my phone for nearly an hour. News from Solv was due any minute and I instructed Ethan not to message me until he heard, because earlier that morning all we kept texting each other was **Any news?** and **Not yet**, back and forth about five thousand times.

Each of us had met with four employees, the last one being the same hiring manager, which suggested our interviews had gone well. The thing that confused me though was that our interviewer was a dev manager, which meant either that he was considering me for a more technical job or that he was the one ultimately in charge of placing all selected candidates. I couldn't even imagine being considered for a technical role. There were far too many people who had superior technical skills and could run laps around my C++ skills.

My phone rang while unlocking Mia's car. "Bitch, it's SOLV don't ignore!!!" flashed on my screen. Mia must've programmed it as a joke, and any other time I would have laughed my ass off, but at that very moment my trembling hands turned frigid when I clicked the green phone icon to answer the call. Too bad Mia and Beth weren't with me for moral support; the two of them had gone to the farmers' market while I opted to go home to rest.

"Hello?" I croaked.

"Hello, may I please speak with Lily Lee?"

My heart thumped against my chest like an EDM bass line. "This is she."

"Hi, it's Donna from Solv Technologies. Is this an okay time to chat?"

My phone buzzed again. I knew it was Ethan with an update, but I didn't dare check.

My gym bag slid off my shoulder and fell into the trunk. "Yes, it's a great time, actually." I sat in the car just so I could get the heater going and the seat warmer on. After taking the cold swim and then stepping into the forty-degree weather with dripping wet shower hair, the last thing I needed was to be like one of those wind-up mouth chatter toys my dentist displayed prominently on his shelf.

Muting the phone, I started the car and let the call migrate via Bluetooth to the car speakers. Donna explained to me that they had more than a hundred candidates from across the country that they'd brought to their offices to interview. Donna's voice boomed over surround sound. "You can imagine how difficult it was to narrow down our list of candidates. But let's cut to the chase, we are thrilled to let you know that you made it to the final round! Since you met with our hiring manager, who is extremely tough on new recruits with his technical screenings, the next round is mainly for fit, and it's only a couple of hours long. During that time, we will try to figure out the best team for you.

We're scheduling the last interviews to take place over the next two weeks. Congratulations!"

She had just shared so much information. But the most important part? I made it to the final round!

"Thank you so much, Donna. I'm so excited to come back to Solv for the next set of interviews. Would these interviews be in California or New York?"

"Well, it's not *official* official yet, but will be soon . . . They're moving more projects to our Manhattan office, and we just signed a lease for another two floors. By the summer, we are aiming to double our headcount in our East Coast hub." I could hear a smile in her voice. "Do you have any preferences on where you'd like to live? New York or California?"

"New York," I answered with no hesitation.

She laughed. "Well, swift decision-making is definitely something we value at Solv. I'll email you a link with a calendar so you can select your interview times. Congratulations again, Lily."

The call ended and I fumbled with my phone as I clicked on Ethan's text.

> Got the call. I made it! I hope you did too!

Yes! We both made the cut!

> I did! NYC or NorCal?

NorCal. You?

NYC. Maybe this improves our
chances if we are from same
school but diff locations?

I hope so! P.S. They are considering
me for dev. Like WHAT. I'm literally
telling everyone I know and
trying to keep my shit together

Amazing! They didn't mention dev
for me. I don't know what group yet

Of course, I had to share my update with Mia and Beth, so I video chatted with them. Both friends joined in on my squealing and shrieking. My hands thawed and shook less. The numbness throughout my body subsided. It was sinking in—in two weeks' time, I might be one of Solv's newest hires.

Not sure how my parents would handle this news if they found out, I decided to wait until I had an offer in hand with a compensation letter before explaining everything to them. No need to add stress to my life, plus, they were plenty busy with my toddler nephews. Based on the Facebook photos they were uploading sporadically, they had their hands full with the twins: one of them loved to run and climb inside the house, the other had a penchant for coloring on walls. Both liked to open the fridge and pull out fruit and veggies.

I typed one more text.

> Got to final round at Solv!
> Please clap for me

I bit my lip and contemplated if it was a good idea to send it. My thumb hovered over the send button for a few seconds, but I finally pressed it.

It was done.

Rather than wait and stare at my phone for a reply, I reversed out of my parking spot and hit the closest bakery. I bought myself a "Congratulations!" red velvet cake and brought it home in the passenger seat. I made it all the way back without sampling the cream cheese frosting, even though I was starving from the swimming lessons.

My phone buzzed again while I barely managed to bring my gym bag, purse, and cake inside in one trip. I didn't dare check it: the last thing I needed was for my cake to cannonball onto the floor.

I checked my messages once I put everything down.

My stomach sank. Just Ethan again.

I'm already drunj

Drunj

Damnit drunj

Fuck it

He sent me ten champagne bottle emojis and an animated gif of a gorilla in a party hat.

I smiled at the messages and responded with more emojis, even though my yearning heart ached. I tried to swallow the sadness lodged in my throat.

As soon as I sent Ethan a reply, the long-awaited text came.

> Congratulations! Busy today,
> but let's celebrate soon!

That was it? No "how about this weekend" or "you pick the date and time"?

Was he blowing me off? Or was he really busy?

What did I really want from him? More than a curt text, that's what. How many words would have satisfied me? I wanted us to be friends and for him to just be happy for me, but I also selfishly wished that he wanted more. Paradoxically, I wanted to have my cake and eat it too.

Beth burst into the apartment and scolded me. "You shouldn't leave the door open! I could have been a burglar here to steal this congratulatory cake I just bought you!" She thrust a cake box toward me so I could view the lovely white tower through the cellophane window. "It's vanilla, from my favorite bakery." Glancing at the counter, she said, "Oh shit, you already have one!"

I nodded and smiled. "I wanted to commemorate this day. And I wanted cake from Sassy Girl's."

Beth laughed. "Mine is from there too!"

Mia peeked over Beth's shoulder. "Did someone say cake? Ta-daaaa! Best chocolate cake in the whole town! From Sassy Girl's!"

My second college journey had started with a sad slice of Sassy Girl's cake pushed underneath a Plexiglas partition.

Now I had three cakes. Three delicious flavors. Three good friends. A wonderful way to enjoy my big day, and a perfect reminder of how far I'd come.

Too bad Jake wasn't here to celebrate with me too.

# Chapter Twenty-Seven

*Twelve Years Ago*

*J*ake draped his arm across my chest while I tried to wiggle out of bed. When I finally managed to extract myself from the cushy comforter cocoon, he stirred in his sleep and grabbed at the air. As I pulled my body off the mattress and exposed it to the cold air, I shivered.

"Come back under the blankets, it's chilly." Jake smiled sleepily and patted my side of the bed.

He was right: it was freezing. Our heater had stopped working in the middle of the night, making a loud thunk that I'd assumed was Jake knocking something off the side table in his sleep. Luckily, I had a thick down blanket in addition to an electric one, so we were able to sleep comfortably for a few hours. It was the first snow of the season, and we were only a couple of degrees away from seeing our own breath inside the apartment.

I slid on my thick fleece bathrobe and grabbed my phone from the nightstand.

Mia had texted from the other room: **Called the HVAC people, they're coming in afternoon to fix the ^#&*$! heat. Too scared to figure out how to work the fireplace, I've never used it. I think there's a raccoon or something living in there and don't want to find out the hard way. There's a space heater on in the living room . . . you can open your door to try to let some heat in but maybe you got plenty of warmth from ya BOI in bed**

I smirked and plugged my phone into the charger. "Heater's broken. Okay if I open the door to let in some heat? Mia has a space heater running out there."

Jake sat up on the bed but kept the comforter on top of him. He peeked his head out while the rest of his body was covered. It looked like he was in a fluffy white igloo. "Orrrr . . . I can wrap you in my Jake tortilla. It's toasty under here!"

I glanced at the door, which seemed too far away, then back at Jake, who had shifted the comforter to his shoulders so it was more like a shawl, and had his arms spread out like he was flashing me.

Come to think of it, he was flashing me. All he had on under there was a pair of boxers.

He rubbed the sleep from his right eye and shot me an irresistible smile. I relented and crawled back under the covers with him, keeping my bathrobe on for added warmth.

We were still in the honeymoon stage. We'd been dating a while and were still annoyingly into each other. Even with his busy schedule, Jake managed to sleep over a few nights a week. I preferred him coming to my place: I was a junior year RA in a large suite with Mia and one of her high school friends, who was a year below us. Jake lived in an Asian fraternity house. I was surprised to find out that Carlthorpe had an Asian frat and sorority. Both of them had Greek names and mottos, which amused me because this seemed so . . . Western. Wasn't anything Greek by definition non-Asian?

In any case, where I lived was more suitable for people who preferred "no questions asked" sleepover events. Jake's Asian brethren were a nosy, gossipy bunch, and the less time I was around them, the better.

Once we were back under the blankets together, he asked, "Are you going to be an RA next year too?"

"Res Life pays for my room and board, plus they offer a monthly stipend, so I'll probably do it again. What about you?"

"My roommate wants to study abroad. It got me thinking about it again." He nibbled my ear and it tickled. "Maybe you should too."

My suitemate Gloria was applying for a semester abroad in Japan. She had studied Japanese in high school and took it in college too, so it made a ton of sense for her to go. "I took two years of Spanish, but it's not nearly enough to justify spending a semester abroad."

He whispered into my ear, "You don't need to study a language to go abroad. Carlthorpe just added a robust network of universities overseas that conduct classes in English. You could go somewhere like Australia."

"Really?" I had looked into study abroad but ruled it out mostly because of the language barrier. When I didn't take advanced Spanish courses my third year of college, I let go of my dream to study overseas.

I rolled over to my nightstand and looked up the exchange program website on my phone. "Oh shit, there are like twenty schools that offer classes I could take, including Spain. And many of them would actually count toward my major! There's an informational session next week. Applications are due end of month to be eligible next fall." Studying abroad my senior year first semester would have its social and academic pros and cons, but to hell with it. What if I could go to Spain? Or Hong Kong? Or Australia?

Jake crept over to my side of the bed and put his hand on my shoulder. "Maybe we could apply to the same places. And if we both got in? It would be cool. And romantic."

I shot him a hopeful smile. "What would you do with all of your side businesses, and all the activities and organizations counting on you for leadership next year?" It was a slight dig at Jake for stretching himself too thin, which I regretted once the words came out of my mouth. But the truth was that Jake always seemed to be going a gajillion miles a minute. He hardly slept. And I'd noticed he was flaking out on others who counted on him when he spent time with me. It sometimes left me wondering if I would be next.

"I'll make it work somehow. I always manage. Plus, you're my girlfriend, so you get first priority."

"Girlfriend?" I murmured. He'd never said that word out loud before. Neither of us was seeing other people, but I'd assumed that was because he was too busy to date anyone else.

He took the phone from my hand and placed it back on the table. Then he kissed me. "Yes. Girlfriend." He kissed

my cheek. "You're." My neck. "My." Left breast. "Girlfriend."
Right breast.

"What special privileges does a girlfriend have after
graduating from friend with benefits?" I asked coyly. "Will
we go to dinner together?"

He laughed. "We already do that. I always sit next to you
in the dining hall."

I raised an eyebrow. "That doesn't count. I mean more
off-campus stuff."

Jake grinned. "Yes. Dates. Movies. And maybe the most
important of all—"

He showed me his phone. I was listed as one of his "favorites" contacts. It was such a funny gesture, but for a guy who
knew, like, a bazillion people, it was a big deal to make it into
his top ten. "If you text me, I'll reply right away. Unless I'm
sleeping, out of cell range, or maimed in a hospital. That's
how much I care about you."

Rolling on top of him, I swept my long hair to my back.
"And you'll always answer my calls if you're not indisposed?
You know I don't like calling anyone, so if I do ring you, it's
probably important."

He nodded and held his hand up. "I care about you so
much that I solemnly swear to answer your calls, especially
because I know you hate being on the phone."

I offered him a light peck on the lips. "One more thing.
You think we could do this boyfriend-girlfriend thing in
Spain maybe?"

"Or South Africa." Jake kissed my lips softly. "Or Scotland."

*My lips pressed his again. "New Zealand maybe?"*

*His hands traveled down to my hips. "Wherever you go, I'll follow."*

*I yanked the plush comforter over our heads so it fully enveloped our bodies. Jake pulled me down on top of him and we molded into the contours of each other's bodies, with plenty of heat flowing between us to keep us warm.*

# Chapter Twenty-Eight

Partying in your thirties was no joke. In my mid-twenties, I could go out on a weeknight and drink to the point of blacking out, then be ready to go for a 9 A.M. conference call. Now? My thirty-two-year-old tongue was coated in sandpaper, my head pounded so hard my brain throbbed, and my eyes could barely open because all the moisture from my tear ducts had been redirected to other critical parts of my body so they could function.

I grabbed a bottle of water on my nightstand and chugged the entire thing.

"That was mine," Mia groaned. She was sleeping on the recliner in the corner of the room. Her arm was draped over her eyes to block the sunlight streaming through the window.

"Can you get water in the kitchen?" I croaked.

"Can't move. Might hurl."

I'd had one fewer drink than Mia because after three consecutive shots, I was on the brink of going to a bad, vomitous place. But she was always one to go for broke, even if it meant suffering the dire consequences a few hours later.

Sliding my feet into fuzzy slippers, I shuffled to the kitchen and brought back two large glasses of water and a bottle of Tylenol.

It took a while for Mia to sit up. "Mental note . . . cake and vodka shots should be consumed in moderation." She took two pills and chased them with desperate gulps of water. "You know, it's a shame we can't talk about Solv on social media. If you get the internship, which I hope you will, we'll need to figure out how to share the news."

Her phone dinged on the dresser. She moaned and glared at it.

It dinged again.

And again.

Snatching Mia's iPhone, I tossed it into her lap. "Can you at least turn down the volume? My brain can't take the noise right now. Especially loud ones that ring and echo in your head. I have to head to class now while you enjoy your restorative beauty sleep."

"Just hearing that you have class right now makes me feel like puking." She fell back onto the chair and moaned.

After a quick wardrobe change and a few pats of powder, I grabbed my backpack and ran out the door. The Global Audience and Influencer Culture class topic of the day was reputation management and cancel culture, and I couldn't wait to go. It would be in full attendance, so I got there early to get a good seat, right in the front row.

The class began promptly, and as the professor began

the lecture, the TA unstacked some chairs and placed three of them in the front, facing the audience.

"The first half of the class we have two special guests to speak about their industries, both Carlthorpe alumni. The second half will be a virtual interview with a popular, longtime YouTuber who will share how he's weathered controversies and difficult moments in his career. Without further ado, I'd like to invite Carlthorpe grads Francesca Clark and Amanda Phillips from Olympus Press to the stage. Francesca is the associate director of social media for the publisher, and Amanda works with authors as an editorial assistant."

The next minute unfolded in dizzying slow motion, both from the shock of seeing Amanda, and from the remaining alcohol in my bloodstream pulsing hard and recirculating throughout my body. There was nowhere to hide because of my prominent front-row position, and I couldn't escape easily because I was smack in the center.

Amanda's eyes fixed on me, a slight head tilt and furrowing brow suggesting vague recollection. But then, bam! It clicked.

All I could do was offer a shrug. Playing it cool (or at least faking it cool) seemed to be the way to go, because flailing and running out of the room screaming wasn't striking me as the right approach.

She managed to stay poised as she spoke about author branding and crisis management, offering the class examples from my own publisher that were nowhere near the level of complexity I was currently navigating. As she expressed how important it was to have transparency and honesty between authors and publishers, I sank low in my chair. Amanda wasn't always looking in my direction, but regardless, those words packed punches. It was like she was talking only to me.

As the professor announced a five-minute intermission, Amanda marched over before I could make a move.

She was tiny, but her overall meticulousness and law-abiding overzealousness scared the living shit out of me. "This is an unexpected place to meet you for the first time in person," she remarked. "Is there a reason that you're here and not . . . writing a book?"

So I tried the transparency approach she had just talked about and came clean, speaking at the speed of an auctioneer, explaining how my life had spiraled, and how I was trying to fix it. That I had an internship almost lined up. And I was only weeks away from getting my degree again. I ended with begging her not to tell anyone.

"It's only three more weeks and I can fix this," I said with as much confidence a hungover, unemployed person could muster. "Please let me try. At a minimum, this would make a funny story for us someday, right?"

"It's time to make it back to our seats for our virtual speaker," the TA announced into the podium microphone.

Offering Amanda my best pleading puppy-dog look, she eventually unscrunched her shoulders. "My reputation is on the line too now. Send me what pages you have so far and what you're proposing to do, and I can talk to Katherine. Just, please, don't make things any worse."

"Believe me, that's the last thing I want. Worseness." I groaned. "I'm sorry, that's not even a word, is it?"

She shook her head and offered me the slightest of smiles. Not once did Amanda mention canceling my contract. Or giving back my advance payment. None of the things I'd feared would happen . . . at least not yet.

Letting out a long sigh, I placed clasped hands against my chest. "I promise, I will fix this. And thank you."

I took my seat again as Amanda walked out with the other guest speaker. For now, my secret was safe.

I walked into my bedroom, surprised to find Mia on the bed, with two laptops, a phone, and a tablet placed around her in a semi-circle. Her cell kept making all sorts of buzzing, vibrating, and pinging sounds while she clicked around on the screen.

"Oh shit." Mia's voice fell to a whisper and her face turned white as a sheet. "Shit, shit, shit."

"Don't puke on my bed," I urged, dropping my backpack and running over to my desk to grab the wastebasket. "Here," I said, dangling it by her side. "Take it."

She shook her head. "No, it's not that. Although, it might be that soon. God, I feel like ass." Mia sighed and handed me her phone. "Don't freak, this is just one media hit I received, I'm hoping it doesn't blow up. When my head isn't foggy, we can figure out a plan."

I stared at the article and read.

## CARLTHORPE COURIER NEWS
### "Celebs Who Walk Among Us"

Carlthorpe has had its fair share of celebrity sightings over the years, due to our low profile, picturesque college town setting and our city's generous production tax benefits. Longtime rumors have been confirmed that an esteemed nonfiction author has been attending classes at Carlthorpe. Lily Lee, a Carlthorpe alum, has been spotted in the science and engineering buildings on campus. One librarian, who asked to remain anonymous, says Lee "is here for several hours, usually by herself, on the weekend."

We're excited about Lee's return to campus and can't wait to find out what special project she's working on to grace us with her presence. Is it a new book? Will she be teaching here? Is she consulting on curriculum? We reached out to her to request an interview but so far no reply. More to come as the story develops.

—Madison Drew, Staff Reporter

Mia took the phone from my hands. "At least they called you a celeb."

It wasn't surprising that my anonymous life on campus might eventually become exposed. I checked my school email and there weren't any messages requesting an interview, but after looking through my social media accounts, I saw a DM from the *Carlthorpe Courier* during exam week, which I'd overlooked. Damn.

I was confident that Mia and I could quickly come up with a viable cover story to explain my campus appearance. We'd already discussed a few options but had never solidified anything official. Once I'd gotten past midterms and had been undetected among the student body for so long, I let my guard down, thinking the coast was clear. But it wasn't. Amanda showing up to my class really shook me.

"Maybe we can order lunch and figure out what our strategy is," I suggested. "Something alarming just happened to me, but I think it's under control."

Mia nodded. "I need something to soak up the alcohol. Why did we think it was a good idea to try sparkling wine from a sixty-four-ounce can just before we went to bed?"

I shook my head. "Please don't mention last night in any capacity. I never want to see red velvet cake again."

She laughed as her phone buzzed three times in a row. "Jesus. How viral could that *Carlthorpe Courier* celebrity sighting blog post be?" She unlocked her phone and clicked a few times, then rubbed her chin. "Okay, so today just turned worse, which I didn't think was possible."

"Is it about me?" I asked.

She nodded. "This might be harder to do than I thought. But don't panic. If I can spin a famous fashion TikToker's rehab and a start-up founder's random hookup as 'self-exploration,' I can help you through this."

Nausea hit me hard when I saw the photo of Ethan and me leaving Solv's Manhattan office building. It was on SpottedinTheBigApple's Instagram account, which was a place where exclusive society news about moderately interesting celeb types who lived in New York could be found. It worked sort of like Reddit, where news stories that received the most likes and engagement would be the stories they showcase on social media. A year ago, it would have been an honor to be featured on SpottedinTheBigApple and I would have died to have a ton of "upvotes." But now? It was a liability. Why was I even on their radar in the first place?

The first part of the caption under the photo poked fun at me for carrying one of those old-school leather portfolios under my arm that people used in TV show legal depositions.

Okay, that was kind of funny.

"At least you and Ethan look hot in the photo," she added.

*Not helpful, Mia. But yes, it is a good picture.*

More concerning than the photo was the rest of the caption. "Spotted: Lily Lee at Solv HQ. Is she working on a secret (!) book? Interviewing employees or . . . interviewing for a position there? We did some sleuthing and scoured the job descriptions on Solv's website and saw an open HEAD OF STRATEGY position, which we think makes total sense given Lee's skill set. But there's more! We also uncovered this recent blog post from *Carlthorpe Courier* about Lily's latest whereabouts on the local campus. Why is she on campus four hours away if she's also in NYC? More news to come (make sure you like and comment to upvote!)."

The post had just gone live in the morning, and unfortu-

nately the engagement was high. There were people speculating on whether I was writing two books: one about tech
companies and one about academia. Others thought I was
consulting. And, of course, the trolls were out doing their
thing, less speculating, more commenting about how I was
an underqualified woman taking jobs away from more qualified men. So far, no one had put two and two together to
actually connect my CS class with my internship candidacy
at Solv. But it was only a matter of time.

I pleaded, "Give it to me straight. In your professional
opinion and as my best friend, how screwed am I?"

She put her phone down. "Professionally speaking, it's
too early to say. I'd recommend that we get ahead of this,
maybe post something in the next twenty-four hours about
why you're back on campus. We should have done that earlier, and damn, that's on me for not thinking it might come
to this. The level of disclosure is up to you, but I'd recommend being as honest as possible without disclosing all the
nitty-gritty details. As a friend, I can offer you a giant hug
and say I have your back no matter what." Mia wrapped her
arms around my body and squeezed. "I think I fucked up,
I'm so sorry."

I swallowed hard. "All of this is not on you. It's on me too.
If there's one thing I've learned in life, it's that adults like us
wing it every day. Even though we pretend to have some
control over our lives and good judgment from years of life
experience, things just go wrong. For me, all the time. Mistakes happen. Risks don't pay off. And we have to somehow
keep going. Sadly, this will go on forever until we die."

She let out a weak laugh. "Well, that was insightful, and disturbingly morbid. Maybe we need Beth in here for a pep talk. Any other ideas on what we can do to make this go away? My brain is not cooperating at the moment."

Usually I was asking her for advice, not the other way around. "Maybe I should just run away, like Maria does in *The Sound of Music*."

She raised an eyebrow. "I hate to break it to you, but there are no convents to run away to within driving distance of Carlthorpe. To be honest, I don't even know if they exist in real life at all in this country, but we have other things to worry about than googling abbey locations right now. Oh! And remember? That crazy-ass Maria came back! I would have ghosted permanently."

My shoulders slumped. "Yeah, true. Okay, how bad is all of this, really, on a scale of one to ten? Be truthful, like you always are." I winced, anticipating her answer.

She flinched. "Ten out of ten. You get a perfect score."

MIA AND I recorded the final take of a short video, coming clean about my college situation, and were trying to upload it when we realized it was too late.

I was tagged in several posts at once. Each headline read like a smack across the face.

IS LILY LEE A FEMINIST OR A FRAUD? *Slap!*

SENIORITIS STRIKES LILY LEE AS SHE RETURNS TO CAMPUS. *Whack!*

HOW LILY LEE'S EDUCATION HOAX FOOLED US ALL: WHY WE SHOULD BAN HER BOOKS. *Punch! Thwack!*

My hands trembled as I continued doomscrolling. Each of these clickbait blog titles and social media grabby posts read like front-page newspaper headlines, shouting directly at me, pronouncing me a huge fake and a pathetic scam artist to the whole world. Every major failure in my life that left me an insecure mess came roaring back into my mind. Getting knocked out of the citywide spelling bee, ironically by the word "disappoint." Being second or third chair in the flute section all throughout high school band, never number one. And let's not forget my sister's MD/PhD, compared to my college dropout status. I couldn't get a job. Couldn't fulfill my book contract. And now I had no life to go back to anymore. Without my reputation and status, I had nothing. What I'd thought about myself for years was exactly how others saw me too.

Fraud.

Imposter.

Fake.

Everything was fully spelled out in the world exactly as I saw it in my head, in pithy sound bites in various news outlets and social media for everyone to see.

It was Mia who broke down crying first. "I'm so, so sorry I let you down. I thought we could get ahead of it."

Mia openly showing her feelings caused me to burst into

tears soon after, and the pressure compressing my chest, plus the sense of doom lodged deep inside me, let up a little as more tears flowed. Crying was more therapeutic than I'd realized.

She took a deep breath and wiped her cheeks. "Let's do damage control and go from there. What do we tackle first? What worries you the most?"

I sniffled and closed my eyes. "God, so many things. Everyone thinks I'm a hack without giving me a chance for a rebuttal. What if my publisher cancels my contract now? And Solv rejects me because of this? What if I've jeopardized my graduation again? And shit, what about my parents?" There was no hierarchy to this list. Everything was equally terrible in its own way, and all the possibilities had increased in likelihood tenfold since morning.

Mia asked, "Are you going to tell your parents?"

My shoulders slumped. "I didn't even think about that. I have to, right?"

"They might guilt-trip you if you don't, but I think you should tell them when you're ready, aiming for sooner rather than later. Otherwise they'll hear it from someone else."

By guilt-trip, Mia meant that my mom and dad would scold me about how they came to the United States when they were in their twenties, fighting for survival and trying to obtain the American dream, only to have me waste time and opportunities. They would read this as my being careless, not appreciating their ultimate immigrant sacrifice, disrespecting them with each and every failure. And having a thirty-something daughter without a college degree? The ultimate disgrace.

It was as if my life had been hit by an 8.0 earthquake, and all I wanted right now was a sliver of hope, a sign that maybe things would work out. I needed something, anything, to believe in. Maybe with that I could see past the wreckage around me.

Mia added, "There are probably other people you want to tell first."

Mia would tell Beth, so it came down to me to let the one person I didn't want to be vulnerable around know about my media exposure.

Truthfully, I wanted to tell him, even if Mia hadn't prodded me. I missed him. And the more time that passed, the more distant Jake and I had become.

I dialed his number. Once upon a time, Jake had promised me that he'd always pick up when I called. What a dumb thing for me to remember and hold sacred after all these years.

An unmistakable feeling of my chest tightening returned. *Hello again, anxiety.*

After three long rings, I heard his voice crackle through the speaker.

"You've reached the voice mail of Jacob Cho. Sorry I missed your call. If you'd like to leave a message—"

My lungs wouldn't fully expand, which cut off my breathing. I hung up.

Mia whispered, "I'm so sorry."

My phone rang before I could respond.

It was Jake.

There was agitation in his voice when I answered. "Hey, I'm walking into an important meeting, but saw you called. Sorry I missed it, the ringer was silenced and I had a feeling that I needed to check my phone when you called. Is it important? Or did you butt dial me by accident?"

It wasn't exactly the movie montage response I wanted, but it was better than getting his voice mail. And the last thing I wanted was to sabotage whatever meeting he had already lined up. But he gave me what I needed at a time I needed him the most.

Hope.

"It's important, but I think it can wait," I said softly.

"Are you sure? It's too late for me to reschedule my thing right now, but if it's an emergency, I can try. This might sound ridiculous, but a long time ago I made a promise to you that if you ever called—"

"I remember," I whispered.

"You do?" he asked, breathing hard.

I smiled. "Yes. And thank you. I'll be fine for now. Good luck with your meeting."

"Thanks. It's a make-or-break moment for me, I'll tell you about if it's *make* instead of *break*. I'll be tied up today but I'll call you soon, I promise."

*He promised.* I glanced at Mia when I hung up. Her mouth tugged at the corners as she spoke. "That sounded optimistic. While you were on the phone, I came up with a couple of ideas I want to run by you. And Beth texted me . . . she'll be popping in here shortly."

Good, I could use some of Beth's optimism. Hopefully without the whistle.

She entered my room carrying a two-tiered frosted chocolate cake. No one had ever entered my room with a two-tiered frosted chocolate cake, but I hoped it wouldn't be the last time. It solved none of my immediate problems and I wasn't really hungry, especially after eating so much dessert the night before, but seeing the cake and Beth's smiling face distracted me enough to help me recognize that I had friends in my corner. My heart fluttered in my chest as Beth set the dessert down.

"I procrasti-baked this brownie cake this morning, maybe my roomie ESP was telling me something." She smiled as she tipped her creation a little so I could see the inscription: *We Believe.* "I ran out of icing. It's supposed to say 'We Believe in You!'"

Mia hugged Beth. "It's beautiful and perfect."

Blushing hard, Beth said, "Thank you. I stayed up all night working on my grad school applications after we drank and I made the brownie layers this morning. I was just going to freeze it for later, but what good timing! I thought you could use some cheering up, and who doesn't love a brownie cake?"

"Wait, you're not hungover?" Mia asked.

She shrugged and sliced into the top layer, revealing chewy, chocolatey goodness. "Good genes, I guess."

Good genes, and a young, sprightly body. Her hydrated skin had the elasticity of a TRX strength band, despite all the Diet Coke she drank. "Your brownie cake is gorgeous, inside and out. Just like you, Beth," I said.

Mia placed one of the slices on a small paper plate and took a bite. "Oh my God, Beth. I thought I couldn't stand looking at this after last night, but this is to die for. I really need you to bake for all my PR events. Let's talk later, when all of this blows over."

"You really think this can blow over?" I asked with a wavering voice.

She licked frosting off her fork. "Have I seen worse than this in my line of work? Maybe not. *But* I have a few ideas now that the shock has worn off a little. Things are going to be bad for a while until the dust settles, so there won't be much down time or"—Mia looked down at her plate—"leisurely eating. But let's eat our brunch brownie cake and brainstorm together, and we can start putting things in motion. How does that sound?"

"It sounds delicious," I said.

# Chapter Twenty-Nine

W hy is Beth wearing a houndstooth blazer with elbow patches and a pair of tortoiseshell reading glasses?"

Mia shushed me. "She's here to help. And it's better than what she was wearing earlier, those CAN YOU FEEL THE LOVE TONIGHT? pajamas, with two soup cans holding hands."

"Are you really one to talk?" I looked down at Mia's novelty tee: I'M GRUMPY CAT IN HUMAN FORM.

She rolled her eyes. "Anyway, Beth's going to present some of her main findings from her senior seminar. I saw what she was studying and thought it could be useful, especially with everything going on." Beth had a 4.0 GPA and was a dual major in psychology and neuroscience.

"Good afternoon, class," Beth said as she handed us some freshly printed pages.

Mia groaned. I laughed.

"Before I begin, I have some questions for you. Who here is in the habit of self-sabotaging?"

Mia and I looked at each other and shrugged.

"Okay, let me put this another way, with more tangible

examples. Please raise your hand if you've ever kept quiet in a meeting or a class even when having a good idea . . . or conformed to a group's way of doing something even though you had an opinion on how to do it better but were too scared to speak up. Has anyone turned down a great opportunity because you didn't think you were good enough?"

Mia raised her hand. Ironically, I was too timid to raise my hand to admit all of this, even though I was here among friends.

Beth looked at me. "Or . . . has anyone praised you for an accomplishment, and you wrote it off as luck? Or have you ever dismissed a compliment, saying 'It was nothing,' or even criticized yourself right after as a way of deflecting praise or showing humility?"

I nodded. *Yes, fine, you got me.* I was guilty of all of it. Slowly, I raised my hand.

Beth nodded at Mia and me. "These are examples of *micro* self-sabotaging events triggered by something researchers noted over forty years ago, imposter phenomenon. There are hundreds, maybe thousands, of other examples of this. But these are the ones that I'm guilty of too."

She continued, "Psychotherapy experts at Georgia State University started studying this in the seventies and honestly, there really should have been many more follow-up studies. We don't have a ton of time to delve deep here, and I'm sharing high-level what I've researched in my classes, but a certified therapist or medical professional would know more. I do have some guidelines to help you think about ways to cope and combat this imposter phenomenon, also known as imposter syndrome, in the meantime."

"Preach, Professor Beth!" Mia closed her eyes and raised both hands in the air. We all laughed.

"First, you need to admit it's a problem. Research suggests that it is more prevalent in women, especially in high-achieving households and in marginalized communities."

Yes, I was in all of those categories. Check, check, and check.

"Many high achievers are both driven and debilitated by the comparison game. Setting goals and targets that you may eventually reach but don't appreciate once you're there is unfortunately common."

Internally, I was screaming. Not at her, but at myself. Beth was so right. I was a successful author and a sought-out career expert. I should be proud of my accomplishments and not feel like I need to show proof of expertise or a certificate of authenticity with every business or professional interaction. I'd carried self-doubts my entire corporate career, and they'd followed me into my author life too.

When would it end?

Mia raised her hand. "How about social media? We're all in the practice of projecting the best version of our lives, our highlight reels of all the good things. And I *still* knowingly compare my *actual* self to other people's perfect online lives, even when I know better, and feel bad about myself for not measuring up."

I nodded and added, "There were lots of bad days when I thought my writing career was already over even when things were going well just because I was comparing myself to others, and seeing my friends who stuck with their jobs rise in the ranks at their companies while I stepped away from corporate life . . . it was a lot."

Would it ever end?

Or . . . maybe it was up to me to end it?

Beth listened and nodded. "I have one more thing to add that's not in my senior thesis. While we've talked about the internalization of bad feelings, let's also note that it's the environments themselves that are set up in a way to perpetuate these feelings."

It was true, this wasn't only about self-esteem and negative thoughts about myself. I nodded. "Yes! Schools, workplaces, and institutional cultures need to be reexamined, because it's not just about *fixing* individual people, right? It's about *fixing* the systemic bias and cultural inertia all around us so that marginalized people can feel like they not only belong but that they can thrive."

Beth exclaimed, "One hundred percent. Full stop." Picking up a legal pad and flipping through it, she concluded, "I think I've covered a lot for today's BethTalk." She tucked a pen behind her ear and looked at Mia. "Is this what you were thinking? How I could help?"

Mia jumped up from the couch and hugged Beth. "It was great! Everything you just said resonated with me so much. What about you, Lily?" Mia asked.

They both looked at me.

I bobbed my head. "It was like you were inside my head with a magnifying glass. I didn't like it one bit. But if there's one thing I can do now, it's start small with the things you've identified and chip away at them. You have to start somewhere, right?"

Mia asked, "What are you going to do first?"

"Well, we're about to navigate uncharted territory with my PR crisis. But I'll start with refraining from my self-limiting, undermining language."

Mia's shoulders slumped. "Honestly, it's so hard to do that, with Korean parents like ours. When you're young, they tell you to be humble and quiet, and to strive for perfection . . . it's just so ingrained in you."

I chimed in. "But they're the worst offenders sometimes—my parents' whole group of friends are constantly bragging and showing off accomplishments. And the comparison game they're always perpetuating is damaging in so many ways."

Mia sighed. "I'm pretty sure my strict dad was the cause of my self-doubts. It was all criticism with that guy, and zero praise. I was never good enough." She leaned back in her chair, contemplative in her thoughts. "But we need to break this cycle somehow."

My parents were the same way. My anxiety first reared its ugly head in high school, and since then, I'd been constantly battling bouts of insecurity, both professionally and romantically. I worked twice as hard to prove to everyone I was a superstar employee, and that left zero time for exploring romantic relationships.

It was time for a change. "I won't downplay my accomplishments, not anymore. I should be proud of what I've done with my life. I had a successful corporate career and took a big chance by leaving it to become a consultant and an author. I worked hard to get to where I am, damn it, and the successes I've had aren't the accomplishments of my parents. They're mine. It's time that I toot my own horn. Others might not like it, but as the saying goes, 'Haters gonna hate.'"

Beth squealed. "You are the walking, talking, real-life version of T-Swizzle's 'Shake It Off' and I'm here for it!"

Mia exchanged glances with me and I cough-laughed. "But this is all good to think about, especially now. Thank you for the helpful, motivational BethTalk."

She beamed. "I'm glad I could help someone with my research."

"Shall we do the cheer?" Mia said, giddy with anticipation.

One drunken night, all three of us had come up with a ridiculous "rah rah" thing that Mia was actually excited about. The timing seemed more appropriate than ever. She put out her hand, Beth stacked her right one on it, and I placed mine on hers.

"On the count of one, two, three!" Mia cheered.

"Let! That! Shit! Go!" we chanted, then broke formation.

# Chapter Thirty

*Eleven Years Ago*

*O*ur bags were packed, the passports were ready, and
I had withdrawn five hundred euros from the bank.
*Strolling down Carlthorpe's main walkway before heading*
*to the airport, I could get one last look at campus before fly-*
*ing to Spain with Jake. Well, we were first flying into Paris*
*for a week, and would then take the train to Madrid, my*
*dream vacation destination, and arrive in Barcelona at the*
*month's end, when classes officially started.*

*Everything we had planned had turned out perfectly. We*
*both got into the study abroad program our first semester*
*senior year at Autonomous University of Barcelona. I had*
*saved enough money so I could travel before and after the*
*semester ended. And I got into all the courses I had wanted.*

*I had never imagined that I, Lily Lee, would be studying*
*abroad in Europe. My only passport stamps were from a*
*trip to Korea, but that was to visit family. This was different.*
*Soon, I would gather my travel gear from Mia's apartment*

and fly across the Atlantic, ready to have the experience of a lifetime.

I shivered with excitement and giddiness.

My phone rang. It was my umma. We'd already said our goodbyes earlier that morning, or rather, I got a lecture about how I was wasting money, slacking off, and I should travel to Europe when I was older instead. I promised my parents that I would study hard and not "play around," as they said.

"It's still not too late to take premed classes and study for MCAT," they managed to squeeze in before we said our good-byes. I hung up knowing I didn't have their support, but it was time to start living my life outside of work-study and my text-books, even if they didn't approve. Three years of adulthood had already flown by, and I had nothing to show for them.

I wanted to break out of my shell and have the time of my life with my boyfriend. Jake and I had fought recently about how he wasn't prioritizing me higher than, say, intramural softball, community gardening, ultimate Frisbee, and a mil-lion other things. He countered by complaining that I was constantly working, studying, or signing up for Res Life ac-tivities. Barcelona would give us time together.

No distractions.

When Umma tried calling three times, I knew it had to be urgent. She'd never tried to contact me like this, not even on the day Carlthorpe sent out their admissions letters, or the day my older sister had gotten into med school, or when Appa had been transferred to a new city for his engineering job and they were selling my childhood home.

"Hello?" I answered with a smidge of fear.

"Lily, good! You're not on the plane. Don't go to Spain."

Actually, I was headed to Paris to spend a week with Jake, stuffing our faces with croissants, steak frites, and macarons. Not Spain. Not yet.

"We've already gone over this," I complained. "My course load there will mostly transfer over and I promise I'll study hard. Financial aid will be the same, and I'll cover any extra spending."

"No, you don't understand," she contested. There was a long pause before she continued. "Did you talk to your sister?"

My sister had, in fact, sent me a travel accessories kit as a bon voyage gift, something my parents hadn't thought to do. "We already said goodbye last night. What is all of this about, anyway?" I checked my watch. "My plane leaves in about four hours." Did my parents tell Sara to talk me out of going, the day of the flight? Now annoyed, especially that they had brought their favorite child into this, I fumed, "Look, I'm going. I've never gotten to travel anywhere other than Korea, and this is a perfect opportunity to do something academic, cultural, and social, all at the same time. I'm heading to the airport now, and I'll let you know I arrived safely."

"No, Lily. You don't listen. You're not going. You can't." Her voice fell faint. "Your appa . . . his company lay him off today, just after we talk on phone. We don't have money for your college, we paying for Sara medical school too, remember?"

I stopped breathing. What did she mean? They didn't have money for college?

She added, "We have enough saving to help paying for

only one semester. And we have to keep paying for Sara medical school. It's a good school, but expensive."

Words fumbled around on my tongue. "So . . . I—I have to stay here?" Queasiness overtook me. I fell onto a bench along the walkway and tried to steady myself.

"Stay at campus and graduate early. You have the AP credit, you can take all of your classes in one semester. We can't pay our share for both semester. We can't take out more student loan right now and it's too late to get low interest. You already borrowing too much."

Her words hit me one after another. I was barely able to process them. Throughout my first three years of college, I'd picked up campus work-study jobs and various other part-time gigs, but increasing my hours wouldn't be enough to pay my parents' portion of tuition. I was in a lot of debt with federal loans already, and although my brain couldn't process what was happening, the math worked: graduating early would help my family financially.

How many classes did I need? Five, maybe six? My schedule would be packed with courses and whatever part-time work I could find to help offset expenses. I would have no life.

My phone beeped. It was Jake calling on the other line. I ignored it.

Rather than apologize or temper this shocking major life change, my mom said, "Well, you can go to Spain another time. When you retire. We didn't want you to go anyway, too much playing."

Boy, she hit a nerve with that one.

I cried out in frustration, "Why do you think I'd go there to play? What do you even mean by that? I wanted to do something on my own for once. Make my own decisions. I didn't even choose Carlthorpe, remember? You and Appa did. And now when I finally have an opportunity to grow up, to figure out how the world works, to enjoy my life . . . I even saved up spending money and tried to do something for myself for once . . . and nothing goes right! And on top of that, I'm the one who has to take the brunt of this money crunch, not future doctor Sara." I let out a frustrated scream as my stomach twisted into a distorted pretzel. A familiar feeling of tightness in my abdomen returned in full force, along with a sense of dread. Could I even get any classes I wanted? Could I get campus housing now? Where would I stay before classes started?

I could hear my mom repeating my name over and over, each time sounding more irritated and impatient. It was too much for me. I ended the call and leaned my head back on the bench.

What a fucking disaster.

A set of large hands covered my eyes from behind. "Guess who?"

I whirled around, my angry fist making immediate contact with Jake's chest.

He held his palms up. "Whoa there! I was just messing with you. And shit, that hurt. I was worried because you were taking such a long time at the bank. We need to leave in a few minutes, so I came looking for you."

"I'm not going," I barely whispered. Tears tumbled down my cheeks and I wiped them away with the palms of my hands.

I repeated those words again. Louder, sadder, and void of hope. "I'm. Not. Going."

Even then, the words still didn't feel real.

He came around to my side of the bench and sat down. "What happened? Did you get cold feet? Did someone get hurt? Is everything okay?"

No point in hiding any of it. I told him about my dad's sudden job loss. How they were paying for my sister's med school too and prioritizing it over my undergraduate studies. He looked stunned as I shuddered and sobbed.

I looked at him. "Could you stay with me?" Just a while. Or longer. Until I figured some things out. "Please?"

Jake's eyes darkened. He hadn't had much time to process what I'd told him, but when his face fell, I knew things were about to get worse.

I pleaded anyway, with more desperation in my voice. "Please don't go. Don't leave."

And this was when a potentially touching moment together turned into another unexpected, life-changing one that would haunt me forever.

Jake didn't offer to stay a few hours, or a day or two to help me get on my feet. Nor did he say he could stay with me for any part of the week when we were supposed to vacation in Paris, when we were going to sightsee together and stuff ourselves with butter-laden pastries.

He proposed none of those things.

His face hardened instead. "I-I'm sorry, I can't flake out on this. You know how you're always on my case about how I do a million things but I never see anything through? My parents say the same thing. They're fed up with me. For switching majors, for changing my mind about summer internships, for not knowing what I want to do after college. They threatened to cut off my college funds, but they said I could go to Spain if I proved I could be responsible. They'll kill me if I bail this time." His eyes became watery but he remained steadfast. "I'm sorry, Lily. I can't back out. I have to go."

The alarms on my phone and watch went off at the same time. A reminder it was exactly four hours prior to the flight departure time. The car service we scheduled to take us to the airport would arrive at any moment.

I withered into a smaller, fragile version of myself. Jake's phone buzzed over and over. "I need to get this. It's my mom. I—I don't know what to say to her. But I should take it."

He hesitated a second, then whispered to me, "I still love you." When I didn't respond, he said it a second time. I still didn't say it back. Instead, I fought back tears and looked away from him.

After the phone rang again, he walked a few steps away from the bench and answered. "Hi, Umma. I'm kind of busy." A pause. "Heading out to the airport soon. Everything's taken care of, I'll call you when I land. Okay, sure, put Appa on the line."

"I need to go," he mumbled to me as he covered the phone receiver. He tried to kiss my forehead, but I shirked away from his touch. His hurried footsteps down the walkway were timed perfectly to the frantic beat of my heart. The aching inside my chest was unbearable, a physical sign of my heart slowly breaking in real time. Jake's silhouette grew smaller and smaller in the distance, and eventually disappeared.

He was gone.

I was alone.

I came back to Mia's apartment a few hours later. Her new roommate, an exchange student from Hong Kong, wasn't arriving for a couple of weeks. So that gave me time to plan around my calamity. Not much time, but some.

I undressed in the bathroom and flicked on the hot water.

Hot showers usually relaxed me and cleared my mind, but not this time. The stream of water hit the back of my neck. My brain played back the worst parts of the afternoon's events. No trip to Spain. Not having money because of my dad's job loss. Jake abandoning me.

No Spain. No money. No Jake. Over and over again.

My mind felt sluggish as the steam from the shower enveloped me. Each breath I drew was more and more shallow.

I needed fresh air.

No, I needed to sit. Sliding my back down the shower wall, I sat knees to chest in the shower. The water temperature transitioned from hot to warm to tepid as I closed my eyes, trying to control my breath.

A squeal above me echoed in the room. The sound of the shower valve cranking to the right. The flow of water stopped.

"Lily? Are you okay?" A familiar voice cut through the fog.

"Mia?" I barely whispered.

She placed a tattered terry-cloth robe around my shivering shoulders. "You think you can get up? Maybe get some rest? Let me help."

"I'm not going to Spain."

With her arms outstretched, Mia grabbed both of my hands and lifted me slowly from the tiled floor. My body weighed a thousand pounds, but by some miracle, I managed to make it to her bedroom with her help. She laid out a few blankets and a pillow on the mattress, placed a mug of water on the nightstand, and dimmed the lights.

I whispered, "Did he call me? To talk about it?"

Mia pulled my phone out of my coat pocket and looked at the screen. "There's nothing from Jake. I'm so sorry."

Mia and I were reunited unexpectedly on the worst day of my life, when I was let down by my family, and my boyfriend became my ex-boyfriend. That night, we formed an eternal bond that could never ever be broken. Mia had my back then, and I would always have hers.

# Chapter Thirty-One

U mma called so many times I finally picked up. Without a doubt, she'd heard the news.

"Umma, I can explain—" I pleaded.

"Make no sense. Thirty-nine dollar wasted! And they say the ice is melted so they can't ship same box again. You need to explain."

But I had no explanation. I had no idea what the hell she was going on about.

"I don't understand, actually," I confessed. "What shipment?"

"Appa and I send you Omaha Steaks gift package as a congratulations on starting new job. Three rib eyes. I wait four month for your big day at your new company, I even marked it on the calendar! I send to Swain and Wallace, where you say you work, and they just call me and say they can't deliver. They say you not working there and no one heard of you."

I swallowed hard. Technically, I never told her I actually worked there, I was careful with my words. But that was beside the point. Like with everything else, I messed this up. There was some possibility I could continue this ruse with my parents, but only with more deceit, and I'd had enough. After taking a deep breath, I told her about my college credit shortage, and how I didn't get the job because of it. And that my book deal was probably also canceled.

I mumbled, "I'm sorry." My natural inclination was to offer an apology for being a disappointment to them, but I stopped myself, my mind jumping back to my recent discussion with Beth and Mia about feeling like I wasn't competent, or skilled, or smart enough. And that my mistakes were evidence of my inadequacy.

But none of this was true. It really wasn't.

I'd moved up the ladder and worked hard to get to where I was. I'd won awards. Gotten performance bonuses. These were facts. And I had receipts.

Going through life striving for perfection, without making any mistakes, wasn't just unsustainable, it was impossible. Admitting as much wasn't showing weakness, it was setting myself up for happiness. Owning my successes was one thing that would help me get there.

And I started by telling my parents the truth.

Then my dad said something that surprised me. It was genuine. Hopeful. Earnest.

"If you go back to college again, this mean you can still go to medical school. Now you have second chance!" Appa said.

Umma chirped, "Law school is okay too!"

I cleared my throat. "Uh, no. That's not happening, and

that's not why I'm doing college again. I will say this though. I'm proud of what I've achieved, even that last semester in college, which was a very dark time for me."

Appa said quietly, "I remember. That was bad time for whole family."

Umma added, "Very hard for your Appa."

Dad whispered, "No, I think more hard for Lily than me. We pushed her too hard because of me."

For once, my mom and dad were disagreeing. I held my tongue, waiting to see how this would play out.

Dad's voice shook as he spoke. "When I lose my job, we can't afford to pay for your school and your sister school. We thought we had to choose."

Anger brewed inside me. "You did choose. You chose your other daughter. I was the one who had to try to graduate early."

Mom's tone changed. It was tinged with sorrow. "We choose wrong. We think because you were stronger person you could handle more pressure. You always have a job, you go to good school, we never worry about you. But now . . . now we worry about you all the time because you change so much after college, working so hard, you have job we don't understand." She sighed. "But maybe you do things we don't know, or don't like, and didn't teach you, and this is okay."

My jaw dropped. For the first time ever, my mom had admitted that not accepting my life choices was a *them* problem, and not a *me* problem.

"Thank you for saying that," I whispered.

Mom added, "We buying your book and tell everyone at church to buy too."

"She good at selling," my dad added. "She sell a lot for you. Very proud umma."

Before I could thank her again, my mom muttered, "We still mad. You waste good steak. But I will ask them for coupon so you can have graduation present. Maybe they will add discount."

Offering a gift of steak coupons meant that they weren't ashamed or disgraced after all. This was as close as I'd ever get to a reconciliation of our past. I'd never known my parents to admit they were wrong, or that they'd made decisions that resulted in adverse consequences. But admitting they'd made a huge, life-affecting decision all those years ago and acknowledging that they didn't have my interests in mind at the time, for some reason that provided me a sense of closure and my heart became less heavy. The regret in my mom's and dad's voices spoke volumes, as did their eagerness to push my books onto their Korean peers. They were sorry. And knowing that went a long way.

# Chapter Thirty-Two

Mia squawked, "Seriously? Still no word from Jake? I thought he—"

*Promised.*

I tried my best to appear calm while I was seething inside. "Not even a text," I said weakly. It had been more than forty hours since I'd spoken to him. Not that I was counting. "I was hoping this time would be different."

It wasn't different.

I was done with Jake. We were done.

I'd officially written him out of my life. Again.

Time to delete his number. Again.

Thanks for letting me down, Jake. Again.

Again, again, again. How stupid was I for thinking I could rely on him this time?

Mia frowned. "I'm so sorry he ghosted you. What a fucking shitty thing to do. Especially now."

Tears pricked the backs of my eyes as I distracted myself with angry-typing an op-ed essay. While revising the short piece, I received an email from my publicist.

"They want me to prepare a video statement and have the O'Haras interview me in a live event this week so I can tell my side of the story," I told Mia.

She raised an eyebrow. "I don't necessarily trust the O'Hara family, do you? But I guess the benefit of doing that event would be that they could bring in a well-connected audience full of media influencers. Plus, it's the devil you know, as they say."

"I can see an event with the O'Haras going either way: it could be beneficial or a total disaster, depending on the crowd and the questions they ask."

Mia took her hands off her keyboard. "Can you get the questions ahead of time? Didn't they request the same from you?"

It was worth a try. I set up an emergency meeting with my editor and publicist that afternoon to discuss urgent book-related matters and requested that the questions from the O'Haras' interview be sent to me beforehand. Mia drafted correspondence for Carlthorpe's dean of students and managed my emails flooding in for media requests. According to her reputation tracking tool, my media hits had gone up instead of plateauing or going down.

She barked out a laugh so loud that it startled me. "Sorry, I checked your follower and subscriber counts. They've doubled in the last day. Maybe this hasn't been all bad."

A crop of pro-Lily articles had appeared, which Mia helped propagate, ones focused on my return to campus, and taking STEM-focused classes, and how the age of undergrad students is higher at Carlthorpe thanks to more gap-year acceptances and transfer students from community colleges. The *Carlthorpe Courier* interviewed various students in my stats and CS classes, and for the most part, the article was positive.

My phone rang as I finished reading.

"Jake?" Mia's eyes begged me for confirmation.

I swallowed hard. "I should have blocked him. I'm going to ignore it."

She grabbed the phone from me. "No. I want you to tell him off. Ten years ago, you two had important things to work out and he left you high and dry. He's a bona fide asshole for not calling you back! Yell at him! Yank his balls off!"

She was right, he needed to hear this. "I might try a slightly different approach, but yeah, I get you." Leaving the living room, I closed the door to my bedroom behind me and answered the call.

"Hey! I'm so sorry it took so long to get back to you," he breathed.

"And I'm sorry I believed you'd call me back. It's been two days." My voice was cold and matter-of-fact.

"Shit, please don't hang up! I said I was sorry, and I can explain," he begged.

I stiffened at his words. "I need you to know how badly you let me down. It's not like it's the first time."

"May I please tell you what happened? Then after that, you can never speak to me again, but I promise you it wasn't for nothing."

I swallowed hard. "Fine," I said flatly. Pulling the phone

away from my ear, I put it on speakerphone, just so I could hover my finger on the end call button.

I heard him gulp. "Damn, I don't even know where to begin. I should have my thoughts more organized, but I haven't slept much. I'm sorry." He took a deep breath. "Okay, when you called, I was meeting with my academic advisor for the last time." Jake paused. "My last time. Can you believe it?"

I couldn't read his tone. How was I supposed to react to this news? Was I supposed to congratulate him? Offer condolences? What did this even mean?

He barreled on, speaking more quickly. "He was preparing me for . . . well . . . I just spent the last day and a half defending my dissertation. I'm exhausted, my brain is fried, but I called you as soon as I finished meeting with the committee. I had to hold two separate sessions, with some people in person, and again in a virtual meeting for a few who were out sick. I left my phone in my advisor's office and he brought it with him to the last meeting. I'm at three percent battery."

My entire body froze, my mouth included. It took a few seconds to regain my speech. "Wait, what did you just say?"

"That I'm at three percent battery? Actually, make that two percent."

"No, before that. Did you say *dissertation*? You mean—" Words scrambled in my brain. "Are you a doctor of computer science now?"

"Yes! Well, informally, but it'll be official soon. And I even wore a tie . . . and dress pants. Can you believe it? I finished my PhD program!"

I couldn't. He'd worn grown-up pants AND finished his dissertation? My body flooded with so many feelings.

Happiness. Excitement. Admiration.

Then anger. Frustration. Annoyance.

"Wait, why didn't you just tell me you were doing this?"

"You had a LOT on your plate, Lily. And I was an emotional mess. Don't be mad, can't you be happy for me that it's all over?"

But I *was* mad. Mad at him for keeping this from me for so long. I was mad at myself for not knowing what he was up to all that time. Mad at both of us for not communicating. It made sense now, why he'd scaled back his office hours. Why he stopped showing up to class. All this time I thought he was a huge flake, but all he was doing was getting his long-overdue degree. Like me.

"Honestly, Lily, I'm just glad it's done. And now that it is, I want to know what's been going on with you while I was out of commission. Please tell me everything. You have my full attention." He coaxed, "Please? What happened?"

I chewed my lower lip, weighing the risk of letting Jake Cho back into my life. But something was different this time with us. The hollowness, resentment, and mistrust deep inside my chest had all but disappeared. I felt a little glow from within, a pilot light ready for a fire.

Hope.

"Is your calendar clear for the day? It's a lot to go over."

"Lily, I'm all yours."

I paused. "You mean it?"

I could feel him grinning through the phone. "More than

anything in the world. Please tell me what I can do to help you."

"I'm going to need all the support I can get," I said, then let out a sigh of relief. "You definitely need to charge that battery. It's a lot."

"I just plugged in the charger and put in my earbuds. Fire when ready."

I got comfy on my bed. It was going to be a long night.

# Chapter Thirty-Three

I sat on a wooden bench along the dew-drenched central lawn. The campus chapel bell rang softly, signaling it was eight in the morning. I checked my watch for the tenth time. He would be here soon.

We'd decided it was easier to meet in person because his phone reception was spotty, and our texts were too numerous and confusing. Jake picked the location. For the life of me, I couldn't figure out why he chose this specific place on the walkway. The last time we were here, my mom had unflinchingly dropped the truth bomb about my dad's unemployment, launching me like a human cannonball straight into adulthood. Then Jake broke my heart on this very bench. I thought back then that it was the most difficult time of my life. But what was happening now rivaled, maybe even surpassed, that experience. My reputation and career were on the line, not to mention that my own health had taken a toll lately, both physically and mentally.

If these life disasters were cyclical, like how cicada seasons occurred every seventeen years in parts of the United States, I would need to plan ahead for the next one in my forties. Hide in a bunker, stock a full bar, and go off the grid.

Jake strolled down the path, wearing far fewer layers than he should have been. He breathed hot air onto his hands and rubbed his palms together. "I forgot my gloves," he said with a lopsided smile. "But I did manage to wear actual pants."

In the sunlight, up close, I could see how his boyish features were now firmer. More striking and handsome. Still youthful, but accented with ruggedness from age. However, the dark circles under his eyes and his deeply hooded eyelids suggested he'd had about as much sleep as I'd had the last few nights. Energy-wise you wouldn't know—he was wide awake and chipper.

He sat on the bench. "Catch me up on the latest," he said. "Lay it on me!"

So I did. I told him about the O'Haras' upcoming event with me. My op-ed that would run in the *Carlthorpe Courier*. Mia's latest crisis management tactics.

He waited until I'd finished before he spoke. He was always good about listening without any mansplainy interruptions.

"I wish I knew how to help you." He looked at me with his warm brown eyes and bit his bottom lip. "Would it be okay if I asked Professor Stevenson to talk with someone at Solv to give you a fair shake at the internship? He's got a ton of influence there and can, at the very least, get them to hold your final interview time. He's also a genius at bringing the energy of the room down a few notches to help people make rational choices. Doc has also helped me through my mental blocks for my PhD dissertation."

"If you could ask Doc to help me out, that would be more than I could have ever thought to ask," I suggested. "Thank you."

His face lit up. "I can also grant you an extension on any homework or classwork assignments, I have the power to do that."

I giggled at his sudden jolt of enthusiasm. "I'm actually all caught up right now, but thanks."

He asked, "Can I walk you back to your apartment? I've been cooped up inside and could use a walk. Plus, I'm getting cold."

"Can we quickly discuss how we're in forty-degree weather, and you're wearing *that*?" My tone sounded harsher than I'd meant it to be, but he was in a flimsy fleece with a waffle-knit Henley underneath. But that wasn't even the worst part—he had no socks on. Just casual slip-on shoes and joggers. I could see his pasty white ankles.

"I see you leering at my sexy anklebones, Lily. My eyes are up here."

My jaw dropped and I let out a shocked laugh. Using all of my willpower, I tried to not stare at Jake, although through my peripheral vision I could see his broad shoulders and chest. His athletic build was hard to miss, especially when seated only a few inches away.

"You're right. I was disrespecting you. I will never, ever drool over your bony ankles ever again."

His eyes sparkled, his charm and exuberance overtaking the tiredness on his face. "Shall we?"

Jake jumped to his feet and held out his hand, pulling me up from the bench. We walked down the central path toward the main gate. As we exited, I asked the question burning in the back of my mind. "Why did you want to meet here? Not at a café, or pretty much anywhere else on campus, but you know, this is where we . . . we—"

"Broke up?"

A lump formed in the back of my throat. I nodded.

"I chose that spot because I wanted to make brand-new memories for us. Instead of it being the place on campus where you remembered I was a selfish, ignorant prick who made poor decisions and didn't take into account your feelings or well-being. I was hoping you'd see me as someone else. Someone better. Someone you're proud of now." He shoved his hands in his pockets. "Maybe now when you pass by that bench on the way to class, you'll remember a person who cares about you deeply and regrets everything about that day we went our separate ways."

I stopped in my tracks.

The temperature had dropped several degrees, and flurries began to scatter and drift all around. It was almost as if we were staging a romantic Hallmark movie scene and the director had cued the snow machines to turn on full blast. It was picturesque and dreamy, a much-needed change from how my life had been spiraling out of control the last three days.

I blurted, "I honestly don't know how to respond. Thank

you for saying all of that." His face brightened a little but fell when I shook my head. "You took off for Spain when I needed you the most. I was at my most vulnerable, and you didn't check up on me to see if I was okay. I went back to Mia's place after we split and had a full-blown panic attack. I don't know if you knew that."

To my therapist, I'd explained that that time in the shower felt like someone had made me wear a bra three sizes too small, tightening my chest and restricting my breathing. That alone was bad enough, but the light-headedness, rapidly beating heart, and hot flashes were also happening at the same time. It was something I never wanted to experience ever again.

I continued. "My anxiety got worse, but I sought out medical help eventually." I lowered my shoulders and sighed. "My life had already been so stressful, but to try to graduate early on top of that, which I clearly didn't accomplish . . . I was a wreck my last semester. And it turned out I went through all of that for nothing. I didn't even finish ahead of schedule, I did the exact opposite."

Close to tears, he scrubbed his hand on his chin. "God, I'm so sorry, Lily. I wish I'd paid more attention. I hate myself every time I think about it. For what it's worth, I'm listening now. And I'm here for you, I mean it."

Reliving that painful time of my life and talking about it with him left half of my body tingling, with the other half numb, like I'd gotten local anesthesia and the shot was wearing off. "I bottled everything inside . . . until I finally broke. It wasn't until Mia took me to the ER for abdominal pains during exam week that last semester that she knew how badly I was silently suffering. I found out that anxiety and stress worsens the ulcers in my stomach, and well, let's just say I'm determined to keep a Zen lifestyle now so I'm not buckled over in pain all the time." I stared into his eyes and held a weak smile. "That was a lot I just unloaded on you. But I wanted to let you know I'm stronger now."

He swallowed hard. "I know I don't deserve it, but if you find it in your heart to forgive me, I'd do anything for a second chance at . . . us. I can never apologize enough for how I acted all those years ago. But I can assure you I'm not the same guy I was back then." Jake averted his eyes to look at the ground. "That day we were leaving for Paris and Spain, I was a total asshole to you. My parents had been on my case all throughout college about how I drop out of everything—first pre-law, then premed—and threatened to cut me off financially if I didn't have a life plan. I panicked. I didn't want them to see me abandon the study abroad opportunity too. It was selfish and I was too preoccupied with showing them I could start and finish something for once in my life. At the very least I should have stayed a while, or called you right away, but I didn't."

I bit my bottom lip. "You were going through a lot too. I'm so sorry about that. I wish everything hadn't spiraled so quickly. They say college is the best time of your life, but that's not true for everyone."

He sighed and peered at me through his dark lashes. "Yes, but some of my best college memories are ones with you. I spent so many years thinking about what I would do or say if

I ever ran into you again. How I'd fall to my knees and ask for your forgiveness. Tell you that ten years ago I missed you so much my chest ached. But when I saw you in the CS class that first day, my heart lodged inside my throat. I could see that you'd moved on, and you were thriving without me."

I coughed. "I'd hardly call it *thriving*."

His eyes lit up. "Are you kidding me? All that you've done, everything you've accomplished, and you still don't see it? You're amazing, Lily. You inspired me with your return to campus. I've made big changes in my life because of you, and I'm hoping they'll all pan out to make a life inside and outside academia, a life with you included, if you'll allow it. And if you'll let me, I want to make you my top priority."

I waved my hand dismissively. "Well, hold on. Let's not forget that you're still technically my TA. The last thing I need is another scandal rocking the campus now. Everything in my life is behaving like a roaring wildfire in unpredictable winds, no need to fuel that with a tornado of Title Nine compliance warnings."

The corner of his mouth pulled into a smile. "Understood. I don't want to distract you from your work and studies, but I would love to start by making things right between us, even if the timing isn't right at the moment. I can wait."

My body shivered. "Really?"

He nodded. "When I saw you on the first day of class, my heart burst wide open. I couldn't believe it. And as we got to know each other again, I thought, what were the odds I'd get a twice-in-a-lifetime chance with you? I was the luckiest man alive."

Maybe he was just being overly sentimental and nostalgic. "And what about your ex? You didn't spend that time on-and-off with her thinking she was your second chance at true love?"

"No way. Gabby was not a good person. She wasn't only cruel to me, she also neglected the pets. She would go on last-minute overnight or multiday trips with her girlfriends when I was away for work, and sometimes she'd forget to feed Sasha and Bandit before she left. She never took Sasha out for walks. Not that I'm a stalker, but I had proof from the front-door camera footage. I had to get out of that relationship, for their sake."

"How could you abandon Sasha and Bandit?" I cried out. "I would never do that!"

"I know." He took a step back to look at my face. Jake brought his hands up to my cheeks. "I told myself if I ever had this chance again, I would be smart enough to never let you go. Lily Lee, I love you, even more than I did back then. I fell for you all over again, really damn hard." His thumbs slid down the curve of my cheekbones to my jaw.

Jake Cho was the first and last person to break my heart. And that was something I couldn't just forget. But time had passed and we had both grown and changed. I wanted this second shot as much as he did.

The words I wanted to say for so long finally came out. "I love you too, Jake."

I stood on my tiptoes, and my lips met his. The light touch of our kiss sent tingles through my entire body.

He grinned. "Can I say one more thing, and then I'll shut

up, I promise. Remember all those years ago, when I added you to the favorites list on my phone?"

I nodded. Because back then, for Jake Cho, that was practically a wedding engagement.

He lifted his shoulders into a barely perceptible shrug. "I never removed you. In Spain, I reached out a few times and hoped you would return my calls. But even after so many years, knowing it was never going to happen, I left your name on the list. It probably doesn't make sense, but it helped me keep my promise to you that if you ever called—"

"You would always pick up." Tears welled in my eyes as I nodded, remembering that when he last took my call, he was walking into his dissertation presentation.

Thinking back to earlier in the semester, he had never asked me for my number. He had it saved in his phone all along.

Jake gathered me into his strong arms, and the moment our bodies connected, my skin pricked as currents of electricity raced through me. "I'm still figuring out a lot of shit about my future, and it may still take a while to get it all sorted out. But one thing I know for damn sure . . . I want you in it."

He clarified, "In my future. Not in my shit."

I choked out a laugh, then wrapped my arms around his waist and squeezed. My cheek pressed against his firm, muscular chest, and I could hear his heart beating hard and fast.

"We better get going." He loosened his grip and shoved his weather-chapped hands into his jacket pockets again. I locked my arm into the crook of his arm and we continued walking. As we stepped onto the sidewalk on Center Street, he bent down to unroll his jogger cuffs.

"Don't worry, I'm keeping any smutty thoughts about your ankles to myself," I joked.

"Much appreciated," he quipped back. "Remember, look up here." Forming a V, he pointed his index and middle fingers at his face.

I gazed into his eyes and sighed. *No problem.*

# Chapter Thirty-Four

The O'Haras picked the venue this time. The Parlor was a wine bar plus bookstore that had recently opened on the Lower East Side. The atmosphere was exactly how you would imagine a secret society's meeting place might look: collegiate-inspired, sort of haunted-looking, and while there were lit candles in actual candelabras throughout the venue, it was hard to see for that very reason. There were overstuffed leather chairs arranged around a fireplace where patrons could grab a drink, buy a book, and read it by the crackling fire.

The hostess led us to a back area that astounded me with its vast size. She explained, "We just opened this area up for events and you're our inaugural guests. Giggles comedy club behind us closed last year and we connected the buildings and converted the space."

"Giggles?" I asked. "I thought that was a strip club. Wasn't it called Jiggles?"

She laughed. "Wow, you remember that? Yes, before Giggles was Jiggles. Needless to say, our owner didn't want to continue with the rhyming names."

As we continued walking, that was all I could think about.

*Wiggles.*

*Squiggles?*

*Wriggles.*

*Pickles?*

She interrupted my train of thought. "I'll take you to the green room, which is actually just our storage room, but with snacks."

We passed through the main room, where the event would be held. Several rows of seats were already claimed by early arrivals, and three chairs with accompanying microphone stands had been arranged on the stage in front. Mia and Jake had just arrived, carrying several plastic grocery bags in their hands, fussing around the tables in the back. I waved hello, but they were so preoccupied that they didn't notice.

It was more comical than anything. *Thanks for blowing me off at my own event, Mia and Jake!*

The green room, aka storage area, was lined with boxes of books. A few were opened and I could see copies of my title as well as the O'Haras' new release in some of them.

After settling on a blue velvety plush chair as my resting place, I used the extra time to look over the latest notes I'd jotted down in Mia's apartment. A wave of nausea hit me as I flipped through the pages, and a short bout of stomach pain jolted me upright. It wasn't likely hunger or low blood sugar, since I had eaten a big lunch and had an apple and a handful of nuts and crackers just before leaving Mia's apartment. More likely, it was anxiety manifesting again, but I ate a piece of a granola bar from my purse just in case. Wiping the crumbs from my blouse to the floor, I looked around to make sure no one saw the mess I'd created.

Ten minutes prior to the start of the event, I received a text from Mia. I'm here in the front row with Jake. If you need me to ask the first Q in the Q&A, shoot me a look

> What look

IDK . . . like someone just took the last good doughnut in the box look

> What???

Like you bit into a cookie thinking it was chocolate chip and it was oatmeal raisin

Cameron came bursting into the green room and scanned the area for somewhere to sit. He grumbled, "Why are there no normal chairs in here? I've been on my feet all day presenting to investors, all I want is to rest my weary feet and to get this event over with."

In a formal and restrained tone, I said hello to him. He didn't greet me back.

Cameron's sister lagged a few steps behind, so I waved at her. The nice O'Hara.

"Hi, Mary," I offered with genuine enthusiasm.

Cameron stomped around the perimeter, offering unsolicited commentary on all the unshelved stacks of books. "Cozy mystery? Historical romance? Are you kidding me? Where are all the *real* books? The business hardcovers?"

He came full circle back to his original spot. "I hope it's okay if I go unscripted. Mary can ask the prepared questions."

She shot him a look. "Wait, Cam, we agreed on the way here that we'd alternate questions."

"And we will—you can ask the scripted ones, and I'll ask whatever I want. And we'll alternate." He scoffed again and crossed his arms. "I'm sure she's great at thinking on her feet. Right, Lily?"

Mary pleaded, "But, Cam. That's not cool—"

The door swung open. "Everyone's seated. It's time to get started and we're right on time. The mics are live and we've done a sound check, so you should be all set. Go have fun!"

A wide grin spread across Cam's smug face. "Yes, let's go have some fun."

THE LAST TIME I'd seen an Asian crowd this big was at my sister's wedding.

I raised an eyebrow at Mia while the events manager read

our author bios. She looked around the room and mouthed back, "Asian invasion!" Sipping from my cup of water hid my approving smile.

There was a wide demographic representation in the audience versus our last event. Mia had done a great job making sure the crowd wasn't stacked with only O'Hara clones. Some of these friendly, eager faces looked familiar too, but I couldn't place them.

Mary grabbed her mic and faced the audience. "It's great seeing everyone this evening, thanks for taking time to come here." Turning to me, she said, "Well, a lot has changed since the last time we saw each other. When Cam heard how the press had created such a hoopla, he thought it would be a good idea to have a forum to chat openly about what's been going on with you the last few months. So thank you, Cam, for being the initiator."

*Yes, thank you, Cameron. Let's see what you have up your sleeve tonight.*

I leaned forward and spoke clearly. "I appreciate the opportunity and look forward to your questions, as well as those from the audience."

"So let's get started." Mary straightened the papers on her lap. "My first question is simple. How did you end up back at school at Carlthorpe?"

"I really missed the dining hall food," I joked. It got a few chuckles from the audience. "But truthfully, it's a long story. What happened to me—"

"What happened was you didn't finish your degree, which

technically makes you a college dropout," Cam blurted into his mic.

"Is there a question in that judgmental statement?" I asked, my tone light but firm.

He rubbed his nose with the back of his hand. "Funny. Okay then, here's a question. Why do you have Carlthorpe listed under education in your LinkedIn profile? Isn't that misleading? When we had our launch event with you, we included you under the assumption that we were having an event with a peer. Someone who was our equal. And what you're doing here is fraudulent!"

I wasn't going to let Cam steer this narrative. I'd already had enough. "I'd like to address what you've both said *and* insinuated, which is actually a lot. If you want to know what happened ten years ago, it was a miscalculation—"

"Lies. More lies." Cam tapped his mic head into the palm of his hand. The thump-thump-thump of his fleshy fingers on the microphone interfered with my thoughts.

Mary growled, "Cam, can you please let her talk without your interrupting and mansplaining!"

The thumping suddenly stopped, so I jumped back in. "Thank you, Mary. Being short on college credits and still getting a diploma happens more often than you realize. Quite a number of people have written me to let me know they had similar stories to mine. They lost their diploma and tried to order a replacement, only to find out they didn't fully earn their degree, resulting in their returning to campus years later to fulfill the requirements. It's amazing that in this day and age, students can still fall through the cracks. Believe it or not, some trolls online have claimed that I made all of this up to seek attention, saying it was a cheap ploy to sell books, and that it's too far-fetched and doesn't actually happen to people. But they're wrong. Like I would go through all of *this* on purpose?"

The crowd nodded along and hung on my words. Something shifted in Cam, his demeanor harsher than before. "Let's move on then and talk about Solv Technologies instead." Cam's mouth curled into a fake smile for the audience. "It was so nice to see you in the Solv lobby. I'd love for you to share what you were doing there when we serendipitously ran into each other. I was under the impression that you were interviewing for a high-level position reporting directly to the CEO. Oh, but I was sorely mistaken." He belly laughed so hard I thought he might choke on his own words. "You were there for an interview all right, and sources at SpottedinTheBigApple say it was for an internship. AN INTERNSHIP. I'd love for you to explain. I'll even hand my mic to Mary, so I can't interject." He passed the microphone to his sister, and she yanked it so fast from his hand it made a *fwwwwp!* sound.

There had been no question in my mind that the Solv interview would come up, and although I was prepared for it, seeing a hundred or so people in the audience intently staring at me sent chills down my spine. My hand quivered as I pulled the mic off the stand. "Yes, you are correct. I was interviewing for an internship at one of the best tech companies in the country. I was the only non-male final candidate for their competitive internship."

Many of the audience members were taking copious notes. Reporters maybe? Bloggers? Whoever they were, they were doing a great job at showing impartiality because their stonelike, serious faces left me in a panic. I visually scoured the room for a quick exit.

"Why were you applying for an internship when you had such a different and promising career trajectory?" Mary asked, with no ill intention in her voice.

I offered an appreciative smile. "For weeks, I kept asking myself why too. Why did I bother? Why should I explore this if I've already invested so many years in something else? Why does it matter? But then I realized I was framing the question wrong. What I needed to ask was, 'Why not?' Why not go for a job like this? Of course, I had so many doubts about even applying. But let me back up a little. When I recently found out I was a few credits short from getting my college degree, I thought I had everything to lose by making this knowledge public. So I kept it quiet, and hoped that after a few months off the grid, I could come back and life would go on as before. But it didn't turn out that way. I took classes that weren't available to me when I was in college and have learned so much. By going back to school, studying something new to me, I had a rare opportunity to apply for an internship at Solv because I had one of the top grades in my computer science class. Even with good grades, I *still* had doubts about my abilities. I thought I was too old to switch careers. I shot myself down without even giving myself the benefit of the doubt. But then I got to the final round of interviews, and it became clear that the only thing getting in my way was me. So why would I not try my best to get a job at a dream company, and see if it's a good fit?"

I took a swig of water and looked at Cam. "The hardest interview I've ever had. But I got a call back for a technical program management internship role."

Cam mumbled, "Lucky, I guess," just loud enough for me to hear because he no longer had a mic, but there was just enough of a questioning tone in it to make my lips tug into a smile.

I addressed his comment anyway. "Well, everyone, Cam here thinks it's luck, and I used to think it was luck too. But it wasn't just that. I've been doing a lot of self-reflection about what people these days call imposter syndrome, which is the *opposite* of what Cam might be more familiar with, a term I coined uniquely for him, 'antagonist superiority syndrome.' It's where someone mediocre by most standards thinks too highly of themselves without cause or merit. It can be shortened to A.S.S." The crowd tittered with laughter while Cam scoffed and crossed his arms.

"It was forty years ago that imposter phenomenon was first studied, at a time when more women were equalizing the workforce and finding tenure in academia. The researchers studying imposter phenomenon noted that self-doubt, especially in women, starts early. For me, it was as early as high school." I glanced over at Mia. She formed a heart in the air with her bent index fingers and thumbs. "The research asks the question, 'How do we undo the ritual of predicting our own failures and instead focus our energy on our successes?' and truly, I wish we could all move in that direction, but it's more than that. How do we undo systemic bias and racism so that marginalized people can be on equal footing? Maybe it's less about the individual and more about workplace environments being hostile and unwelcoming and needing a cultural overhaul."

The audience clapped. A lady in the back yelled, "Amen, sister!"

I smiled at that comment. "I've learned a lot about myself my second time at Carlthorpe. That being confident and believing in myself is absolutely necessary to achieve my full potential. Without doing that, in my own mind, I can never truly be enough." I looked over to Jake, who sent warm pricks of heat through me with his coy smile. "There have been times I was too scared to try to get what I wanted, out of fear that I couldn't have it or didn't deserve it. But I'm taking more risks now, even trying things a second time, and seeing what happens."

A silence fell over the room. Mary dropped Cam's mic by my foot. She muttered, "I'm sorry, I was just shocked by how it sounded like you were in my head, Lily."

A hum of chatter in the audience swelled so loud that I had to tap my mic to get the attention back to the conversation on the stage.

Mary asked the audience, "How many of you can relate?" Every single hand shot in the air.

Well, except Cam's of course.

"I hope that by opening up dialogue about the workplace, and with writing books like mine, I can help in some way. To help others feel seen and less alone."

I blushed as the audience clapped again. More *amen, sisters* this time too. "Related to this, I'm excited to share some new book news with you." I glanced over at the junior publicist from Olympus Press, who gave me a thumbs-up to continue.

"My next book isn't going to be like my previous one. It will be a memoir about my present-day journey, letting you in on my own day-to-day struggles with anxiety and the challenges I face at work. I'll share my career exploration with you, including key findings and learnings discovered during the interview process and on the job, so you can see some of my failures as well as my successes. I also want to incorporate my personal experiences with therapy, journaling ideas, and mindfulness exercises. My editors, Amanda and Katherine, have been brainstorming and crafting chapter ideas with me, and none of this would be possible without them. The working title of the book is *Type A Minus*, and the main takeaway is how no one is born an expert."

A hand in the back shot in the air. "Can we preorder that now?"

"Yes, you can! This is my official book announcement, and it's on my publisher's website as of an hour ago. And this indie bookstore will have signed copies on release day."

Just when things were ending well and wrapping up, Cameron grabbed his mic off the floor. "Before we leave, I want to offer an opinion, rather than a question. I find it disgraceful that you had this career ruse going for ten whole years before that news tip finally exposed you for the fraud that you are. I hope your readers find out you're a college dropout. Again, there's no question there, it's just my personal thoughts."

I bit my lip. This was the other topic I knew Cameron would bring up today. It went without saying that this was not on the approved list of questions, like all his other rude outbursts.

Looking directly at him, I said, "I do feel bad about that and I have apologized publicly. I honestly didn't know I didn't complete my BA degree, and I haven't logged in to LinkedIn in years, so I haven't updated my bio in a long time. I'll fix that right away. There is one thing I'd like to point out though that hasn't been discussed yet, but now is as good a time as any. The PR job I took straight out of college didn't require a BA or BS degree. They accepted work experience in lieu of that, which I had because of my various jobs in college. So if you think about it, it's pretty amazing I got as far as I did, by using your own words, only being a *college dropout*. And I'm proud of myself for going back to school to get my college degree. It wasn't an easy decision to make for many reasons, but I'm glad I did it. Not everyone would have the guts to go back to college ten years later with no family support and no financial safety net. Could you?"

Cameron's mic rolled off his lap and hit the floor. I don't think he meant to drop it, but it happened.

The events manager walked up the aisle from the back of the room. "Wow, okay, let's end with that. Does anyone have any final questions?"

Nearly half of the audience shot hands in the air. This was

going to be a long night. But for the first time in what seemed like ages, pure relief radiated through my whole body.

Jake, Mia, and Beth were waiting for me by the Parlor bar when the event ended. Tears filled my eyes as I hugged each of them.

"You really inspired everyone, I'm in awe of you," Jake said. "We should celebrate! I have some of my own news to celebrate too, but I'll tell you later."

"Thank you," I said. "And I can't wait to hear about it."

I turned to Mia. "Okay, so explain to me why there were so many press-type people in the audience and, separately, why the room was packed with so many Asian brothers and sisters."

Mia laughed. "The press were there because it's a juicy story. Popular nonfiction career author gets busted for not even having a college degree? C'mon. But how you spun it at the end, saying you did all that without a college degree and asking Cam if he'd have the guts to do it? Genius! I have a few more interviews lined up for you next week too. As for all the Asians, I sent an email to the Carlthorpe ASA alumni list. So many people showed up! I also said there'd be free food, which was all supplied by Beth. And free books, which were supplied by your publisher."

Beth chimed in, "Mia had an idea to make an assortment of gourmet inspirational fortune cookies, with quotes from female thought leaders and pioneers from all around the world. People are scanning my fortune QR codes and putting in orders for your book! I've gotten a few corporate order requests from this too."

"You are amazing, Mia. And you too, Beth. I volunteer for kitchen duty when I get home."

I looked at Jake. "And then there's the matter of your good news." I reached for his hand and squeezed.

"Wait!" Mia blurted. "How about we all head back to my place and you can share the good news there? Beth can help me load up my car with the extra cookies and books left over from the event. You two go ahead, we'll catch up. You have my key, right?"

I nodded. "Okay, I hope you have champagne or something at your apartment; if not we can pick some up on the way."

She smirked. "My apartment is fully stocked, so no need to worry about that. See you later."

The cold air whipped hard as Jake and I walked quickly to Mia's apartment. My teeth chattered and my cheeks grew numb, but I hadn't felt this alive in months. Jake offered me his thick striped scarf, which I gratefully accepted. It was nice, being enveloped by his uniquely clean, woodsy scent around my neck, but I would have rather had his arms gathered around my body, holding me close to him.

I fumbled with the building keys, and after a few attempts, we made it inside. He held the door to the elevator open; I'd never noticed how small it was until we both stepped inside and his backpack alone took up most of the space.

"Jesus, what do you have in there?" I tugged on one of his shoulder straps.

"I bought some books before the event. And I've also started scrapbooking." He shot me a wry smile and wriggled his backside.

Before I could ask if he was joking or not, the rickety elevator lurched, then ascended at the speed of me crawling up five flights of stairs. My shoulder pressed into Jake's arm because of the limited space.

"Cozy," he whispered in my ear. I turned my body to face him.

"Very," I agreed. "This death trap is always out of order. Now that I've been on it, I'm not surprised."

The elevator approached the apartment floor. Once we got the door open, the aroma of Beth's cookies welcomed us in the entryway. The lights were dim but I knew the layout so well I didn't need to fumble with the overhead lights or lamp switches to make my way inside.

On the coffee table, Mia had not only laid out a plate of cured meat, hard cheese, and olives, but she also had created a dessert charcuterie board, with an assortment of chocolates, cookies, brownies, and fruit.

Jake discovered something best described as a vodka shot charcuterie board on the dining table. Two flights of spirits in tiny glasses in an assortment of colors. With adrenaline still coursing through my body after the event, I raised a glass. "Bottoms up!"

Jake grinned. "Down the hatch!"

We ate, drank, and laughed for fifteen minutes before I received a text from Mia.

> Oops, sorry, not going
> to make it home tonight.
> Have fun with Dr. Jake!

I plunked down on the couch and made room. "I think we've been stood up."

He sat next to me and read the text. "Or we've been set up."

By this time, the vodka had kicked in and warmth spread to my entire body. I said, "I'm sorry I'm the only audience for your big news, but I promise I'll cheer extra loud." I put my drink down and offered him my full attention.

His eyes twinkled. "Ready? I'm leaving Carlthorpe!"

"What?" I blinked rapidly. "How is that good?"

Jake laughed. "I got official word that I graduated! You inspired me to believe in myself, is that corny? It really fueled me to work toward my goal of finishing my graduate degree and moving on. And I did!"

I grinned. "Okay, but speaking from personal experience, are you SURE you have the credits to graduate?"

After a fit of laughter, he said, "I'm positive, but honestly, because of what happened to you, I confirmed it with the registrar. I asked for a printout."

Jake lowered his eyes. "I was invited to stay as a post-doctoral research assistant and TA through the end of the semester, but I declined. Want to know why?"

I shuddered as his breathing became heavier.

He lifted his hand to brush my cheek. "I did it so I wouldn't have to be your TA anymore."

"Was it really that bad being my TA?" I placed my hand on what I thought was his lower chest, but I hit a solid set of abs. *Damn, Jake.*

His lips curved into a playful smile. "Being your TA was definitely a conflict of interest. For two reasons. One, I didn't want to jeopardize your chances at getting the internship at Solv. If people knew we used to date, there might be claims of favoritism."

I sighed. "True. And the second?"

"Well, I'm definitely interested in someone in the class. She's about your height."

I deflected. "My height? Right now I'm maybe three feet tall sitting down."

"Well, your height when you're standing," he clarified. "She also has winter accessory thievery issues, but we're working on it."

Jake tugged on my scarf. His scarf.

He leaned forward to loosen it.

"Hey, you let me borrow that." I whispered in his ear, "But fine, I'll give it back, Dr. Cho. Hey, that sounds pretty sexy."

His eyes filled with mischief. "You want to hear something *really* sexy? And nerdy?"

My heart pounded inside my chest. I nodded.

He leaned in and whispered into my ear, "You'll *always* have the highest priority in my queue. You always come first."

I gulped. "So . . . are you saying you'll show me your *source code*?"

Jake laughed and tipped my chin, rubbing up and down with his thumb. "Yes. Would it be okay if I kissed you?"

"How about I help?" Our bodies instinctively drew together like north-south magnets. I reached for the back of his neck, and my heart pounded as he leaned down and his lips met mine. It was a well-acquainted kiss that sent a shiver down to my toes.

My mouth parted as his lips descended on mine again with more longing and aching, this time inviting a deeper, intense, intimate closeness between us. We were different people now, and the next kiss proved it. The sweetness, timidness, and carefulness of our youth were gone. He kissed me with an intense hunger, like he'd been waiting forever and this was his only shot in the world.

"I've wanted to do that for so long," he breathed. "I have more good news. I'll be teaching at Columbia in the fall, so I'll be in the city, and we can do this anytime you want."

I unraveled his scarf, and like a lasso, wrapped it around his wrists.

"I like where this is going," he said.

I motioned for him to follow me to Mia's bedroom. She wouldn't mind. In fact, she wanted this to happen.

The bed was made, there were LED tea light candles on her windowsills, and Janet Jackson's "That's the Way Love Goes," was playing on her Bluetooth speakers.

I pushed him onto the bed. "Wait there. One second."

Mia wouldn't be home anytime soon, but just in case, I locked the door.

# Chapter Thirty-Five

I ended the semester with all As. The only thing left between me and my diploma was the swim test.

That goddamned swim test.

It was now or never. Do or die. Sink or swim.

Literally.

The test proctor explained, "When I blow the whistle, you
can go at your own pace. Remember, no holding on to the
walls, and no flotation devices. Some of our engineers like to
test the limitations of the rules, so this year we've also added
'no riding on anyone's backs,' and 'no motors of any kind.'
Any questions?"

No questions. I knew what I had to do.

As I checked out the other calm and collected seniors
in my swim lane, the queasiness in my stomach turned to
full-blown nausea. I glanced at the pool entrance and the
emergency exit. *Remember, Lily, this isn't a race, you're just
trying to pass. And also to not drown.*

The shriek of the whistle startled me, but what really
made everything so much more unpleasant was all the

splashing that immediately ensued. The other students had no regard for personal space, dousing me in water with all their aggressive, propeller-like kicking.

I clung to the wall. My fingers wouldn't uncurl. I was frozen in place, too scared to make a move.

"Okay, Lily, no more second-guessing yourself. It's just like we practiced. Let's go go go!" Beth appeared above me with a megaphone hanging by her side.

She clicked a button and spoke into it, pointing the speaker down at my head. "Sorry I'm late. The battery ran out and the line at the drugstore was ridiculous. It takes a nine-volt, so annoying. Anyway, I'm here. And you said no whistle. You ready?"

I nodded.

"As we practiced, Lily! Let go in . . . three, two, one!"

I pushed off the wall and glided on my back, and I could hear the muffled sound of Beth arguing with the swim test proctor. Desperate to hear more, I stayed floating on my back as long as I could before kicking and circling my arms to prevent me from sinking.

Beth shouted into her megaphone, "Sorry, Coach, let's read the swim test requirements then, I have them printed from the website. There's absolutely nothing in the rules that says she can't do the elementary backstroke."

Muffled, muted mumbling. More arguing. Then I heard Beth's voice.

"It's a modified elementary backstroke. And it's mostly floating and drifting, but the rules state she just needs to refrain from holding the edges of the pool or the ropes."

Pause. "All you said was she can't use flotation devices or be on anyone's back."

Mumbling.

My hand scratched against the concrete wall. I'd made it to the other side.

I turned around and float-drifted the other way, carefully avoiding holding on to anything.

More megaphone shouting. "Sorry, Coach, I have my whole day cleared for this. There's no time limit, I triple-checked, so looks like it's just us three here until whenever she finishes."

Circle. Kick. Circle. Kick. I was done with the second lap. One more to go.

I moved faster than ever before, knowing I was past the halfway point. All of this was so embarrassing, especially knowing Beth and the proctor were watching me and arguing about my unconventional approach to the swim test. The one good thing about getting out of the water last was that no one other than Beth and the proctor could see me barely finish.

Poolside cheers from a few new voices confused me as I kicked my way down the lane. I briefly turned my head toward Beth and saw PJ, Grace, and Ethan.

"You can do it!"

"Half a lap left!"

"Let's goooo, Lily, let's go!" It was Jake's voice on the megaphone. I glanced over and there he was, next to Beth, grinning at me with tousled hair and sleepy eyes. It looked like he'd just woken up and come here in a hurry. Just for my laps of shame.

The blue flags lined above my head meant one thing. A few kicks more and I'd be done.

And done meant I would graduate.

My hand scraped the end of the concrete pool, and yes, there was some blood. It wasn't exactly an elegant way to end, needing Neosporin and a bandage, but you know what? I did what I needed to do.

When I pulled myself out of the pool, Beth was ready for me with my terry-cloth robe, like that Rocky Balboa coach in *Creed*. "Congratulations, Roomie!"

Through heaving breaths, I managed to say, "We did it!"

She laughed and helped me pull the robe over my shoulders. "*You* did it, Lily."

I did.

I did it.

"Thanks, Coach," I said.

My friends gathered around to hug me. "I'm dripping all over you," I apologized. "Thank you for coming. Please make sure you delete all video and photographic evidence of this embarrassing event."

Ethan asked, "Did you get the internship? I just got the email!"

I shivered as I pulled out my phone from my gym bag. "Oh wow! Yes! Holy shit . . . I'm going to work at Solv!"

We laughed and hugged, then Ethan, Grace, and PJ agreed to meet up with me for a celebration dinner later that evening. They headed out for brunch at a new Asian fusion café and waved goodbye to me.

Jake pulled me into him and held me tight. "You were

awesome," he whispered into my ear. "Congratulations to my favorite intern!"

Beth asked Jake, "Mind taking her back? She might want a shower."

I nodded and leaned my head against his chest. "I'm dying to go home." A shower sounded good. A hot shower with Jake sounded even better.

Heading back to his car, I said, "Thank you for showing up today. I wasn't expecting you, but it really meant a lot to me."

Jake stopped walking and turned to me. Placing his strong, warm hands on my shoulders, he looked into my eyes. "I will always show up for you." He ran his fingers down the length of my arms, then kissed me gently on the lips. Then to my surprise, he grabbed my hands and kissed each of them, even the scratched and bloody-knuckled one. "Mmm. Chlorine. Blood. Very sexy. Very wet."

I laughed. "So, my place?" I suggested as he pulled me closer to his body.

I knew what he had on his mind and beat him to the punch. "Wanna take me home and get me out of these wet clothes?"

Jake tugged on the belt tie of my robe. "I can't wait," he murmured.

## Chapter Thirty-Six

**M**y parents showed up at my apartment the day of graduation with a box of oranges, a Hallmark card, and my old commencement gown from ten years ago.

I hadn't invited them. I didn't think they'd want to come.

"Why didn't you tell us which day is your big day? We ask your sister. Sara tell us you graduate today." Umma clucked her tongue and looked at my dad as if to say, "Youngest daughter. She'll never learn."

As annoying as it was that they showed up unannounced with a heavy box of citrus from Costco, I could see it was their own way of showing their love.

My mom and dad marveled at the farm decor. I'd gotten so used to it that I had forgotten what my initial reaction had been. They held hands and said a prayer in Korean, blessing my home. After taking off their shoes, my mom and dad wandered around, examining each room.

Dad fell into the recliner and leaned back, then flipped on the TV.

"Just make yourself at home, Appa," I joked.

He muttered, "Your sister kids, they are too much work. We are tired grandparents. We need a break."

My mom nodded vigorously. "They asking so much. 'Help me, Halmoni!' Cry all the time. Picky eating." She shook her head. "Make us realize how easy you were. Your sister too."

Had they . . . softened by becoming grandparents? It had never occurred to me that they could change at all. Even so, they always managed to cause some degree of drama, and on this graduation morning, that was the last thing I wanted.

"I don't have graduation tickets for you, I'm sorry. I wasn't expecting anyone other than Mia and—" Shit, they didn't know about Jake.

"And God." *Good one, Lily.*

"God is everywhere," Mom agreed.

I wiped my brow with the back of my hand. "Indeed, He is," I said.

Dad said, "We tell everyone you working at Solv now. That's good company."

I'd started my job at Solv virtually, with the goal of transitioning to the NYC office at the start of summer, and that had temporarily put me in my parents' good graces. But that was just it . . . it was only temporary. I knew to not let their opinions dictate who I was, not anymore. I had thought their love was what was most important. It was a well-meaning love, but too callously brutal and unhealthy to become fixated on. It wasn't the only type of love in the world.

Self-love was what I needed most. And I had that now.

I extended an olive branch. "Maybe we can grab a late lunch after graduation, or tomorrow. You can buy me that steak you promised me," I joked.

Mom held up my old gown encased in a thin dry-cleaner plastic bag. "It's okay if we don't go to ceremony. We saw you do before anyway ten years ago. Maybe if you wear this one you can give other one back for refund. Save money."

I laughed and examined the material. It hadn't faded at all. They'd brought it all the way from Virginia, where they lived now to be close to the grandkids. Bringing this gown was their way of showing they cared. Why not wear it?

I pulled it over my head, and luckily it still fit. The cap did too. "How do I look?"

I immediately regretted the open invitation to discuss my appearance. This could go in any direction, and the odds were 75 percent bad, 20 percent neutral, 5 percent good, with a margin of error of 5 percent.

My mom stifled a yawn and took an off-center photo of me in my gown, then shared it with my sister. Neither parent said anything about how I looked. They were too tired and probably forgot what we were discussing. But this was a much better outcome than I had hoped. I didn't dare ask a second time.

My mom's phone dinged twice. "Your sister write back." She handed me her cell.

Tell her we're all proud of her

Congratulations!

I beamed and made plans to meet my parents later in the day at my favorite café. They went back to their hotel to rest while I finished getting ready.

As I glided on the finishing touch of lip gloss, I noticed a white shirt box on my bed. At first, I thought it might be a graduation gown accessory from my parents, but it was too heavy. Lifting the lid and peeling back the tissue, I uncovered a plum-colored T-shirt with WORLD CLASS STEMINISTA in white lettering across the front with a card from Mia and Beth. I couldn't wait to wear it.

Also enclosed was a scrapbook from Jake, with "Lily's Greatest Hits" on the cover. Inside, he had filled it with photos and news articles from the last ten years, showcasing all my professional accomplishments, leaving blank pages in the back to add more. Creating a bound portfolio of my successes was something I had been meaning to do one day, to reflect on my personal and professional wins so I didn't focus so much on all my screwups. So Jake *wasn't* joking about his most recent scrapbooking endeavor. It was skillfully crafted, wonderfully curated, and, most important, thoughtful. This project must have taken him weeks. Maybe even months.

Flipping through page after page, I blinked back tears when I saw collages of photos and articles from my past and present, including old and new pictures from campus, my 30 Under 30 award, and an official book announcement for *Type A Minus* in *Publishers Digest*. By the time I got to the last page, the waterworks were unrelenting. The worst timing too, because I'd just finished all my makeup touch-

ups. Luckily, I'd worn water-resistant eyeliner and the powder and blush were easy to reapply.

I ran out the door, thinking unironically how this was
already turning out to be the best graduation I'd ever had.

I had officially graduated in December, but I had the
option of walking with the rest of the senior class in May,
which I gladly did. College graduation the second time
around was just as exhilarating as the first. Beach balls
bounced back and forth from the student body to the specta-
tors. A few NSFW inflatable women and men were passed
back and forth among the graduating class. Airhorns blared
and noisemakers rattled. Ethan, Grace, and PJ brought bottles of vodka under their gowns and snuck occasional sips.

Walking the stage again as a real graduate felt especially
important this time. When I shook Dean Balmer-Collins's
hand, she held it a little longer than expected. "I wanted to
say how sorry I am about everything. Ten years ago I was
so caught up in getting ahead and getting promoted that
I—" Her voice hitched, her words catching in her throat.
"You were right. I was selfish and made so many mistakes
that I regret deeply. I owe you a huge apology. I will try to
do better, I promise. By the way, I preordered your next
book and will be following your journey."

My heart lifted, knowing this feeling of injustice from
my past had resolved to an outcome I could accept. "Take
it from me, don't let mistakes define you. Who you are isn't
your history of mistakes. It's how you genuinely learn from
them rather than making excuses and offering insincere
apologies. The goal is to become a better person, right?" I

took her other hand and offered her a courteous smile. "I appreciate your support and wish you well, Dean. Thank you."

She nodded. "You offer wise words that I promise to take to heart. Truly."

When I got back to my seat, Beth asked, "What was that all about?"

I relished the moment. "Just a normal human making mistakes and finally learning from them."

# Epilogue

*One Year Later*

"Do you think we'll ever get sick of eating paella?" I asked as we settled the check.

"Honestly, no. Do you think you'll ever stop taking more than your share of shrimp?"

I narrowed my eyes. "You always take more clams and mussels. So it's only fair."

"Touché. So what's next?" Jake asked as we exited the restaurant. A leisurely lunch after strolling through the Picasso Museum had been on my bucket list for years and we'd finally done it.

Jake didn't seem to have a strong opinion about our afternoon plans.

"Dessert at Boqueria Market? Then maybe we can go to Barceloneta Beach for an afternoon swim so I can use all those aquatic skills Beth taught me?" I suggested.

He smirked. "You know I'm not going to say no to that."

On the bus ride to the marketplace, Mia sent us the latest

photos from her dog- and cat-sitting adventures: Sasha and Bandit basking lazily in the sunlight streaming through the windows of Jake's brownstone. It was such a relief to know those two were in such good hands while we were away on a much-needed vacation.

When we arrived at La Boqueria, we were met with vibrantly colored booths and tantalizing aromas of sweet and savory foods. Zigzagging from stall to stall, we were lured by the fragrant and visually stunning fresh-pressed fruit juices, produce, and desserts. Spanish specialties surrounded us, making us want to have a second lunch of jamón ibérico, Manchego cheese, and bacalao. Thank God we arrived with full stomachs, otherwise we would have gone broke from trying a little of everything.

I went with a crema catalana: a custard pudding topped with a coating of burnt caramel, which to me looked like crème brûlée, one of my all-time favorite desserts. Jake opted for a red juice that looked like strawberry but tasted more like mango and pomegranate.

As Jake chatted in Spanish with the vendor, I grinned to myself, thinking about how different my life was just a year ago. And how over a decade ago, I thought I'd never make it to Barcelona, and here I was with Jake, all these years later.

He came to me wearing a sly grin, holding a second juice.

"You got me one too?"

"It was on the house. He remembered me from back in college, can you believe it? He called me Señor Triste back then, because I looked so sad." He handed me the drink.

I raised the cup and said loudly to the man at the drinks stall, "Gracias, Señor!"

Jake leaned in and kissed me, and all the bustle around us disappeared. He tasted sweet and earnest. I closed my eyes and let the world continue to melt away as his lips pressed against mine a second time. "He said the drink is for you, for making me so happy."

I took a sip. "You make me happy too."

# Acknowledgments

I'm writing these acknowledgments as I stare at the back of my daughter's head. She's sitting on the couch right in front of me, participating in a summer online Zoom art camp. It's unbelievable how long this pandemic has gone on, and how much our lives have changed as a result. I released my first book during lockdown, and thought for sure when I released this sixth book we'd be out of this by now (looks like I know as much about epidemiology and pathology as I know about spelling). As you can imagine, I've had a lot of ups and downs during my pandemic author career, but honestly, it's been mostly ups thanks to my supportive friends, family, and colleagues.

I'd like to start by thanking my husband for all of his encouragement throughout my writing journey, and for writing a computer science book (with Dustin B), because it was the perfect resource for me when researching CS college coursework for this novel. He also helped with manuscript proofreading, and as always, caught a number of things. Thank you for being amazing.

Speaking of amazing, I want to send love to my kiddo, CJ, who has cheered her mama on and offered to fix my grammar mistakes when she is allowed to read my adult books. Only six more years to go!

Many thanks to my visionary editor, Carrie Feron, who helped me center this book on what was most important. For the first time ever, I had to cut thousands of words, and the novel is so much better now. Enormous thanks to Asanté Simons, Amanda Lara, Beatrice Jason, DJ DeSmyter, Yeon Kim, Decue Yu, Diahann Sturge, and all of the Avon production, marketing, and sales teams for being so wonderful during this process. Much appreciation to Brent Taylor, my agent extraordinaire, for all your encouraging words over the years and continuing to champion my work. Kathleen Carter, thank you for continuing to be on this journey with me—you're wonderful!

Lots of love to my family who have been so encouraging and enthusiastic about my writing career. My UCLA Anderson friends, Columbia buds, Lincoln moms, Julie Kim, my Korean language guru, my writing group, my author and writer friends, librarians, booksellers, podcasters, IG live interviewers, and my lovely bookstagrammer buddies (especially the OC/LA/API fam), thank you so much for the cheerleading! Special thanks to Helen Hoang, and also Roselle Lim, who continue to be my go-to people for raves and rants. ILU! Alexa Martin, Alison Hammer, Liz Lawson, Dante Medema, Jeff Bishop, Stephan Lee, and Qs writing retreaters (Kathleen Barber, Chelsea Resnick, and Kristin Rockaway) have all graciously responded to my "yay!" and "huh???" messages and texts in a timely manner . . . thank you to you all.

Huge thanks to the bookstores, libraries, and festivals who have hosted me, and to anyone who has attended my in-person and virtual events. As someone who once awkwardly performed stand-up comedy in front of an audience of three people, I'll admit this is one of the things I fear the most about being an author: that no one will show up to anything, even if I bring delicious cookies. I really appreciate my lovely eventgoers, and I'll do my part to keep the panels, conversations, and interviews fun and engaging.

Much appreciation (and admiration) to Emily Henry, Christina Lauren, Emily Giffin, and Harlan Coben, who plucked my last adult book *So We Meet Again* from their towering TBR stacks and championed the heck out of it. I'm still so grateful for that over a year later.

And finally, a huge thank-you to my readers. I know my quirky books aren't everyone's cup of tea, but thank you for buying, consuming, and sharing this tea with others. You are the best!

## About the Author

## About the book

Insights,
Interviews
& More . . .

# Meet Suzanne Park

SUZANNE PARK is a Korean American writer who was born and raised in Tennessee.

In her former life as a stand-up comedian, Suzanne appeared on BET's *Coming to the Stage*, was the winner of the Seattle Sierra Mist Comedy Competition, and was a semifinalist in NBC's "StandUp for Diversity" showcase in San Francisco. Her novels have been featured in "best of" lists in NPR, PopSugar, *Real Simple*, *Country Living*, Bustle, Buzzfeed, *Marie Claire*, *Parade*, Shondaland, and the *Today Show*.

Suzanne graduated from Columbia University and received an MBA degree from UCLA. She currently resides in Los Angeles with her husband, female offspring, and a sneaky rat that creeps around on her back patio. In her spare time, she procrastinates. ∿

# Letter from the Author

Funny story: the idea for this novel came from a recurring nightmare. My most frequent hellish dream is one where I walk into class on the last day of school and need to take a final exam for a course I've never attended. During the earlier months of the pandemic, I had this exact same dream several days in a row and knew I had to try to do something to get this out of my head, so I wrote down what I was thinking and feeling on paper (and in MS Word). When I journaled my worries and concerns over the course of a week . . . voila! I discovered the kernel of the idea for *The Do-Over*.

Like with my other adult contemporary novels, in this book I wanted to incorporate themes of women's empowerment, self-discovery, and the pursuit of love. I tried to do something a little different this time by including glimpses of Lily's past to show how much she'd changed since college, and to also give her room to explore the notion that there is still plenty of room to grow as adults. Adding in a frat party, a challenging swim test requirement, and other nods to campus life were all in good fun and enjoyable to write about, even during the pandemic.

Although I've included serious topics in this story (imposter syndrome and mental health), *The Do-Over* is meant to be a feel-good, heartwarming read about how the future we think we want when we're younger might turn out very different than we ever imagined. As someone who became an author after a long corporate career in the travel and technology industries, I am a firm believer that it's never too late to try something new.

I hope you enjoy reading the book as much as I loved writing it.

With love,
Suzanne ෴

# Reading Group Guide

1. If you had the chance to re-do any part of school, what would it be and why?

2. Have you had any relationship that ended in a way that you wish you could get a second chance at reconciliation or a complete do-over?

3. Lily has moments of "imposter syndrome" aka imposter phenomenon in the story. Have you experienced imposter syndrome? How did you (or do you) handle it?

4. Throughout her life, Lily struggles with parental expectations and breaking free from them. Have you dealt with this, and how did you get past it?

5. Jake re-enters Lily's life after ten years of being apart. Have you ever had someone you didn't expect come back into your life years later?

6. Lily and Jake had planned to do study abroad together in college. Do you think their relationship would have survived through the rest of college and beyond had they not broken up?

7. Beth and Mia are Lily's "found family." What role did they play in Lily's life?

8. The story is told from Lily's point of view. What moments in the story would you have liked to know what Jake was thinking?

9. Discuss the structure of the novel: how do the glimpses of Lily's past college life impact your understanding of Lily and Jake?

10. Do you think Lily and Jake will stay together? ⌒